"This house is awesome," Skye said.

"I was just thinking the same thing about you," Terrance said in a for-her-ears-only whisper.

His comment caught Skye off guard. She wasn't sure how or if she should respond. After all, this was the man her friends had warned her about. His reputation was legendary, and it spelled caution any way you looked at it. He probably still had all of his bad habits, she thought. Some men never grew up, never relinquished their "playa" cards.

Just then, Terrance stepped closer and held out his hand.

"It's been extremely nice meeting you," he said, clasping her hand warmly between his. He held her hand a little longer than seemed necessary.

"You, too," she said. "Looks like we're almost roommates."

"Now that would be asking for way too much," he said with a slow and heart-stopping smile.

Skye quickly entered her room and closed her door. She was trembling as she leaned back against it. She closed her eyes and tried to gather her wits. He was only a man, after all.

But, wow, what a man he was....

LINDA WALTERS

has been a photojournalist, and has worked for both national and local publications, covering celebrity profiles and jazz festivals, etc., around the world for many years. Nothing inspires her like love, though. Romance novels are like fuel for the soul if you are able to be inspired by the possibility of "what if." Even if you aren't an eternal optimist, you no doubt can still be moved by stories that capture the imagination and the indefatigable strength of the human spirit.

Writing romance novels is the perfect balance for Linda as she is also a wholesale account executive with one of the nation's top mortgage-banking institutions, giving her the opportunity to use both the intuitive and analytical aspects of the thought process.

LET ME
Love you

LINDA WALTERS

KIMANI™
ROMANCE

 KIMANI PRESS™

ISBN-13: 978-0-373-86038-8
ISBN-10:   0-373-86038-2

LET ME LOVE YOU

www.kimanipress.com

Printed in U.S.A.

Dear Reader,

In today's world of fast-food restaurants, instant access to everything tangible and romance via the Internet, it is oftentimes a challenge to find a solid commitment to the work and energy it takes to truly build anything from the foundation up. Even the construction of both commercial and residential projects now often begins with prefabricated walls, thereby dismissing the need for the time-consuming task of laying the foundation brick by brick. In today's time-sensitive environment, most of us don't have the luxury of indulging in time-consuming activities. This realization led me to the exploration of a relationship bound by that kind of restriction.

Let Me Love You is the exploration of a relationship that starts in an almost prefabricated environment, but then is allowed to develop and grow into something substantial and even worthwhile.

Thank you sincerely for the continued interest, the solid commitment and the solid love you exhibit each time you pick up another one of my novels.

Keep reading! It means more than you know.

Linda Y. Walters

Acknowledgment

I'd like to acknowledge all the folks who continually encourage and support my efforts to bring stories to light that somehow display the human spirit in its finest element. I truly believe that love is the answer.

Thank you to my family, my sisters, my nieces and nephews, and of course, to the many friends who have been there along the way. Donna Hill—you are my muse and my mentor.

Thanks especially to Nikki, Lance and Teylor, who guide me, encourage me, push me, elevate me and love me— you guys are the wings beneath my wings!!!!

And most importantly, thanks to the Lord above, whose presence is felt throughout my day 24/7, 365 days a year.

Blessings to all.

Love,

Linda Walters

Chapter 1

Skye Thompson picked up the ringing telephone, reached for a Form 1003 and began to take the necessary information which would ultimately lead to the purchase of a new home or result in one very disappointed client. The final decision would be up to her employer, the Bank for Residential Lending.

In the next forty-five minutes, she completed the application documents, ran the borrower's credit and calculated the applicant's debt-to-income ratios. After checking the incoming fax machine, Skye pulled off the bank statements that had been sent in and began to complete the necessary paperwork which would, hopefully, culminate in a complete file being turned in. She immediately recognized that the client had good credit, standardized pay stubs and bank statements which showed a substantial amount of assets, along with an acceptable amount of seasoning. There had been no large deposits, no unexplainable spikes or dips in the balances shown during the most recent months.

Skye breathed an audible sigh of relief as she acknowledged that the client qualified for more than one program. She also realized they would qualify for several of the low interest rate loans which they, as a first-time home buyer, would also benefit from. The phone rang again.

Skye picked it up after only two rings. "Skye Thompson, Bank for Residential Lending," she said quickly, poised to reach for another application.

"Girl, how are you doing?"

The voice caught Skye off guard for a quick moment, then the familiar tone was recognized. They'd been best friends forever, starting with a double Dutch contest in the third grade. After challenging one another, they'd tied the contest in knots and became best friends from that day on. Even after Skye's family had moved from New York to Atlanta, the friendship had continued.

Nita, as she'd been called since she turned sixteen, did not wait for an answer and continued speaking. "I know you're busy, girl, but I had to call you. My crazed husband has just decreed an edict that all members of the wedding party are supposed to show up here on Friday of next week. Don' ask me what he's up to. I just know that it will entail me cooking my butt off. I don't know why I married him. On second thought, yes I do," she said, then laughed deeply.

Skye joined her, their voices mingling, as the meaning behind the unspoken washed over them both. The joke worked in more ways than one as there had been many occasions when Nita had referred to Branch as a very skilled lover. She claimed he made all others before him look like amateurs. It didn't hurt that he was also her soul mate.

Skye had been Nita's only bridesmaid, with her older sister, Monica, serving as the maid of honor. Skye's memory of the day only two months earlier, when Nita and Branch had pledged their love for one another in a beautiful ceremony, was still fresh. The small church had been filled with family and friends from both sides of the couple.

It would have been difficult to imagine anyone in the wedding party being happier for Nita than Skye. Marriage was something they'd both talked about, dreamed about and fantasized about all throughout their years of growing up. Many times, they'd even discussed planning a double wedding. When Nita announced her engagement to Branch, Skye's happiness for her was bittersweet with the knowledge that she would not be joining her best friend as she walked down the aisle as a bride. It took a minute, then Skye realized that she was genuinely happy for Nita. Her time would come. She was sure of it though she couldn't put her finger on who, what, when and where.

"I'm up to my ears in work, girl, but you know I'll be there. Should I bring anything? And just what is the occasion this time?" Skye asked, laughter in her voice. She knew that neither Nita or Branch really needed an excuse for a gathering. They both loved people, including friends and relatives, as much as they loved one another.

"Don't ask. And, no, you don't have to bring anything. Just try and get here by next Friday evening—

say about seven or seven-thirty. I think Branch felt badly about a couple of his friends not being able to attend the wedding so he's doing the catch-up thing with the photos. They just came back from the photographer," Nita added.

"Oh, I can't wait to see them. How'd they come out?" Skye asked, her breath coming in a rush from the excitement she felt. It would be the first time she would get to see the new home in Fort Lauderdale that Branch and Nita had purchased. They'd moved in only two weeks after the wedding ceremony.

Her mind was also still concentrating on figuring out what pieces of information might be missing from the file she was putting together. Daniel Drake, the branch manager, always seemed to find something she hadn't thought of which would be necessary before a file was acceptable for submission.

"Girl, they are gorgeous. With the exception of one or two, they all came out perfectly. Of course, Lorenzo can mess up anything at any time. How many times did we have to tell that boy to look straight ahead?" she said, referring to her husband's younger brother. "If I didn't know better, I'd think he was looking down Monica's dress in a couple of the pictures," Nita added, laughing.

Skye sat back in her chair and laughed, too. "Girl, you are too much. Lorenzo seems to have a one-track mind, but Monica was way ahead of him. She probably knew what he was up to and was just taunting him."

"Oh, you are so right. That would be just like her. Anyway, I'll let you go. See you next Friday night—use our travel agent again. She can get you a special deal on the flights. I'll e-mail you her information right now."

"Okay. I'll do it right now, before I move on to the next thing in the pile on my desk. Then I'll e-mail you with the flight's information."

"Good. Just be sure to get there before seven o'clock. We're doing to dinner and I don't want you to be late," Nita added as she hung up.

Skye almost gave her standard retort, "Then it wouldn't be me," but instead placed the receiver in the cradle. She then began recalculating the debt-to-income ratios of her latest clients and finished the work necessary for the file to be submitted to underwriting. Her day moved forward quickly and before she knew it, the clock read six forty-five.

Dreading the traffic ahead of her on Memorial Drive, Skye delayed leaving the office.

Skye checked her e-mail, called the travel agency which Branch and Nita had an account with and booked her round-trip ticket.

After sending an e-mail to Nita, she repacked her briefcase and headed toward the elevators. Her car was parked in the company parking lot and as she approached it, her mind once again returned to the conversation she and Nita had shared earlier. Skye smiled, knowing the weekend would be a good change of pace for her. Lately, she'd given up on clubs and the local watering holes which only seemed to feature the same faces and even clichéd tactics.

Dating had offered some significant challenges right after college, with the pool of available men appearing to be inexhaustible. Now, some five years later, the novelty had worn off and the whole thing seemed to be one huge joke.

She'd stopped going out on occasional dates which seemed a test of her people-handling skills of late. The last time she'd had any kind of relationship was with Aldon Scott, co-owner of Triad, one of the largest title companies in Atlanta. That eight-month liaison ended when he disappeared for two weeks without a single phone call. Skye had been devastated when the truth behind his absence had come out…and the woman who she'd never known existed. Determined to put Aldon— and his double life—behind her, she immersed herself in work, decorating her apartment and selecting the pieces she wanted to pull the condo together. She refused to answer his phone call some three weeks later.

Sometimes, you have to give a brother the "Forget my name, number and information" act, she reasoned and vowed to never again speak to him again. When she heard he'd gotten married some months later after getting his assistant pregnant, it only confirmed her stance, making her even more committed to putting her career on the fast track.

The corporate offices of the Bank for Residential Lending were located on the fourteenth floor of a building on Peachtree Street which had been recently renovated. The marble and glass lobby, topped by an exquisitely ornate atrium ceiling, had been painstakingly brought to life incorporating Old World Federal style and New World elegance. She loved the feel of the building with its light airiness, and its corporate atmosphere. Daily, it buzzed with the best and brightest that the booming city of Atlanta, Georgia had to offer.

Skye's five-foot-six-inch frame, shoulder-length hair and milk-chocolate skin often caused heads to turn. She had grown accustomed to the double take which some-times preceded the approach of total strangers but never understood the reaction she seemed to cause. She often wondered what the fuss was all about.

Skye didn't realize that her curvaceous body, her flawless skin and her sensuous lips were a drawing card. In her mind, it was all just part of an average-looking existence.

On most business days, Skye wore her hair pulled back into a tight knot and found it annoying when her hairdresser insisted on blowing it out. It seemed to draw too much attention in Skye's mind, so she would wait until she arrived home, secure it with one of the many ponytail bands she owned and once again feel in control. In Skye's world, control was a very important element.

She loved her work as a mortgage banker. It satis-fied a need to help others that had been ingrained in her by her mother, Lillian Thompson, years before she'd moved to Atlanta.

Lillian Thompson had been a practical nurse in one of New York City's fastest growing metropolitan hos-pitals. She'd seen it all in her time there. Everything from hopelessness, violent crime, domestic abuse and people dying of AIDS had been her constant reality for the thirty-three years she worked there.

Now, as Skye headed for the apartment she'd recently purchased in an eight-unit building, she thought of her mother and made a mental note to call her, realizing she was due in from a trip she'd taken to Arizona. Travel seemed to be the one thing that gave Lillian Thompson great enjoyment in her senior years. Thankfully, her health remained solid.

Skye drove quickly to her Stone Mountain neighborhood and pulled into her parking space. Rod's space was empty and she wondered if he would be working late for the remainder of the week. He normally worked long hours and was also in the industry.

Mortgage broker of his own Federal Housing Administration–licensed shop, he did a sizable business in both conventional and government loans. Luckily, Skye represented one of his most frequently used lenders.

Skye knew that Rod's insistence on her trying the industry out had been instrumental in her current success. She again thanked both him and the Lord. She knew it had been fate which had brought her to the building and to Rod.

In the beginning, when he'd first approached her, Skye figured he was trying to hit on her. His friendliness had caught her off guard, making it awkward at times when they ran into each other in the parking lot, or in the elevator.

It was only after he'd introduced himself, invited her over for a *welcome to the neighborhood* drink and she'd turned him down repeatedly, that he'd laughingly said, "Girl, you don't have to worry—you're safe with me. I'm not into fishing in my own pond," he'd added, a huge grin on his face. Somehow, his sincerity was established with that one statement and Skye realized he was genuinely trying to be friendly. She relaxed for the first time since she'd moved into the complex and began to enjoy her stance as a new home owner, even if the home was a condominium.

In the ensuing months, they'd gotten together several times for impromptu dinners and sometimes even watched rented movies together. He'd never made a move on her.

Rod had a fantastic sense of design which was apparent by his use of color, texture and form throughout his three-bedroom, two-bathroom unit. Done in brown, beige, white with black accents throughout, it was warm yet elegant. He'd used distinctive African accents in the bathrooms and also in several of the prints which hung on the walls lining the hallway. Mocha-brown walls greeted you immediately upon entering the foyer which was accentuated by starkly framed black-and-white prints. White carpeting lined the hallway and covered the floors in both the living room and dining area.

Skye wondered how he kept it so clean and thought of her own single-bedroom apartment. In contrast, it was comfortable, but unremarkable. Her color palette ranged from pale blues, to an even paler palette of pastels. The one concession she'd allowed herself was to paint her bedroom a warm yellow. The stark white down-filled comforter and other white accents she'd pulled together made the room appear even larger than it was. She'd done the adjoining bathroom in the opposite color scheme with orange accents, leaving everything else stark white including the towels, rugs and shower curtain. A small bowl of tangerines occupied one corner of the countertop and a vase filled with eucalyptus tied with orange twine sat at the opposite corner. The fruit served a few purposes, reminding Skye each day to take her vitamins, eat plenty of fruits and vegetables and to live a healthful existence. The eucalyptus reminded her to live in the present and to appreciate each day for what it represented—another chance to live life to its fullest.

Three years before, Skye would not have been cognizant of any of these things. It had taken a life-threatening episode, advanced technology and an act of God to deliver her whole and resolved to move forward. One of the first things she'd done was to purchase the condominium she now lived in.

Renovation had taken more than six months. New kitchen cabinets carved from warm maple wood with brass accents lined both walls and the entire kitchen had been painted linen-white. Skye purchased light blue kitchen towels, a set of wooden canisters and decided to paint one wall a vibrant shade of blue.

When Rod saw what she'd done, he hugged her and shook his head. "I knew you had it in you, girl. This is good: Your decorating instincts are alive and well, which I suspected all the time. Now, we can pick out some other stuff whenever you're ready. And you have to allow me to take you to some of my favorite haunts," he added, grinning in triumph.

"Don't get carried away. I still think that a funky look without all this coordinating is the way to go. I just painted the bedroom and the one wall in the kitchen 'cause I was bored," she said, unconvincingly.

Rod looked at her, closed one eye and smiled seductively. "Yeah, and you don't really expect me to believe that, now do you?"

Skye laughed then, knowing she'd never fully convince him of her lack of interest in something he loved passionately.

"Look, can we just change the subject? You'll never admit that I don't have a decorating bone in my body 'cause you want to believe otherwise. And that's fine with me—as long as you don't insist on my shopping at Linens 'n Things every week. How're things going on the broker side of the industry?" she asked quickly.

"You know. It's either feast or famine. I'm still working on getting the sales force to get their act together. They either chase the clients away with some of their tactics during the applications process, or they overload them with too much information. Either way, I find we have about a fifty-fifty pull through ratio. Everybody except Pablo. Now, that guy knows how to market himself and the loan programs."

Rod laughed then and Skye joined him. Images of Pablo, who was tall, thin, handsome and well dressed, were present in both their minds, but for different reasons. Pablo appealed to Rod as the quintessential recruit. Although he knew him to be happily hetero-sexual, if ever there was a change, he wanted to be the first to know.

"I guess you need to identify what it is that Pablo does, bottle it and market it throughout the territory that your company is covering. Sounds like you need that winning formula," Skye added then, wondering if anything like what she suggested had ever been tried.

"If it wasn't so simple, it would be diabolical. You're absolutely right—it just can't be done. Every mortgage person acts from his own strengths and, let's face it, his or her own weaknesses, as well. I don't have to tell you that, though. You've become an expert."

Rod's reference to Skye's success was delivered with pride. In his mind, he'd shown her the path and could take credit for that much, at least. Her continued ability to originate and close a substantial number of loans was totally her own, though.

"Look, I'll always remember that your input made a terrific difference in my ability. I think of you daily whenever I'm faced with anything that offers resistance. I also recognize the personal insights you contributed from the time I entered the industry over two years ago right up to this very moment," Skye said, without a hint of laughter in her demeanor.

Rod watched her, shook his head and then smiled slowly. "Don't even try and play yourself, girl. You were ready from the moment I said go. Your instincts are good, your people skills are excellent and you took to the industry's standards including programs, products, etc., like a duck to a pond. You're a born mortgage professional. My only claim to fame is that I discovered you," he added, grinning in triumph. "A distinct coup was staged the first day you walked through the door."

Skye laughed and put an arm around him in a leisurely hug. His summation of her talent, her abilities and her knowledge of the industry made her feel accepted and accomplished. After what she'd gone through in the past few years, the feeling was a welcome one.

Now, as Skye headed for the building, she wondered just what Nita and Branch had up their sleeves. She walked in, checked her messages, then made an appointment for a wash and blow dry. The weekend seemed far away, but a girl could never go wrong with a clean head of hair.

Chapter 2

Terrance Marshall placed the phone into the cradle and waited. It took two minutes for it to ring again. He hesitated for another twenty seconds, his patience growing shorter by the moment. Contrary to his wishes, the phone continued to ring. Picking it up slowly, he spoke into the receiver quickly.

"Hello…" There was silence on the other end and his temper flared.

"If you're not going to speak, you should stop wasting both your time and mine," he said sternly, then placed the receiver into the cradle. He walked out of the room hoping to avoid what he knew would be a senseless exchange.

"Women…" he muttered under his breath. His instincts told him that his caller had to be Brianna. Who else would call him repeatedly, refuse to speak to him and hang up without saying a single word. He knew she was angry, and perhaps, rightfully so, but her anger was a moot point. Their marriage was over.

They'd tried their best to avoid divorce, but it hadn't worked. In the scheme of things, too much time had lapsed as he'd avoided giving her honest answers to the questions she posed on a daily basis. There really were no clear-cut answers.

Besides, he'd learned long ago that honesty was over-rated. They'd only been married for four years but in that time, they'd created something of beauty. Jacqueline. If it were not for their daughter, he'd have split long ago.

Terrance took off his tie, turned on the television and tried to figure out what he should do for dinner. Sorting through the many takeout menus he kept in a kitchen drawer, he decided to order in. He made the call, hung up and it rang immediately. "Here we go again," he muttered under his breath.

Unable to stop himself, he cursed under his breath and barked into the receiver. "Yeah, what is it now?"

On the other end, Branch laughed, then said, "Man, didn't your mama teach you to answer a phone any better than that?"

Terrance snorted, then breathed a sigh of relief. "Actually, you'd better be glad you said something 'cause my next comment would have been a solid insult. Someone's been playing phone games since I walked through the door. I'm hungry and not in the mood for nonsense," he added, then chuckled. "Guess you caught me at a bad time. What's up, dude?"

"Not a thing. Just calling to save your tired life is all."

"Now, what's that supposed to mean?"

"Well, you were the one who vowed to make amends for having missed the wedding. My bride has almost forgiven you, but you'll have to do a lot more than apologize before you can enter my good graces again. Thought I'd let you know that next weekend is your redemption, buddy."

"Do you want to explain yourself properly or do I have to revert to King's English just to get you to spell it out for me?" Terrance knew his buddy was giving him a hard time and he also knew that no matter what, he'd end up on the short end of the stick. Branch usually had a way of making good on any promise he'd made and Terrance was sure this would be no exception.

"Okay, here it is, dude. Nita has invited all of the members of the wedding party for a fun-filled weekend here in Fort Lauderdale. The house can accommodate all of you, so it's not a problem. Most are coming in on Friday evening, but some can't get here until Saturday morning. No matter what, the party is kicking off Saturday evening. Be here or be square," he said.

"Party, huh? And just what's the party celebrating, may I ask?"

"Sure, you may ask, but I really am not in a position to answer. You'd have to ask Nita and she's not really speaking to you right now. Her stance is the same as mine—be here or be square. Now, before you start making excuses, let me tell you that you missed a jamming party with our nuptials being the significant excuse for folks to act up. I don't think this event will be any less intense, just significantly less formal," Branch said, laughter in his voice.

"I see. It doesn't sound like something I'd wish on

my worst enemy but you may have caught me at a time of weakness. Okay, I'm in. I think I could use the getaway." They talked for another five minutes, exchanged the pertinent information and then hung up.

Terrance's statement, though brief, told Branch more than Terrance realized. In college, Terrance had always gotten the girl, dropped the girl, then sung a song of woe for the next week before hooking up with the next honey in line. Then, in his sophomore year, he'd met Zoie.

Sophomore year at Temple University had been tough. Declaring a major, keeping your grades above the basement level and establishing your coolness ratio were daunting tasks. Both Terrance and Branch had been dedicated to the cause. Avoiding the unwritten rules of college life was definitely a major part of the deal with the number one rule being no dating of freshmen.

Enter, Zoie. Temple's freshmen class had a number of delectable entries but Zoie Anderson was noticed almost immediately. Tall, thin and shapely, sure of herself and extremely intelligent, Zoie exuded sensuality. When she walked into a room, heads turned. When she spoke out in class, students listened. And when she moved off campus, got an apartment with two other freshmen and it became part of the campus knowledge, it also became the stuff of which Temple University legends were made.

The two met on a rainy night at a noisy off-campus party that neither one really was enjoying. They left together and became instantly inseparable. In the next months, they were seen on campus together, off campus together, and if one was spotted without the other, the next question asked was, "Where is your copilot?" That lasted for the next two years. It seemed that Terrance had been taken off the available list by a freshman. There wasn't anything anybody could do about it. Not even him.

He wasn't able to explain it, couldn't seem to stop it and was powerless to change her influence on him. She commanded his attention, his concentration and most of all, his loyalty. It was a different kind of existence for him coming from a family which had been functionally inadequate. Terrance was unaccustomed to having to give answers on his whereabouts from the time he'd turned twelve. No one ever thought to ask, "Where are you going and how long will you be gone?"

Unbeknownst to him, that information had suddenly become common fodder for a daily planner which Zoie kept in her locked duffel bag. By the time Terrance realized he'd become the pet rock of a freshman zookeeper, it was too late. Precedents had already been set, limitations already established. Oddly, it felt right.

It was fine for a while. Actually, it was lovely for a long time with quiet walks in the park, movies when they could afford it and lovemaking at any time the notion hit them. That is, until the day when the blinders were lifted after he decided to try having an in-depth conversation with a graduate student about the coming election of a new city council leader. Zoie walked in on them sitting at a conference table in study hall and had a midday meltdown. The fact that the girl was an unknown entity, a sophisticated upperclassman killed the deal—at least for Zoie. She assumed, correctly, that an upperclassman would possess the ability to outrank, outclass and outmaneuver her.

Terrance was still under the misguided impression

that he could handle things, so the young couple continued to see each other even after the initial crack in the
relationship's exterior. Originally enrolled as a science
major, Terrance realized his real passion was medicine
at around the same time as Zoie's freak-out. He switched
majors but tried, unsuccessfully, to remain consistent
with his dating partner.

Six months later when Zoie saw him with the same
female student as before, she showed up at his dorm
room armed with a can of spray paint, an armful of
flyers and proceeded to paint her way into Temple University history.

She spray painted obscenities, accusations about his
masculinity and several badly spelled expletives all
across the campus, concentrating her efforts at Xenon
Hall where he shared a room with an economics major
from Buffalo.

Then she proceeded to cross the campus from one
end to the other stapling posters to each tree or any
other standing element which would allow punctures.
She also covered many of the existing billboards. The
flyers contained a photo of Terrance with the word
"PLAYER" sprawled across the front and a huge red
line through his picture.

Needless to say, the incident curtailed his dating
efforts for the remainder of his tenure at the school. His
name had become part of the public consciousness on
Temple University's main campus. Ironically, Zoie's
legacy included being called up on charges by the
school's administration and a psychiatric evaluation.
She quietly left Temple soon after and returned to Pitts-
burgh, her hometown.

Now, looking back on it, he wondered if he hadn't had that experience, if things would have turned out differently.

After being dateless for a full year, he'd met Brianna. Determined to take his time getting to know her, it dawned on him pretty quickly that they had more in common than not. The fact that he'd never noticed her, although she was in his graduating class, stunned him. That she also came from the Caribbean pleased him, although he'd always wondered what Trinidad had on his home, Paradise Island.

Aside from being several times the size of the Bahamas and reportedly one of the wealthiest islands in the Caribbean, Trinidad's existence had never posed any real interest for him. Suddenly, he found it important to know as much as he could.

Small, petite with coal-black hair, Brianna was pretty with an added touch of exotic flair. She also possessed both the talent and brains to become a top-notch M.D. Terrance was immediately struck by the reality that she was different from anyone he'd ever met before. Although she studied a great deal and partied very little, she still managed to be more fun than many of the party animals he knew. Something about her inspired confidence, a quality he found refreshing. Ironically, on their second date, he began calling her Bree without knowing her entire family did, too.

They were married one year after graduation. Brianna passed the examinations necessary to become a registered nurse in the Bahamas and they set up housekeeping there. Around the same time, Terrance finished up his premed courses and entered into an internship

with Nassau Medical Center, a state-of-the-art hospital
which had only been built three years before. They were
owned in part by a medical conglomerate located in the
United Kingdom.

They'd discussed Brianna's change of heart about becoming a doctor many times. Terrance did his best to
convince her that it was still possible, but she no longer
felt it was necessary.

"One doctor in the house is enough. I'll continue in
nursing. It's fine," she'd said.

The marriage was solid for the first year and a half.
Then all hell broke loose. It started with small things,
then mushroomed as each month passed. Brianna complained incessantly about every birth-control product on
the market. Everything from bloating, headaches, diz-
ziness and real or imagined weight gain plagued her.

Terrance attributed much of the complaints to her not
wanting to take the Pill; hence he concluded she wanted
to be pregnant. For some unfathomable reason, the
thought of becoming a father bothered him. And the
thought of Brianna becoming pregnant terrified him.

One Sunday afternoon, as Terrance polished his
silver-gray BMW 535, Brianna walked outside, came
around to him and put her arm around his waistline. Not
one to be prone to intimate gestures in public, Terrance
put down the cloth he was using, looked at her briefly
and asked, "What gives?" He had already come to the
realization that any uncharacteristic gesture from her
usually meant that something was up.

"I think you might want to sit down for this," she said
softly, then took his hand and led him into the small house
they'd leased for the past two years. As they both sat down

on the dark green sofa which filled the den, she'd looked at him quickly then whispered, "I think I'm pregnant."

Silence reigned supreme for the next moment as Terrance remained speechless.

"Well, say something," she offered.

"I'm not sure I understand. You said you think. When will you know?" he asked quickly, not wanting to react before there was certainty.

"Well, I'm late and I took one of those home tests a little while ago. According to the test, I'm pregnant," she ended, her face showing a mixture of emotions.

Terrance held his breath, took one of her hands into his and said slowly, "I thought we agreed we would wait."

"I know but I can't help it if it happened. I didn't see you saying anything at the time it was occurring, so don't start now," she snapped, then jumped up and ran into the bedroom.

Terrance continued to sit in the same spot for the next twenty minutes, unable to go to her. A baby would change things, that much he was certain of. They'd barely made a dent in the mountain of bills they'd each brought to the marital table, not to mention the student loans they each carried. His concern was strictly practical although he also wondered if he possessed the parenting skills necessary to produce a well-rounded human being. As the sun went down, that thought plagued him as he washed, waxed and buffed both of their vehicles. He focused on the task at hand, not allowing his mind to acknowledge any of the thoughts which threatened to break through.

By the time he came back inside, Brianna had dinner on the table and seemed to have also put the exchange

behind her. Two days later, the test results were confirmed by her physician. A baby was on the way.

Meanwhile, Terrance avoided the discussion,
avoided his wife and did his best to ignore the obvious.
Although Brianna hadn't brought the subject up again,
he recognized that the longer it took for them to hash
out their differences, the more entrenched she would be
when the time finally arrived. And so, from the start, he
knew that his stance was a moot point.

Brianna went through the nine months of pregnancy
without incident, but the couple had already suffered a
crushing blow. They spoke rarely and discussed things
pertinent to the baby only when necessary. The irony of
it was that once Brianna gave birth to their daughter, Jacqueline, the feud was inexplicably over.

As soon as he held his daughter in his arms for the
first time, Terrance realized he had never known uncon-
ditional love. What he felt for the bundle within his
arms was and would probably always be unsurpassed
by anything he felt for anyone else on the planet.

Months passed, but Brianna never forgave him. And
he never forgave himself for second-guessing Jacquline's
entry into the world.

The doorbell rang then, breaking Terrance's thought
pattern. A dinner of brown stewed chicken, steamed
vegetables and salad was delivered from a local restaurant he'd called. Terrance ate slowly while watching
the evening news. His mind was still on the conversation with Branch.

He also wrote out a check for the monthly child
support, then went online to make a round-trip airline
reservation to Fort Lauderdale.

Branch's statement stayed with him and he wondered when, if ever, he'd be done with playing catch-up to all the people he owed some form of consideration to. He'd been alone for the past months, but felt good about it. Twice monthly weekend visits with his daughter kept him going and for that much, he was grateful. He'd always wondered why couples fought so bitterly for child custody when they could more easily share the burdens and joys. It simply made sense to him.

With that thought, Terrance picked up the phone and dialed. Brianna answered on the second ring and he took a deep breath before speaking.

"Hi—it's me."

"Hello, Terrance—Jacqueline is asleep already," she responded, shortly.

"Have I gotten you at a bad time?" He wanted to ask why she sounded so winded, then caught himself. It was no longer his business what she did, when she did it and with whom. So he just waited for her to respond to his question as asked.

"I was exercising. Listen, can you call back tomorrow night, but before eight o'clock? I try to get her into bed by then or otherwise, it's a fight to get her up in the morning."

"Yeah, I know she's not a morning kid, at least not yet," he said, wanting to lighten the conversation. What he really wanted to do was to talk to her, but he sensed she was not willing to engage in that kind of exchange, so he continued to hold the phone in his hand, wondering why on earth he was feeling so melancholy.

"I don't know that she'll ever be. Kids just need more sleep. Anyway, I'll let her know that you called. She gets excited whenever your name is mentioned."

Terrance smiled then and relaxed a little. "Does she? So, she's still Daddy's little girl, hmm?" He couldn't help himself. The thought of Jacqueline's face when she smiled almost broke his heart, but he'd already done his crying, already had his meltdown and now was not the time to revisit that place.

"Absolutely, but isn't that always the way? Mommy gets to do all the hard work and Daddy gets all the glory. It's a story that's as old as time," Brianna ended, an edge of bitterness creeping into her voice.

Terrance figured it was time to end the conversation then, knowing he was in no mood to hear charges of recriminations or to have a guilt trip laid at his feet.

"Well, I'll keep the eight o'clock slot in mind and be sure to call before then from now on. You take care of yourself, Bree," he added, wondering why she'd hung up on him before.

"You, too. And I will remember to tell her that you called," she added. She wanted to say more but something stopped her.

They both hung up then, aware that there were things left unsaid, but grateful that they had been able to leave it that way.

Terrance showered, turned the radio to his favorite jazz station, killed the lights and got into bed. Just before he closed his eyes, the thought of Jacqueline's smile entered his mind.

Chapter 3

Days later, the weather forecast for the entire peninsula of Florida was ominous. On Thursday, Tropical Storm Charley was off the shore of Florida and it looked like it could be upgraded to a category four storm.

After carefully deliberating the wisdom of traveling under such conditions, Skye was en route to Atlanta's Hartsfield Airport. In the end, it was still out at sea and she decided to take the chance that it wouldn't hit. She'd wrapped up all the loose ends on several loan applications she'd been working on, changed her voice mail, notified her assistant of any possible emergency contingencies and left detailed instructions on how to handle each scenario. She was also reachable by both cell phone and BlackBerry. Current technology left nothing to chance.

Skye breathed a sigh of relief as the cab stopped at the central terminal building of the sprawling airport. All during the ride, she'd listened as the driver's radio blasted an ominous weather forecast.

The cabbie shook his head, his corduroy shirt seeming to suggest that milder temperatures were just around the corner. Skye wondered if he realized it was sixty degrees.

"Storms like this one seem to keep happening this year," he said, his voice filled with something close to awe and curiosity. Even though he never took his eyes from the road, Skye could still hear the mixed emotions coming from the driver's statements. It was apparent by his voice that he, too, was less than thrilled about the current forecast.

"Yeah, this is the third time we've been under a tropical storm watch in less than two months. Fort Lauderdale hasn't been hit hard but I'm still worried. Do you think the flight schedules will be affected?" she asked quickly. She'd thought of canceling the trip, then realized that weather prediction was still an uneven science. There was a chance that the storm would never reach the United States, much less Florida.

"You'll see in a minute. If you want me to wait, I will," he added, turning suddenly to reveal a lopsided grin.

Skye thanked him and reached into her wallet for the fare. She knew that he was being considerate in his offer.

"I'd appreciate that. Thanks."

"No problem."

The departures level of the airport was bustling with travelers being dropped off, bags being checked and traffic tied up by all the comings and goings. Skye was able to check her bags in at curbside, confirm that the flight was slated on time and hurry back to the cab, leaving a healthy tip. She breathed a sigh of relief as she watched him pull off, knowing that the trip could have been cancelled or possibly delayed by the weather front which threatened the southeast corridor of the country, but instead, she'd been spared—thus far.

Skye fell asleep as the flight became airborne and did not wake until the captain announced the plane's final descent into the Fort Lauderdale airport.

Nita waited at the curbside as Skye exited the airport. Waving frantically, she laughed as her best friend approached, one single piece of luggage in tow.

"Girl, what took you so long?"

"When I called you from the cell phone, I hadn't gotten down to the baggage carousel yet. Little did I know it would take another fifteen minutes for them to unload the plane and for the luggage to circulate," she added, hugging Nita fiercely.

"Well, let me see what you've got going on, girl," Nita laughed. She stepped away from Skye, did an exaggerated once-over and then smiled approvingly.

"Yep—you've still got it together alright. That's what I figured. You're probably scaring the men off at this point," she said as they both got into Nita's four-year-old Honda Accord.

"Now, you need to stop. You don't look half-bad yourself," she returned, giving her friend a long, exaggerated stare that took in her sleek ponytail, skin-revealing halter top and cropped white pants. Red lizard sandals picked up the stripes of the halter top and Skye remembered that they both shared a love of fashion.

"Look, girl. You know there are lots of tired men on the planet—at least the last time I checked," Skye continued. "If a woman looks good, has her stuff together and knows how to earn a living equals a scary thing, then so be it. I'm tired of making excuses for people," she added, then sat back into the seat and fastened the seat belt.

Nita watched her, began to laugh, caught herself, then started the car and pulled out into the traffic.

"Girl, you're right, but you've also got to admit that we're living in a different age. Men are still a hot commodity. Why do you think most women want one? The average brotha doesn't know how to respond to a serious, responsible female or to a relationship that's going to make them accountable."

"Point made. So, what was your secret? How did you and Branch make it through the foolishness that seems to accompany dating?"

Anita thought for a moment but continued to keep her eyes on the roadway. As she approached the airport exit signs, she turned to Skye with a perplexed look on her pretty face.

"Honestly, hon, I don't really know. I just know that we were both not trying to play any games. Branch took one look at me behind the library's information counter and that was it. He asked me out and I said no. But he kept coming back for the next two weeks and each time he'd ask me out again. Finally, I gave in. He had no idea I was set to graduate with honors from the program I was enrolled in, hadn't a clue that in six months I would be an X-ray technician, but he pursued me anyway. I just think it was fate. We laugh about it all the time," she said, now turning to look at Skye with a grin on her face. "Nova Southeast University gave me just what I needed," she added proudly.

"Wow, look at you. You're still beaming and the honeymoon was more than two months ago. I'm happy for you, Nita. I really am." Skye realized with that statement that she was feeling a little sorry for herself. She also knew it was not the right time for that kind of reflection. The weekend was to be a tribute to the happy couple, a revisiting of the day they'd joined hands and hearts. It was inappropriate to point out how miserable she'd become, or how disappointing the quest for a solid love life really was.

"The storm has me a little concerned, though. What's the latest weather forecast?" Skye's face showed genuine concern and Nita realized she'd probably given the storm a lot of thought.

"Honestly, we're keeping watch on it and hoping it will either lose strength or move in a different direction. Look, just relax and enjoy yourself this weekend. Branch has some fun things planned and the house will be overrun with some great people, including many of those who were at the wedding and some who were not. Don't worry, we should be fine."

"Okay—it's just that lately, these storms are so unpredictable. I'll try my best to take your advice—at least we're all in the company of good friends." Skye found herself reassuring both herself as well as Nita.

"You know, sometimes I worry about you, thinking that your job takes too much energy and concentration. You need something you can forget about as soon as you walk through the door at night. That, and a good man to take your mind off the day's frustrations would put you in the right frame of mind," she added, a mischievous grin on her face.

"Yeah, well, when you find the two-legged creature that can fill that bill, please let me know. I haven't been on a date in more than three months, by choice," Skye commented, shaking her head.

Nita and Skye both broke into laughter then, knowing they probably sounded like two frustrated dilettantes.

"Remember when we used to actually screen guys before our dates? We never let them know if we liked them, and didn't even care if they really liked us or not. All we were interested in at that time was dinner, a movie and possibly a good-night kiss. Anything more was scandalous. Then, about sophomore year, things changed. That's when all hell broke loose," Anita laughed.

"You're right. But tell me more about who will be there this weekend. I'm trying to live in the present, not dwell on the past. You said some interesting things back there about the other folks you guys invited. Anyone I don't know? Anyone I should be trying to get to know?" There would not be a dull moment during the coming weekend, that much she was sure of.

"Girl, you haven't changed one bit. Sure, there'll be one or two in attendance that you've probably missed meeting somehow, but don't worry. Everyone we invited this weekend is either one of Branch's tightest posse, or an old homey of mine you somehow never got the opportunity to meet. Either way, they're all good people. Relax."

Skye watched her best friend as she operated the car expertly through the crowded streets of Fort Lauderdale and marveled at the change in Nita's personality. She was still Nita, only calmer, more sure of herself. Her tactfully delivered statement had included just the right touch of assertiveness and caring.

Watching her, Skye wondered if marriage had a similar effect on all people. Then she wondered if she'd ever get the opportunity to find out.

Anita pulled into the driveway of the sprawling ranch home just as the front door was opening. Branch walked out, turned around and continued talking with two other guys who were following him. Skye recognized Lorenzo, Branch's younger brother, immediately. He'd matured since the last time she'd seen him and she wondered if the mustache he'd grown had anything to do with the change in his appearance. Although he was just graduating from college, he was definitely fine and Skye watched him as he walked toward the car, a huge grin on his face. Behind him walked another guy, obviously one of Branch's friends, whom Skye had never met.

Lorenzo reached her, engaged her in a bear hug and Skye laughed as she begged to be set free.

"Man, you don't know your own strength. And what's that growing above your lip?"

"Hey, you know what this is, so don't even try it. Damn, girl, you are looking good. If I didn't know you were an older woman, I'd hit on you myself," he said, laughing as he continued to embrace her. Meanwhile, the stranger looked on—no smile on his face, his eyes hidden by dark shades. He'd displayed a decidedly nonchalant stance and Skye wondered who he was.

Anita began to unload the car as Branch walked up, hugged Skye and helped her with the shopping bags she had in the car when she had picked up Skye from the airport. Branch gave Skye a quick once-over, hung his arm around his bride and smiled. "You still look exactly like all the photos Nita has of you from college. You haven't changed at all," he added.

Skye wasn't sure if his statement was a compliment or simply an off-the-cuff remark, but decided it would be best to think positively.

"Thanks, Branch. I'm trying to work on my professional image but it's so much easier to run around in jeans and loafers pretending to still be a collegiate," she responded.

Branch grinned and shook his head. "You don't have to pretend. You're still as cute as you were in college. Hey, meet my right-hand man, Terrance." Branch picked up some bags and headed toward the house, leaving Skye and Terrance in the midst of a quick introduction. Meanwhile, Lorenzo grabbed the rest of the bags and prepared to head toward the house, but stopped and looked back at Skye. She had met him at Nita's wedding months before and he had developed something of a crush on her, although he acknowledged that she was totally out of his league.

At the moment, Skye's senses were totally engaged with the man whom Branch had introduced as his right-hand man.

He appeared to be no-nonsense in character. His clothing suggested careful consideration, lots of money spent on the finest of fabrics and something else—self-confidence. A tobacco colored raw silk shirt topped off tan slacks. He hadn't bothered to wear a belt, but his loafers were expensive, his expression guarded.

Terrance stepped forward, held out his hand and Skye took it with a businesslike grasp. He held it a few seconds longer than was necessary, then let it go with a smile. The warmth that transmitted was felt by both.

"Terrance Marshall," he said, and though he never removed his sunglasses, Skye could feel his gaze on her face. It unnerved her because she realized she wanted to see his expression.

"Well, I'm glad we all made it this time," Lorenzo said, then turned and walked back toward the house.

"Yeah, me, too. I mean, I haven't seen you for a while so I'll catch up with you later," Terrance called out to him. He then turned his attention to the lovely creature standing next to him as she watched him with an unreadable expression. He could not ignore the signals she was unconsciously sending. The way she stood, the way she avoided making eye contact, even the fact that she remained silent although he was aware of her scrutiny, told him that she felt the same radar impulses he was getting.

Terrance suddenly grabbed the one suitcase left in the car's trunk and turned to her. "Is this all you have?" His short-sleeved shirt revealed arms that were well muscled and sinewy. He was tall, maybe six feet two inches and built like an athlete. Skye took in his physique, his unspoken words and his pointed stare without comment. She knew trouble when she was in the midst of it.

"Yes. Thanks, but you don't have to do that. I can roll it," she offered.

"No, it's okay. I want to. It'll give me more time to get to know you. I'm sorry I didn't get to meet you at the wedding. My daughter came down with something and her fever spiked. I hated not to be there for Branch, but I just couldn't leave town with her fever that high. It was a scary few days," he added quickly.

"Oh, I had heard about that. Nita's been talking about you for a long time now."

She waited for him to respond, then thought maybe she'd said too much.

"Yeah, we've been buddies since college. Nita probably also told you that I'm the reason for his scandalous bachelor days, too," he said with a questioning stare.

Skye ignored the comment. She figured he didn't really expect an answer. Instead, she smiled. "Yes, I do seem to remember a few things, but you know how it goes." She couldn't bring herself to admit that if she'd known he was so fine, her memory would have definitely been sharper. At that moment, Skye planned to revisit the subject with Nita the first chance she got.

They entered the ranch-style house and Skye's focus shifted. Branch and Nita had remodeled extensively in the past months. They'd painted, refinished the floors and modernized the kitchen and bathrooms. The four-thousand-square-foot ranch house was open, airy and contemporary, yet it offered expansive comfort to all who entered its doors.

"Come on in, girl," Nita interrupted. "That sun and heat can get to you if you're not used to it," she added. "Here, let me show you to your room," she said as she directed Terrance and Skye toward the back of the two-story structure.

"Four thousand square feet of casual elegance supported by functionality is what our design consultants describe it as," Nita offered as they passed three bedrooms.

"Wow, that's a lot of space," Skye squealed as she passed the rooms and the adjoining bathrooms which lined the hallway.

"Branch was adamant when we looked for a house

that it should be able to accommodate friends, family, whatever."

"By family, I am assuming you're referring to any children you two have. I know my man was not trying to encourage the onslaught of relatives that a five-bedroom house can summon," Terrance offered, smiling.

"I'll give you one thing—you definitely know my husband very well," Nita laughed.

"You're darned right I do, but that's Husband 101— do not encourage the in-laws to move in," he added.

Skye shook her head, then joined them in laughter. "No matter what or who comes to visit, this house is awesome," she said, still looking around in wonder.

"Yes, it is, and I was just thinking the same thing about you," Terrance suddenly whispered so that only Skye would hear. Nita had walked on toward the fourth bedroom and was chattering on about dinner being served at seven-thirty that evening.

His comment caught Skye off guard. She wasn't sure how—or if—she should respond. She also wasn't at all sure she wanted to. After all, this was a man whom she'd heard stories about from the time her best friend had met her newly acquired husband.

His reputation from his early college days was legendary and it spelled *caution* any way you looked at it. Temple University had been his stomping grounds. She realized that he could have very well kept his old habits intact. Some men never grew up, never relinquished their player cards. In her mind, the pending divorce Nita had mentioned was, in all likelihood, something to which he'd contributed wholeheartedly.

Terrance wheeled Skye's suitcase just inside the

doorway to the bedroom she would occupy and then quickly turned around, holding out his hand once more.

"It's been extremely nice meeting you," he said, clasping it warmly between his two hands for a brief moment, which somehow seemed to last far longer than was necessary.

"You, too. Looks like we're almost roommates," Skye added, nodding toward his room which was just across the hallway.

"Now that would be asking for way too much," he said and walked toward the door. "But a guy can hope," he added, laughing as Skye quickly closed her door. She was trembling as she leaned back against it. She closed her eyes and tried to gather her wits about her. He was only a man. But, *what a man.* His body, his face, his voice, his eyes, his shoulders and his walk all came together in her mind and Skye opened her eyes in an effort to try and regain her composure.

It was the first time she'd seen a room done in shades of red. The walls were red, the café curtains at the window were red and the framed prints lining the walls were all in red themes. The furniture, the bed's comforter and the area rug which sat next to a black leather chair were stark white, lending both contrast and a feeling of extreme space.

Skye's breathing slowed as she composed herself. She vowed to keep herself under better control for the remainder of the weekend, trying to ignore the fact that the object of her undoing was housed less than ten feet away.

She unpacked, brushed her teeth, changed her blouse and wondered if she'd make it through the next forty-eight hours. Then, she bravely made her way toward the huge living room where Nita, Branch and the rest of the weekend's company had already assembled.

Nita's younger sister, Monica, and her current boy-friend, Patterson, were seated on the long sectional sofa looking through the wedding photo album. Lorenzo was pouring drinks, and Branch's cousin, Ellie, also had a separate book of photos she was engrossed in.

Skye walked into the room, was quickly reintroduced to everyone with hugs, kisses and small talk. It took her several seconds to realize that Terrance was nowhere in sight. It took another minute for her to admit her disap-pointment, even if it was only to herself.

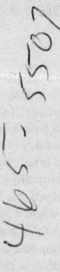

Chapter 4

Terrance looked down at his cell phone, thought about turning it off and realized it was not an option. If anything happened to Jacqueline, if there was any type of emergency, he wanted to be available. The fact that this left him open to the possibility of Brianna's constant monitoring, harassment and other displays of annoying behavior did not escape him. He left the phone on, turned the ringer off and prayed that he would not hear from the one woman in the world who could effectively ruin his day from more than three hundred miles away.

The past eighteen months had been a living hell, ~~ugh~~ he'd remained steadfast in his determination to ~~forward.~~ The two-bedroom condominium he'd ~~signed~~ a contract to purchase was something ~~thought of~~ as a temporary haven. After ~~essentials,~~ establishing a fairly efficient way of doing things and coming to the conclusion that moving again would be too much of a hassle, he realized that he liked the easy access the apartment provided. Located in a newly renovated section of Nassau township where tourists were seldom found, it contained all new appliances, upgrades in the things that mattered and a sweeping view of a small coastal waterway. Many of his evenings were now spent having dinner alone on the tiny veranda just outside his living/dining room as he watched the boats enter and leave the small harbor in his view.

His everyday existence consisted of work, work and more work. Which was why he'd had no qualms or second thoughts when Branch issued the weekend invitation. At the moment, Terrance was doing his best to forget the face and body of the shorty now assigned to the room across the hall from him for the weekend. Still, her smile lingered in his thoughts. Something about her made him want to see her again and he found himself eager to rejoin the group for their first night of reminiscing.

Terrance checked his watch, noted the time and decided it wouldn't hurt to change his shirt and freshen up a bit. Fort Lauderdale sunshine and heat were different from what he was used to experiencing in Nassau. The humidity of the Florida environment took getting used to, even for him. Just as he finished brushing his teeth, his cell phone vibrated. He looked at it, shook his head and reached for it.

"Hello."

"Hi, Terrance. I hope I didn't catch you at a bad time," Brianna said, her breath coming in gasps.

"No, not at all. Is anything wrong?" Terrance's pulse raced suddenly. He spit toothpaste into the sink, as adrenaline surged through his body. In the seconds that followed, he tried to tell himself that the call was probably just an unnecessary interruption, but he also realized that he stood frozen waiting for Brianna to answer his question.

"No, actually I just thought I'd call to give you some good news for a change."

The voice on the other end of the phone suddenly sounded soft, sweetly feminine and decidedly friendly. Warning bells went off in his head and he looked at himself in the mirror. Suddenly, the whole episode seemed funny and he laughed, putting the toothbrush back into its case.

"And what would that be?" His relief was so thorough that he was caught off guard, feeling an immediate sense of relief, which was followed by an abrupt shift to curiosity.

"Oh, it's just that Jacqueline has decided she wants to be just like her daddy and be a doctor. I thought it was the cutest thing. I also thought you'd get a kick out of hearing about it." She laughed deeply, the intimacy of sharing their daughter's dreams and hopes coming through in her voice.

Terrance joined her for a moment, then was brought back to present-day reality when he remembered that this was the same woman whose moods could change on a dime—and usually Terrance was the scapegoat.

The fact that their two-and-a-half-year-old daughter was still unable to speak coherently also made him realize Brianna's statement had to be taken with a grain of salt.

In his mind, this was a woman who alternated between existences, never knowing what she really wanted or what she needed, especially when it came to him and their marriage.

Shortly after Jacqueline's birth, Brianna had insisted that she return to work. They hadn't really needed the money, but in the end, he'd agreed just to keep her from being miserable. As an emergency room nurse, the hours she'd picked up had taken them from simply getting by to doing very nicely. But he'd noticed a change in Brianna's personality immediately and wondered if this was what he'd have to contend with forever. He'd also wondered if her behavior was the result of too much pressure, not enough support or just a lack of maturity. It hadn't taken long for him to get an answer.

Daily complaints about not having enough time to be herself, not enough room to have any space and not enough air to breathe soon became a mantra. Brianna began staying out even when she wasn't scheduled to work and often came in the following morning.

Terrance had attributed it all to stress, both on the job and in her new role as a mother. It wasn't until he realized that they were no longer making love, no longer spending real time together and no longer communicating in any meaningful way that he began to suspect otherwise.

The arguments began including accusations, recriminations, denials and worst of all, threats which very often left him shaking his head in amazement. He'd never realized that she had been unhappy. In his mind, the baby had rounded out any rough edges the marriage had contained. In the arguments Brianna presented, their daughter's birth had only served as a catalyst. Now, in her mind, she felt like her life, her identity and her youth were slipping away.

Terrance was unsure as to Brianna's real motivations but one thing was sure—they would never be able to go on if the current daily tirades continued.

He'd made it clear, stood his ground and waited for Brianna's response. He remembered the evening they'd argued and then Brianna had retired to the bedroom, emerging some twenty minutes later, dressed in a flowery tank top, white shorts and white sandals.

She'd let her hair fall down around her face, curled the ends slightly, and despite their argument earlier, Terrance couldn't help but notice that she was still a beautiful woman. At that moment, though, the fact that his wife was looking decidedly hot in a way that reminded him of college, only angered him.

"Where the hell do you think you're going?" he asked, ready to do battle again to defend his home, his family, his life.

"I'm going out. There's no sense in sticking around here watching you. I already know how you feel about this so save your breath. I'll be back in time for you to leave for work. The baby is asleep." Her words sounded hollow, flat—and they appeared to echo in his head as he watched her saunter over to the door.

"You have got to be kidding. Bree, we just talked about this stuff. You cannot just hang out whenever you choose to. You are a married woman, a wife, a mother—I mean, this is unheard of," he said, his breath coming in short gasps as he struggled to keep his anger under control.

"Look, Terrance. We've already had this discussion. I can do anything I damn well please. I contribute to this household, I keep this place running, I take care of our daughter, I do it all." Her voice raised with each additional chore she listed and in the end, she was almost screaming. Color rose in her cheeks and the pretty that Terrance had assigned to her only moments before, somehow now took on a grotesque quality that made him turn away.

This was his wife, the mother of his child, the woman he'd held in his arms on many nights and made love to. The woman who stood before him now no longer resembled anyone he'd ever loved or would continue to love. She was a stranger, both in emotion and intention.

He realized at that moment that their marriage was disintegrating before his eyes and the realization shook him to his core. The foundation they'd built was crumbling.

"Fine. If you feel the answer to our problems is for you to continue to run the streets each time we have words, go right ahead. I hope you find something out there that will offer you what you already have—but I sincerely doubt it," he ended, his voice filled with emotion.

"I'm not *looking* for anything," she replied curtly, then left the apartment quickly.

Several months later, with the same scene playing out over and over again, including an escalation in arguments over the same unacceptable behavior, they'd agreed to separate.

Terrance was devastated. In his mind, there was no plausible reason their marriage had failed. He attributed it to Brianna's immaturity and his lack of ability to control her.

She'd requested the apartment, the furniture, the car and half their bank accounts. They would share custody of Jacqueline. He'd acquiesced because of one thing—guilt. He felt guilty each time he realized that his daughter had been cheated out of growing up with both her parents in the same home, and that he'd been powerless to change that eventuality.

In the end, Brianna won simply because he hadn't wanted to drag things out any longer. He'd had to start anew, from scratch, on everything. He'd consoled himself with the fact that his daughter would benefit somehow. Seeing and hearing her parents tear one another apart couldn't possibly be healthy or beneficial.

On a more practical note, months later, he still felt disgruntled each time he thought of the furniture they'd purchased together, or items he needed to replace, which he realized he was doing for the second time.

These thoughts and more rambled through his head quickly as he held the phone to his ear, putting one arm into a white button-down shirt, which he quickly rolled the sleeves up on.

"Listen, I just wanted you to know that your daughter is a chip off the old block. Jacqueline may have been born to two parents who were in the midst of a marital meltdown, but the genes are still there."

"I suspect she's a powerful mix of us both. Where is the little princess?"

"Actually, Godmother Grace just picked her up about half an hour ago. They were headed to the mall. I almost went, but decided I could get more mileage out of staying at home and catching up on a few things. I never seem to be able to catch up." Once again, her voice edged him toward compliance, almost as if they were comrades in arms and Terrance wondered what the real reason for her call was. And then, just as if she'd read his mind, she cleared her throat and took a deep breath.

"Listen, Terry, I wanted to talk to you anyway."

The use of the shortened version of his name stopped him cold. In the past, she'd only used that name when she either wanted something badly, or was in the throes of passion. He suspected the former and prepared himself.

"Go ahead," he forced himself to say. It was too late to end the call or to pretend he hadn't time to listen. He sat on the bed, his senses heightened, his mind fully ready to do combat if necessary, or to offer support if called upon.

"Well, I've been doing a lot of thinking lately. I mean, we broke up and it was like a hurricane hit. There were a lot of things said, a lot of very hastily made decisions and most importantly, a lot of extremely painful moments. If I could take any of it back, I would. But that's not what I called you to say."

"Okay—go on."

"Terry, I think we made a mistake. I know it's late, I know we've both said and done some things that are unforgettable. I've been doing a lot of thinking." Her voice trailed off then and Terrance let the breath he'd been holding in out of his lungs in a silent rush. His body was no longer tense, just alert. What he'd suspected had just been confirmed. And he knew in his heart that there was no way he was going back. He also recognized that the next words spoken would make all the difference, so he chose them with extreme care. Brianna was no fool, but neither was he. If she'd come calling with her tail between her legs, he suspected there was an agenda in place.

"Bree, everything you've just said is probably true.

Everything but the last part. I don't think it was a mistake at all. I think we both botched up the relationship and I certainly don't blame you for any of it, 'cause I did my share, too. Truthfully, I just think it wasn't meant to be. Not for the long run anyway." His last words echoed in his head as he counted the seconds, waiting for Brianna's reply.

"Why do you think that it's too late? I mean, is it too late for us because we never had it to begin with, or is it too late because you've already moved on?"

Her questions lay heavily on his heart, her voice having taken on a tone of intimacy and eagerness he'd only heard a few times in their years together. It told him of her seriousness, told him that she had indeed thought it through and, more importantly, told him that his next words could possibly be crucial to both their lives.

Terrance hesitated, gathered his thoughts, then cleared his throat.

"Brianna, I can't tell you that I'm surprised to hear you say that you've thought this out because I have, too. The truth is that I think we did the right thing by initiating the divorce. For many reasons, we just weren't right together. I'm sorry, but that's the way I feel. You'll always be the mother of my daughter, someone I love very dearly and hopefully, a close friend forever, but I don't think it would work."

He ended the sentence and felt an illuminating moment of regret. He also felt tremendous relief at having told the truth. He inwardly wondered if that would buy him points, then realized that no one was really keeping score.

Brianna was silent for a moment, then took a deep

breath. "I'm sorry you feel that way. For the record, I disagree, but then we always did have different answers. I guess that was part of the problem. We also had a different approach, and a hell of a different way at looking at life. I guess that's how we got to where we are," she added, a hint of cynicism in her voice.

Her tone waved a red flag to him and he wondered if she was just having a bad day or truly felt they would do things better if given a second chance.

"I want to thank you, Terrance, for being honest."

He could hear the disappointment in her voice and wondered if he'd ever be able to forgive himself for putting it there. Then, in a moment of clarity, he chastised himself. He hadn't fallen out of love with her—not until she had begun to run the street, stay out all night, and not before she'd made it painfully clear to him that the marriage was no longer a priority for her.

"No problem. Hell, I'm surprised that you picked up the phone to call me. That took guts. You're one unpredictable woman, Brianna."

"Thanks. Sometimes I'm not sure how to separate the present from the past. Our lives are tangled like the branches from a vine, intertwined. Hey, I don't mean to get deep on you but I have given this some degree of thought."

Terrance didn't respond. There was nothing left to say.

Brianna had gone over each and every point to see if there was any one factor which she could use to turn his decisions around. If not now, then perhaps later, was her resolve. It wouldn't be over until she said so. In her mind, that was the final answer, so she switched gears instead.

"Hey, listen, I really wanted to let you know your

daughter is showing definite signs of your personality. That made it a little easier to pick up the phone." Her voice had taken on an edge of pride when she spoke of Jacqueline. In that moment, Terrance recognized that they'd always share the bond of being parents to a terrific kid.

"I'm going to hang up and go on back to my assigned chores for the day. I want to have accomplished something by the time Godmother Grace returns with Jacqueline." Though she did her best to mask it, the stress of having gone through the last few moments was evident in her voice. For his part, Terrance was relieved to be able to put the subject to rest.

"Sure. You go on ahead and handle your business. Give my sweet pumpkin a kiss for me." He sighed as he thought of Jacqueline's tiny face, her deep brown eyes and the dimples she'd inherited from her mother.

"Sure thing," she said.

Terrance said goodbye softly into the phone and ended his call with Brianna.

As he closed his cell phone, he breathed a huge sigh of relief knowing that he'd managed to handle a major hurdle in their relationship. He prayed that going forward, Brianna would be far less inclined to bring up any kind of reconciliation.

For the first time since he'd met with a divorce attorney, Terrance felt capable of handling whatever was coming his way. He finished dressing, put a belt through his pants, slid his feet into a pair of black leather loafers and headed for the living room. He could hear the laughter, smell the dinner which had just been prepared and knew that the evening ahead was most certainly not part of his past. The thought made him smile briefly, though it also made him nervous to think about his future.

Chapter 5

Terrance entered the room and looked around. He recognized the faces of many of those present as longtime friends, but knew that Branch's open-door policy would have gathered folks who were merely acquaintances, too.

Roger, whom they'd both met while still in college, held center stage in one corner. Nita's younger sister, Monica, now all grown up and looking dangerously close to being a heartbreaker, was all ears as the older, more experienced women in the room spun tales of their last heartbreak or some newly sprouted romance.

Terrance gave a perfunctory wave to all, nodded to those who made eye contact and made his way across the oversized family room. Although one wall held a fireplace framed in stone, the afternoon warmth made it extremely unlikely the hearth would be lit any time soon. Fourteen-foot ceilings with a skylight on either side of the fireplace provided light and an ambiance which elicited banter, laughter and a solid exchange of stories fraught with creativity. And the bride and groom beamed. Legitimately in love, they continued to exhibit behavior which confirmed their absolute belief in one another.

Terrance's heart beat heavily in his chest as the conversation he'd just ended seasoned his mood. No one had told him he'd have the regrets he now dealt with every day. No one had warned him that he'd have so many memories. And no one could have predicted with any amount of accuracy that in only four short years, it would become necessary to take the final steps to end his marriage.

Terrance's eyes swept the room uncertainly, timidly, as he unconsciously sought the face of the woman who had garnered his attention earlier. He wanted to get to know Skye better, wanted to find out what made her tick, wanted to know if she was as incredible as she looked. His thoughts were interrupted by a heavy hand pounding on his back which almost made him choke. He turned around quickly, wondering if he'd encountered an enemy in his midst.

"Damn, man, it's good to see you. Remember the time we were all scouring the streets of Nassau searching for a soul mate for the night?" Lorenzo said, laughter in his voice as Terrance turned toward him.

"Yeah, and you were almost jail bait so we decided to postpone the operation and instead, went out dancing. Man, has anybody told you that you're really heavy-handed?" Terrance added as he threw one arm around his best friend's brother in a mock choke hold. The rivalry between the two had been in play since the first day they'd met. Today was no different but for some reason, Terrance felt somewhat awkward. He imagined Skye watching, wondering if she'd think their exchange immature, then figured it didn't matter since she didn't know him anyway.

He still hadn't seen her, but was sure that she was somewhere within the room, was certain that she would perceive the masculine interchange between him and Lorenzo as immature, which immediately made him want to end it.

Lorenzo, on the other hand, had no such qualms about tussling with the man he thought of as his most prominent adversary.

"Man, where the hell have you been for the past couple of years? It sucked that you missed the wedding." He continued without waiting for a response, as Terrance wondered how he'd managed to remain exactly the same for so long.

"You know, I'm surprised that Branch invited you this weekend. But then, you could always talk your way in or out of anything. I know he was disappointed when you didn't show up, that's for sure."

"My daughter was sick, Lorenzo. You know that. And as for Branch not inviting me, you know he couldn't do that—I'm his boy."

Lorenzo nodded in agreement, then hugged Terrance again, confirming the statement. "Oh yeah, I forgot," he mumbled. This was his brother's best friend, his favorite adversary and someone whom he'd always envied.

In actuality, Branch had reached out to Terrance at the last minute, insisted he show up and he'd done as he'd been told. In part, he'd made the trip because he really wanted to be there, but in a small way, he'd come because he did feel guilty about not attending the actual wedding.

Branch was aware of the difficulties he'd faced at the time and that was all that really mattered. He continued to make small talk with Lorenzo, his eyes unconsciously scanning the room.

Suddenly, he caught sight of Skye in one of the far corners laughing and talking with a somewhat quiet couple from Washington, D.C. and he swallowed hard. She sat at one end of a long sofa covered in Haitian cotton, one leg tucked under her. The white camisole top, white shorts and sandals she wore made him think of the wedding they were all there to celebrate for the second time. In his mind, the woman who sat across the room looked suspiciously like an advertisement for a bride in an extremely relaxed setting. Her ponytail and sandals reminded him of a casual dress rehearsal.

With an open magazine resting in her lap, she appeared poised and totally at ease. The two young women engaged in conversation to her right seemed oddly out of sync with the picture of serenity she presented. Anyone else in a similar setting would have appeared distant, aloof, incompatible. Skye simply appeared to be engrossed in the enormity of it all, unwilling to commit herself to any one grouping or sampling of those present. Looking up suddenly, her eyes met his across the room and his throat went dry. He swallowed, then tore his gaze away.

This was crazy. Insane. He'd only met her less than an hour ago. So what if she was beautiful? So what if she was apparently single? It didn't matter, because the ink was not even dry on his divorce papers yet. In his mind, it should be months before he was free to actually pursue another relationship. Emotionally, he was a wreck and he knew it. The thought crossed his mind that this was not to be a relationship, it was merely an attraction, and he immediately relaxed.

Across the room, Skye felt herself warm under Terrance's watchful gaze. He'd been staring at her from the time he'd entered the room. She knew she should have been flattered, but instead felt unnerved. Her reaction did not really make sense, even to her, so she continued to browse the magazine, though the articles were unintelligible. She looked up after a few moments, allowed her eyes to find him, and realized that he was still watching her. They made eye contact and Skye smiled slightly, not wanting to appear unfriendly.

Terrance needed no further reason to end his conversation with Lorenzo and, after clasping him in a quick breakaway embrace, made his way across the room.

"What're you drinking?" Terrance called out as he walked toward her with ease. He waited for an answer, then turned toward the small bar their hosts had so thoughtfully set up. It held a full spectrum of spirits, wines and coolers, all encased in a cart which could be wheeled to another location. The wet bar, adjoined by a sink and mini refrigerator, had also been well stocked with ice, lemon slices, olives and two platters of hors d'oeuvres.

Skye watched his approach and wondered how far the flirtation would go. She vowed to be cordial, but careful. If her instincts were right, Terrance spelled trouble with a capital T.

"Oh, I don't know. How about a wine spritzer?" she asked, wondering how he managed to look so cool, so clean, so calm when her nerves felt on edge just watching him.

"Sure thing—one white wine spritzer coming up. Anyone else want something?" Terrance asked, flashing a broad grin. To the others who were present, exchanging updates on the latest in their daily lives, he appeared his normal friendly self. No one would have suspected the rapid beat of his heart, the determination in his gait or the inner thoughts he repressed.

Skye's eyes did not waiver as he finished pouring, mixing and adding ice to the drinks he mixed. He walked toward her, toasted her glass quickly and said, "To brides everywhere," before he took the seat next to her. The statement was not lost on her and she swallowed deeply, taking in too much of her drink, which caused her to choke.

Skye coughed nervously, covered her mouth, then sipped again. She wanted to look at him but felt it would be too risky, so she continued to sip the drink.

"Are you okay?" he asked, wondering if he'd made the drink too strong. The combination of wine and club soda was not a potent combination, so he figured she had probably swallowed too quickly.

She placed the drink on the coffee table, coughed a little more, then stopped.

Skye decided to look at him directly, figuring if she just faced her fears, they would be easier to overcome. The awkward moment she'd just gotten though made her feel as if they shared something and she wondered if she was simply looking for a reason to bond with the man seated beside her. She lifted her eyes to his then, ready to face whatever challenge he offered.

It was a mistake. Her stomach lurched as she realized she wanted to touch his mustache, wanted to run her fingers across the broad planes of his chest, wanted to feel his lips against her own. She looked around her and was grateful that no one could possibly have noticed the inner turmoil she was experiencing. They were all engaged in friendly banter and the exchange of wedding day stories. It felt as if a cocoon of sorts had been woven around the two of them only, binding them together and closing out the world.

"Cat got your tongue?" Terrance asked, stretching long legs out before him. The pants he wore clung to his muscular thighs as if by design and Skye tore her eyes away reluctantly. Picking up her glass and bringing it up to her lips, she drained it quickly. She reached forward to put it on the coffee table again, then turned to him boldly.

"I'm from the school of minimalism. I don't believe in doing anything idly and I especially don't believe in chatter," she replied with a slight toss of her head.

Terrance noticed the way her ponytail moved with the action and smiled. The defiant gesture was a surprise to him, but it registered that he'd no doubt just been issued a challenge.

"What's the formality for? I just want to get to know you better."

"Really? What for? Odds are we'll never even see each other again. We live hundreds of miles from one another."

"Hey, it doesn't really matter where you live. Anywhere in the United States is just a hop, skip and a plane ride away from the Bahamas. I've got plenty of frequent flyer miles."

"Really?" She wanted to say more, but did not feel comfortable encouraging the line of conversation, so she stopped herself.

"Yeah, and a two- or three-hour plane ride is just long enough for me to get a good nap, regain my composure and regain my strength," he added, the implied meaning coming through instantly and with crystal clarity.

His eyes flashed in an unspoken conspiracy and Skye's mind raced. When had he begun to flirt so openly with her? She wondered, for a quick moment, if she should get up and leave the area, then told herself they were both adults.

"I think you probably have overestimated your abilities," she deadpanned. A moment of silence ensued and Skye wondered if she'd hit a sore spot. To try and soften her last statement, she turned to him casually, put on her best smile and tried to reestablish civility.

"So, what exactly do you do? Obviously you fly often," she found herself saying, though she wanted to kick herself for asking something she already knew the answer to. Nita had mentioned he was a doctor in one of her recent stories about him.

"Yeah, actually I visit the States quite often. I also go back and forth to the Bahamas where my home is and sometimes abroad, to England. As a doctor I travel a lot," he ended.

Terrance realized as he spoke that for some unknown reason, his body felt tense, almost as if he'd been on guard the entire time. They'd only been talking, laughing and sharing a wine spritzer, but he felt the effects as plainly as if they'd engaged in a battle of some sorts.

Now, with Skye's glass empty, he realized he didn't want her to drink anymore. He wanted to get to know her without the benefit of inebriation, without the assistance of anything or anyone. He also realized that if he ever did get to try and seduce her, he wanted them both lucid so that they would remember each and every detail, down to the most minute aspect. He recognized all of this in a split second, then excused himself and headed toward the kitchen. He wanted to end their interaction before anything negative could enter it, before he could spoil it in any way and before she could come to the conclusion that she no longer wanted to share his company.

Skye watched him walk away and smiled. "Punk," she whispered under her breath.

Branch and Nita were both in the huge kitchen, each consumed with instructing their young kitchen helper, a teenager from the neighborhood. Though he had a decided and demonstrated knack for the preparation of simple, functional foods, it wasn't easy to get him to do so in a timely fashion. Nina had purchased more food than would be necessary even if they were under a two-week siege.

The grill held several tilapia fillets, salmon steaks and at least two pounds of jumbo shrimp. On the other side, steak kabobs and delicately seasoned chicken breasts were also slowly cooking. Side dishes included potato salad, green beans almondine, and a salad of mixed greens tossed with lemon juice, garlic, extra-virgin olive oil and red onion cut into thin slices.

Terrance, who hadn't eaten since morning, felt his stomach churn as he looked over the enticing party fare. "Damn, man, you sure know how to throw a dinner party."

"Hey, don't give me all the credit. Nita put her heart and soul into this gathering. Everything from the house being meticulously maintained, to the shrimp cocktail, is all her doing. Nita is on the money when it comes to handling this stuff. And that's only one of the reasons I married this woman," he added, throwing one arm possessively around her shoulders, drawing her close to him. He kissed her on the cheek, looked her in the eye and whispered, "I love you."

Terrance watched the interplay between the two and thought of the conversation he and Brianna had just had. He had vowed to move forward with his life, hoping that she would do the same, but now knew that regret would probably accompany them both for years to come. He didn't feel the need to revisit the marriage as she'd suggested. There was no compelling reason for them to try and rekindle their relationship except Jacqueline and, in his mind, she'd probably fare better with them being apart. He'd never believed the old adage of children growing up in a two-parent home; not if neither of the parties truly wanted to be there.

He wondered if Skye would understand his thinking, then realized that it didn't matter. His burdens were his own. He vowed to get through the weekend without embarrassing himself but also wanted to do so without annoying any of the other guests.

In an effort to maintain that stance for the remainder of the evening, he kept his distance from Skye, doing everything in his power to remain outside her presence. It was all for naught because it only made him more acutely aware of her existence.

Somewhere around midnight, Terrance switched to

martinis. He drank too much, laughed too loudly, and went to bed at two o'clock in the morning wondering how he'd make it through the remainder of the weekend.

Skye slept like a baby, dreaming about airplanes, blue skies and crystal clear water.

Awakening at her usual hour of 6:30 a.m., she put on orange running shorts, a white tank top and sneakers. Adjusting her earphones on her MP3 player, she hesitated, then put her cell phone into her pocket before she left the house. There were no signs that anyone else had arisen. The day was overcast, but it seemed as if it wouldn't rain for several hours.

Thoughts of her job, her new condo and last night's encounter rambled through her mind as she headed north on University Boulevard. She always did her best thinking as she covered the two miles she ran each morning. In her mind, today would be no different except for the route.

The busy boulevard hadn't begun to be impregnated by its usual heavy traffic patterns early on a Saturday morning. Most of Fort Lauderdale's residents were still asleep, others were still indoors, glad to put the former week solidly to bed.

After jogging for a few blocks, Skye crossed a large intersection, being careful to watch for any oncoming vehicles or turning cars. The curb was just in front of her and she made the mental calculation to step up higher to accommodate it. As she did so, her ankle twisted sharply, causing her to momentarily lose her balance. The pavement seemed to come up to meet her, and she braced her fall with her left hand. Her knee took the weight with the fall knocking the wind out of her diaphragm.

She came to a heap just outside the crosswalk, wondering if she'd broken a bone or anything else. Her ankle throbbed, her wrist hurt but her pride was even more injured. Looking around quickly, she realized no one had witnessed the fall and was grateful.

Willing herself to her feet, Skye realized she'd probably sprained the ankle as she made several attempts to put weight on it. The quarter mile she'd already run made it impossible for her to hobble back the same distance without difficulty.

Suddenly, she remembered she'd put her cell phone into the tiny pocket of the shorts. She reluctantly pulled it out. Lowering herself to a sitting position at the curbside, she dialed Nita's number.

After two rings, Branch growled into the phone. "Yeah."

Skye knew she'd probably never live it down but she had no choice. "Branch, I hate to wake you, but I need some help."

"Skye? What's the matter?" Obvious confusion could be heard in his voice and she wondered if anyone at all realized she'd left the house.

"Branch, I went jogging like I do every morning, only I tripped and fell."

"What? Why didn't you tell someone you were going out? Where are you?" he asked.

"I'm at the intersection of University and SW Sixth Street. I hate to ask, but could you come and get me with the car? I don't think my ankle can support my weight right now," she ended, her voice suddenly cracking.

"Yeah, sure. Don't move. Stay right there. I'm on my way," he said as he placed the phone into its cradle.

Nita turned over, flung an arm over his pillow and snuggled more deeply into the bedcovers. Branch watched her for a moment, thought of waking her, then walked toward his closet. He pulled on a pair of jeans, threw on the shirt he'd worn the night before and left the bedroom, closing the door quietly behind him so as not to awaken his wife. She deserved to rest after playing hostess until two a.m.

He passed the kitchen, thought he heard a sound and looked into it. Terrance was standing over the sink, a glass of juice in one hand, bottle of Motrin in the other, looking very much like a train wreck.

"Damn, man. What happened to you?"

"Had a rough night, my man. What the hell are you doing up so early, dressed and looking as if you're sneaking out?" Terrance's questions were issued with a degree of real pain. Every effort he made to move his lips was rewarded with a quiver somewhere in his head and the Motrin he'd just swallowed had not yet begun to do its work.

"Dude, take a ride with me. One of our guests has had an accident and I'm the resident EMT." It took a moment for the statement to register, then Terrance put the glass down.

"Sure, I'll take the ride. Who the hell is dumb enough to be out this early in the morning though? Wait, don't answer. Probably Lorenzo on his way to a beer run or some other self-serving errand," he added as they walked toward Branch's Escalade. The oversized vehicle looked formidable in the early-morning light, its black exterior adding class and elegance to a sports utility vehicle that ranked among the best.

"No, actually it was Skye. I take it she runs every morning at home. Probably figured she'd do it here but I think she fell or something. I don't know—she just called and said she's at an intersection about twelve blocks away."

His words knocked the wind out of Terrance's lungs and for a moment, he felt sick to his stomach. He wanted to ask several questions at once, then thought better of it. He'd know soon enough and in the interim, he didn't want Branch to know that he was struggling with a growing interest in his wife's best friend.

When they pulled up some moments later, Skye was still sitting at the curb, looking very much like a woman who'd made up her mind to run a marathon that morning. Wearing no makeup, hair pulled back into an uncombed ponytail, the orange shorts and white tank top bearing road dirt and grime, she still appeared to be serious about her sportsmanship. She also looked embarrassed.

Terrance and Branch walked toward her and Skye fought to keep the tears from coming. She hadn't expected to cry but seeing the formidable rescue squad affected her sensibilities, confirming that without having had the cell phone, the outcome of a minor accident could have been much worse.

"Thanks for coming. I don't know what I would have done if you hadn't answered," she said as they stepped to either side of her.

"Stop thanking me. Nita would never forgive me if I don't take good care of you. By the way, I didn't try and wake her just now, knowing you'd be there soon enough to fill her in. I suspect she's gonna give you hell for leaving the house without telling anybody though," Branch said, a smile playing across his mouth.

He hadn't meant to scold Skye, but was concerned that she'd left without telling anyone. In his mind, the weekend meant that all their guests were his responsibility until they were well on their way back home. Accidents aside, he wanted to avoid anything bad happening to anyone in their midst, especially without him knowing about it.

Terrance had remained silent until then. "Did you hurt any other part of your body?" he asked, pointing to her upper torso.

"My wrist hurts a little, but this ankle is killing me," Skye answered quickly.

Terrance nodded, reached over and examined the wrist. "I think you just twisted it a little. Let me take a look at the ankle. This may hurt a little, but I have to make sure you don't have any breaks." He bent down then and reached for her injured foot.

Skye watched as he expertly ran his hand along the shin bone, being careful not to cause her any additional pain. Only when he reached the ankle did he see her flinch.

He stood up then, and instructed her to continue sitting.

"Here," he said as he stood up and lifted the injured foot, placing it against his thigh. Slowly, he removed her sneaker, then gently peeled the sock down the ankle and removed it from her foot. His large hands quickly and expertly examined the bones around her ankle, feeling for any swelling and signs of bruising. He felt no trepidation in performing the tasks, his medical training kicking in instantly.

Skye flinched as he pressed the skin, but was encouraged when she noticed it had not begun to swell. She knew that was a good sign and began to breathe a little easier.

"I don't think it's broken. Maybe just a slight sprain," Terrance announced as he stuffed the sock into her sneaker. Motioning Branch around to Skye's other side, they each took her weight onto themselves as they walked her to the car parked at the curb.

Terrance was unusually quiet, not sure of whether he wanted to step in or draw the line. Suddenly, he noticed tears in Skye's eyes and realized that she was probably either in pain or just plain scared.

"It's okay. You were lucky. Both on the fall and in having that cell phone with you," he assured her.

Skye nodded without speaking and wished she could have avoided the whole episode. She was grateful that the man whom she'd flirted with, dreamt about and avoided for much of the evening, was a medical professional.

Skye hobbled on one foot as he held the door open and Branch moved the seat up to facilitate easier access.

As they pulled away from the scene of the early-morning accident, Skye whispered, "I feel so silly. I never trip, never fall. I don't know what happened but I just lost my balance as I stepped up on the curb." Her voice was soft.

Terrance's heart lurched as he realized she blamed herself for the fall. "Listen, anything can happen. Falling is something that we don't have any control over. Your running shoes look brand-new so you can't say you weren't outfitted properly. I'm sure if you run every day, you're in good shape, too. It was simply an accident, unpreventable," he ended.

Branch listened and noticed that his friend was being extremely polite. He wondered when he'd heard him sound so concerned before. Either his bedside manner contained an extra dose of nice or his friend was somehow interested in his wife's best buddy. He knew there had been trouble on the horizon for Terrance's marriage long before the divorce was filed. But he didn't anticipate his buddy being interested in dating again yet. Terrance was unusually tight-lipped about his personal life, but then that was Terrance. He'd always been that way.

"I appreciate your trying to make me feel better but I still feel pretty ridiculous. I just hope this thing is not sprained, or that the ligaments are not torn. That stuff takes a lot of time to heal," Skye said, sitting back into the seat comfortably. Her wrist still hurt, but the pain in her ankle was what really worried her.

"Don't worry—we'll get you back to the house, put some ice on it, elevate it and see what the next few hours bring. If it continues to give trouble, then we'll have to visit the nearest emergency room," Branch replied, his matter-of-fact nature kicking in.

"Let's hope we don't have to go that far—I am not prepared to spend the weekend in and out of a hospital waiting room," Skye added nervously.

Terrance heard the concern in her voice and shot Branch a look. "Hey, don't worry, Skye. I think you'll be fine. Let's just take this one step at a time," he said firmly.

She liked the way he seemed to take charge, liked the way he made her feel. She'd liked the way he looked totally comfortable taking off her running shoe and holding her now throbbing ankle in his large, firm hands. If the pain she felt at the time hadn't been present, she wondered how his fingers would have felt against her flesh.

It was in that moment that Skye realized that she wanted more than anything in the world for Terrance to touch her again. The thought surprised her, disturbed her and made her even more agitated than the thought of a badly sprained ankle. Conversely, it also made her smile.

Chapter 6

The house was still quiet when they returned. Terrance, Branch and Skye entered the great room with Skye balanced between them, her injured leg dangling oddly as they made their way to a sofa.

Nita, the consummate hostess, was already in the kitchen preparing a buffet-style breakfast. She'd wondered where Branch could have gone and was even a little miffed that he hadn't wakened her. Knowing he was super excited about Terrance's arrival only one day earlier, she'd dismissed it as guy stuff.

Hearing the commotion in the great room as they entered, she hurried toward the oddly balanced trio. She immediately saw that they were balancing Skye's weight between them. Each time she had tried to put her right foot down and stand, a pained expression crossed her features.

Nita saw the look on her friend's face and almost panicked.

"My God, and here I was wondering where you'd gone. I had no idea you guys were even out of your beds so early. What happened?" Her voice rose as she asked the question and Branch realized he should have awakened her before leaving.

Terrance offered a quick version of Skye's fall as he helped her sit down. Nita continued to listen as the story unfolded. Finally, she could hold her thoughts in no more and the words spilled out.

"Girl, I'm just glad you had the good sense to have your cell phone with you," Nita said, worry etched into her face. "And, I have to tell you that I am more than a little upset with you, missy, for not even letting any one of us know that you were going running. What if you had been hit by a car, or attacked? You are still the same daredevil you were when we first met. You always tempted fate," Nita said, her voice tinged with worry.

Skye wanted to defend herself against Nita's charges, but the pain in her ankle, the concern on her friend's face and the two men standing in her midst who'd come to her rescue, all added up to a powerful argument for the prosecution.

So, she remained silent instead and murmured a soft, "I know and I'm sorry." She dared not add anything more because she knew tears would find their way to the front of her eyes. She'd already embarrassed herself totally in front of a man she'd only met less than twenty-four hours earlier but who seemed to somehow matter. She dared not add any additional insight into her frailties—at least not until she had gotten back on her own two feet.

These thoughts were at the forefront of Skye's mind as Nita stood in front of her, reached down, took one of Skye's hands into her own and then sat quickly beside her.

"Look, I don't want to lecture you—you know I'm not like that. But for God's sake, Skye, be careful. Now, let's forget about all this and try and have the wonderful day that both Branch and I have looked forward to ever since we decided to plan this crazy weekend."

Branch smiled, reached for his wife's hand to help her up and quickly pulled her into a loose embrace.

"See, this is why I married her. She's fiery, practical and most of all, likes to stay the course. Guess I'm in for a lifetime of pure heaven, huh?" he teased as Nita laughed.

Terrance watched the two people in front of him and wondered if he'd ever loved Brianna that way, then stopped himself. He'd always believed there were varying degrees of love. If that were true, the measure of what he'd felt for Brianna would have paled in comparison to what Branch and Nita shared, but that alone would not have been grounds to end the union. In his opinion, they had both allowed their time together to drag out longer than either had felt necessary, thinking that Jacqueline would benefit. In the long run, she had sensed the tension anyway, behaving as if she were worried or even anxious at times.

His thoughts were interrupted by Branch. "Man, let's move this into the kitchen—I am starving. Plus we should get you some ice for that ankle," he added as they headed toward the massive eat-in kitchen. Terrance hadn't realized how worried he'd become when they first spotted Skye sitting curbside. It was only when he heard the scolding that Nita delivered that he realized he, too, was genuinely upset by Skye's accident. He also came to the conclusion that now would not be the time to deliver that information to Skye. She looked totally indefensible as she sat gingerly on the sofa, one sneaker on, one off and an ankle that had been compromised.

"Okay, let's check this thing out thoroughly," he announced with authority. Terrance dropped down onto one knee to give further inspection to an ankle that was now somewhat swollen. He expertly pressed his fingers against the area which he suspected had incurred the most damage, moved farther up, to the left and right side and silently came to a conclusion.

Skye winced, then bit her lip. It took much of her conscious willpower to keep tears from her eyes but the last thing she felt she needed to do was create more drama, more concern. She was in a great deal of pain, but dared not complain, feeling she had brought it on herself.

Terrance wanted to offer her as much comfort as possible but also knew that medically, the ankle should be X-rayed if it continued to give her pain and the swelling remained in place.

"Should we call a doctor or go to the emergency room? I mean, it looks pretty bad to me but I'm not the most experienced in medical stuff," Skye admitted.

"I think we should put some ice on it, keep it elevated and wait a couple of hours. If the swelling hasn't gone down, if it continues to give you a lot of pain and seems to be getting worse, then it's time to take it to the next level," Terrance announced authoritatively.

Skye now watched Terrance more closely. He'd taken charge, given clear direction and was obviously totally comfortable with the entire medical effort. He must be an excellent doctor.

"You've been great through all of this. I'm sure you know what you're doing and I don't want to jeopardize a speedy recovery if that's really not the case," Skye said softly.

Branch smiled and hunched down at that moment, placing an ice pack on Skye's ankle. "Actually, internal medicine is his specialty but he probably knows something about bones as well," Branch added quickly.

All the air seemed to leave Skye's lungs at once and the room spun. She hadn't eaten anything that morning, the adrenaline which had been released with the fall was now diminished and she was now experiencing low blood sugar levels.

Terrance saw the color leave Skye's face, noticed that she couldn't seem to inhale deeply enough and recognized the signs of shock. He stepped forward, placing his hand at the back of Skye's neck and lowered her head between her legs. She wanted to protest but felt too weak to do so, so she remained silent. The warmth of his hand at the back of her neck reminded her of moments before as she'd been forced to sit curbside at the intersection. She wondered if Terrance also felt the heat generated between them, then chided herself for being foolish. The man was a doctor, for God's sake and no doubt touched thousands of patients in the course of treatment.

Skye closed her eyes and willed away the feelings threatening to overtake her body. Moments passed and she felt a cold glass being thrust into her hand.

"Drink it," Terrance urged her, his voice coming almost as a whisper in her ear.

The icy cold orange juice slid down her throat and she gratefully drained the glass.

"Better?" Terrance asked, taking the glass from her hand. He waited for an answer and watched her closely as she seemed to regain her composure.

"Yes. Definitely. Where's the bacon, eggs and toast?" Skye uttered to everyone's surprise.

Nita laughed, Branch smiled and shook his head and Terrance realized that his patient was turning out to be quite a handful. He also realized that he was definitely attracted to her, but more importantly, liked the way she handled herself.

"I think she's going to be fine. We could probably all do with some breakfast at this point," he added.

"Coming right up," Nita and Branch both chimed in.

"Let's head for the kitchen," Branch said as they marched down the corridor connecting the great room and the cavernous kitchen.

Skye looked up as Terrance stood before her, offering his arm in assistance. She grabbed it, braced herself and pulled herself up quickly, making sure to keep the one leg up off the floor.

They made their way toward the kitchen as one. Skye leaned on Terrance as she hobbled on one foot. By the time they reached the room, Branch and Nita were already reaching for pots and pans from the multitude of cabinets which lined the kitchen's perimeter.

"Never thought I'd see the day when you were eager to help in the kitchen, man," Terrance laughed, having discovered a new side to his best friend.

"Well, I didn't expect to be called to an episode of 911 this early in the day, either. It's the stuff that appetites are made of," Branch responded, a smile playing at the corners of his mouth.

Terrance led Skye to a large wicker chair which sat in the corner, placed her into it carefully and looked around for something which he could elevate her foot on. Looking around the fully equipped kitchen, he noted a set of square rattan ottomans which matched the high-backed kitchen chairs. He pulled one toward her, then lifted the injured foot carefully, placing it onto the seating element.

Turning toward Nita, he issued one word. "Ice."

"No problem," she answered quickly. She retrieved Skye's ice pack from the great room and handed it to Terrance.

Terrance placed the homemade ice pack onto Skye's ankles.

"Keep this on it, keep it elevated and you should be fine in about six to eight hours. If not, we'll have it X-rayed," he stated authoritatively.

Skye wanted nothing to do with emergency rooms, hospitals or the possibility of anything further. She shook her head in agreement and offered a smile.

"I'm sorry I'm unable to help with the breakfast today, but don't count me out just yet." Her effervescent attitude, combined with the ridiculous picture she made sitting squarely in the kitchen's midst, huge ice pack on her leg and an ottoman serving as her footstool, made everyone present laugh.

"Yeah, we're really gonna sit around and wait for that. Just relax yourself and take advantage of an unfortunate situation," Branch advised.

"Aye, aye," Skye answered with a mock salute of her

right palm. The other wrist which she'd scratched in the fall was already starting to feel better.

The smell of hickory bacon cooking wafted through the house, making it impossible for the remaining guests to continue to sleep. It wasn't long before they stumbled into the kitchen, some in better condition than others.

Lorenzo offered to help and wound up making coffee, the most requested item. Some of the other guests were too engaged in recapping the events of the evening before to notice that their breakfast was already in preparation.

Terrance had pulled out the matching ottoman to Skye's newly designated footstool and sat only inches from her. Every once in a while, his gaze returned to the swollen foot and he realized he wanted nothing more than for Skye to be under his care, even if it was only for a weekend.

Everyone wanted to know what had happened and Branch immediately set up a control mechanism, fearing that Skye would have to recount the details of her early-morning mishap a dozen times.

"Look, when breakfast is on the table, we'll say our blessings and include Skye's mishap in it. After that, she can tell you guys all, part or none of the story. I just don't think she should have to tell it over and over again is all," Branch added as he continued to flip pancakes.

Meanwhile, Nita was busy scrambling eggs and frying bacon. She shook her head in agreement, adding, "Branch is right. Let's wait until we're all settled, then we'll give you guys the 411 on this morning's sunrise events."

Nita's description set off a wave of laughter with Skye joining in. She continued to sit right where

Terrance had placed her, watching the morning's activities unfold around her. Moments later, the food was set up buffet style. Everyone took plates in hand, helping themselves, and breakfast was under way. To Skye's surprise, Terrance handed her a plate he'd put together, with another glass of orange juice.

"Coffee?" he asked, looking down at her.

"No. I mean, yes. Thanks. Listen, you don't have to wait on me. I really appreciate this and everything, but it makes me feel guilty. I'll be fine," she said quickly, not sure of what her answer would be if he challenged her.

"Not with this crew you won't. I know these guys and food is a commodity where most of them come from. Not that they can't afford it, they don't know how to properly cook it," he added, then laughed. Lorenzo shot him a look and several of the other guests just shook their heads.

Branch confirmed Terrance's statement by nodding his head in the affirmative. "He's absolutely right. There's plenty here. Let the man do his thing. Don't you know about being spoiled?"

Nita laughed then and wound one arm around her husband's waist. "Baby, you're one of a kind. You spoil me just for the sake of doing it and you know that I love it. Most guys are afraid to show their women that kind of attention," she said as he leaned down and kissed her quickly on the lips.

"Okay, you newlywed lovebirds. Give the rest of us a break. We're trying to handle this stuff on an empty stomach," Lorenzo stated with mock disgust.

"Just you wait, my man. I'm not saying anything 'cause I know you're about two minutes from being caught out there. The rest of you clowns just sit down and eat your breakfast that I and my lovely wife have prepared. Lunch is on you. We have the grill set up, the salads are in the fridge and the rest is history. Every man for himself and every woman for every man," he added, laughing.

"Hey, that's cool. I like the thought of helping out somewhat. You and Nita have been phenomenal. We're all here to celebrate your union and the wedding but instead, you guys are making us feel as though we're on some kind of weekend getaway," Terrance said as he filled a plate for himself.

"Well, that's the way we wanted to handle it. We figured you guys had all been so great to us throughout the wedding, the gifts, the cooperation and all, we just had to do something to bring us together again and also to let you know how much we appreciated your friendship."

"Toast, toast," somebody shouted and someone else held up several slices.

They all laughed, but Lorenzo actually held up his glass in tribute to his older brother's marriage, cleared his throat and spoke quickly.

"Here's to longevity. It's not often that two people find one another and are able to stick it out. In today's world of instant gratification, may you both find peace and serenity in the presence of one another, and unending love and acceptance in one another's eyes."

Silence ensued as everyone reached for their glasses, lifting them high in unison. Skye awkwardly held her glass up, carefully balancing her body in the chair so that the one foot which was elevated remained in place on the ottoman.

Terrance watched her and wondered how he was

going to avoid any emotional entanglements with her. He decided to take it one day at a time. He only had two days left.

Meanwhile, at the National Weather Center, with winds reaching one hundred and ten miles per hour and rainfall becoming increasingly more heavy, the tropical storm had been upgraded to Hurricane Charley, and was moving toward South Florida. It seemed that Miami and all of Southern Florida could be in its path.

Chapter 7

"Twelve o'clock pool party my foot," Lorenzo shouted as he proceeded to lead the way through the French doors leading to the patio/pool area. The remaining guests watched him with mild amusement, knowing that Lorenzo had always been the class clown.

"I'm not waiting for noon. I'm going in now. Come on," he added, encouraging those who were just waking up, just finishing breakfast and some who were only half dressed, to join him.

Landscaped with palm trees, lush vegetation and huge tropical plants natural to the region, the patio was enclosed by a forty-five-foot-high screen, an enhancement which Branch swore kept out mosquitoes, gnats, wasps and any other creatures which happened to be in the vicinity.

The air felt saturated with moisture and the sun still

made its presence known with a weak light which created moderate sunshine. And still, there was no rain in Fort Lauderdale.

Nita laughed at Lorenzo's leadership comment, and added her own interpretation of the day's scheduled activities. "Listen. You of all people should know that my husband is very finicky about who goes into this pool. You guys have definitely been designated special. I suggest you take advantage while you can." She laughed, then winked across the room at her husband.

Branch nodded in consent, not ashamed of his known status as a person with extremely discriminating tastes.

"Nita is right. I pride myself on taking care of the pool. We don't have a designated pool boy, so for all intents and purposes, I'm it. Keeping the chlorine levels just right is not an easy task. Just make sure you use the shower on the side of the deck before and after entering the pool. That way, you don't add as many lotions, oils and other stuff. Especially you ladies," he added as everyone laughed.

"Hey, I'm serious, you guys. The showering also takes most of the chlorine off your skin as quickly as possible when you come out," he said, a note of sincerity in his voice. "See, I'm looking out for you guys, too. Don't want you to have irritated skin or any complaints," he added.

"Okay, old man. I think we have the picture. Don't worry, we won't pollute your pool," Roger said then, half-serious, half-joking as he peeled off the khaki shorts he was wearing to reveal blue-and-beige striped bathing trunks. He moved quickly toward the diving board, climbed onto it and slid into the pool with both elegance and grace.

Lorenzo watched with his arms folded and mumbled, "Show-off," before he, too, decided to trim down to his bathing trunks. Neither of them had bothered to take the shower which Branch had alluded to only moments before, but he remained silent.

Skye watched the goings on and decided to remain quiet, wondering if she should bother to change. Her ankle still throbbed, though the swelling seemed to have subsided somewhat. She continued to hold the ice pack against it. A bottle of water, which she sipped every so often, sat at her feet.

Almost as if he'd read her mind, Terrance walked over, bent down and lifted the ice pack from her ankle. He peered at the ankle with a studied eye.

"Hmm, looks like there's some improvement. You may only have a simple sprain after all," he said convincingly. He looked up at Skye then and smiled, wondering how she'd look in her bathing suit.

He noticed that her skin had taken on a honeyed glow and shone with a light sheen of perspiration. Under the overcast skies, her skin matched the color of smooth pecans left in the sun. Terrance found himself swallowing hard. She radiated good health, a quality he had always found to be a powerful attraction. He remembered that she constantly drank water and wondered if that was her secret.

"So, are you joining us around the pool?" he asked.

"I don't know if it makes any sense. I don't think I can risk going into the water right now, so what's the point?" Her question was delivered with a slight degree of frustration which was not lost on Terrance's ear. As a medical practitioner, he was familiar with the many sides of patient care and knew that Skye's mental state would be important to her healing process, even if she had only suffered a minor sprain.

Terrance wanted her to enjoy as much of the afternoon's activities as was possible. For reasons even he was unable to understand, he wanted her to remember the weekend as a positive experience, even if it was overshadowed by a minor accident.

"Look, why don't you at least put on your suit and just sit around the pool? You'll feel better, you'll look great and you'll definitely improve my overall outlook," he suggested, a smile playing at the corners of his mouth.

Skye watched him, shook her head, then laughed.

"Your bedside manner is questionable. Are you this persuasive with all your patients?" She also wanted to ask if he was as attentive, but thought the question would be in poor taste, so she relented.

"You haven't seen anything yet. I have been known to convince patients back to good health with a healthy dose of my in-office consultation. If you're interested in trying that method, though, you'll have to visit me in the Bahamas."

Skye watched him as he said the words and pondered his real meaning. She also considered the man standing before her and realized that he truly posed a threat. That was the second T she'd assigned to him in less than twenty-four hours. But another voice which seemed to have taken up residence inside her psyche overrode her pragmatic side. *It's just a weekend,* she kept thinking. *Go with the flow, have some fun, relax.*

The morning passed quickly as the pool party got under way. Nita had changed into a black-and-white striped two-piece bathing suit which emphasized her full hips and ample bosom to perfection. She pulled a white collared shirt over the bathing ensemble and tied the shirt at the waist.

Branch watched, his face full of love. He walked toward her, put an arm around her shoulders and kissed her temple.

"You look amazing, lady." Then he whispered something into her ear and they both laughed. She wound one arm around his waist as they presented another facet of their united front to their guests.

"Okay, you guys. Remember, lunch is hosted by Nita and I, but you're all responsible for its preparation. Lorenzo, you're in charge of the barbecue grill. Roger, drinks are your thing. And, ladies, you can handle bringing the salads out, setting up everything, et cetera. I don't want my wife all tired out from serving you cats all weekend," Branch said with mischievous grin.

"Okay, man, we get the point and we'll handle our business. Listen, aren't we all going out tonight?" Terrance asked.

"Yeah—we have dinner reservations at a club called the Harbor Bay. It's on the water, the food is great and they have a reggae band that plays some mean stuff. You can even dance there. You guys will love it," Branch added.

Nita nodded her head in agreement. "Branch wanted you all to experience Fort Lauderdale's best. We really like this club, especially the band."

"Well, I'm up for it," shouted Lorenzo as he made his way out of the pool after having done several quick laps.

"What about the storm? I just heard on CNN that it's been upgraded to hurricane status," Roger said, nodding to his weekend date, a somewhat quiet, serious young woman named Simone. He'd recently broken it off with a longtime girlfriend whom he'd dated, dumped and dated since college.

Meanwhile, some guests headed back to their rooms to don their swimsuits, while others decided to just hang out poolside with shorts on.

"I think we'll be okay. It's still miles off the shoreline and very often they turn in a different direction. We'll keep our eyes on it but I think it's a safe bet to say that we're in no danger," Branch said with assurance.

Meanwhile, Terrance watched as Skye tried to gather herself in an effort to move. He wanted to offer his help, but also didn't want to appear to be crowding her. Chivalry won out though as he crossed to her, offering his arm.

Skye took it to brace herself as she stood up and noted its strength and muscular composition. From the strength she could feel in his arms, she realized that he probably worked out religiously. That would also explain the definition in his chest, the strong flat abdominal muscles she saw displayed under his open shirt and the tight rear end she'd been eyeing since she met him.

Instead, she said, "Thanks, I am not used to having to ask for assistance." Her voice was filled with a slight tinge of annoyance. "I hope this is not going to be a long, drawn-out process. And I don't like the sound of this storm stuff, either," she added.

"Actually, both conditions will probably clear up in days. On the matter of your ankle, I've seen it happen. The swelling seems to be subsiding and you're not in an elevated level of pain. Believe me, if it's more than just a mild sprain, you will know it by this evening. And the storm will probably pass us by. We seldom have hurricanes in the Bahamas," he added.

Meanwhile, Skye leaned on the firm arm of Terrance as he guided them both into the coolness of the air-conditioned house.

"Well, I hope you're right—on both counts. Mmm, that feel's good. I mean, the sun does, too, but the cool air feels delicious against my skin," Skye murmured as she closed her eyes for a moment to savor the cool, dry air of the interior of the house.

Terrance watched her face and found himself fighting the temptation to kiss her. He'd watched her all morning, thinking what it would feel like to touch her. As he reached one hand out to caress the side of her face, he acknowledged he was fighting a losing battle. Slowly, he eased his lips toward Skye's and kissed her softly. She was surprised and opened her eyes, raising one hand to her lips.

"Wh-why did you do that?" she asked, looking at him in amazement.

"Because you wanted me to," he answered brazenly.

"What? Okay—you are clearly tripping. I didn't want you to, didn't ask you to, didn't expect you to," she said quickly, anger filling her as she tried to pull away.

She'd forgotten, for that moment, that she was a woman who was currently unbalanced, with one foot on the ground, the other held high in the air as she braced herself against the nearest wall for support. The clumsiness which accompanied this position caused her to be off balance and she had to reach out to Terrance to right herself.

Their heads almost came together awkwardly but

Terrance was quicker than Skye and once again used the unexpectedness of the moment to look deeply into her eyes. The explosive current which she felt was unexplainable, but also undeniable. This time, their lips came together as if by design. The electric current which raced through them both held Skye transfixed; she could not pull away. She didn't want to.

Instead, her lips softened and warmed, parting with a definite goal in mind. Terrance's arms, which had earlier been used as a brace, now snaked their way around her body, forming a steel-like embrace.

Despite her initial resistance, Skye found herself responding to the pure maleness of him. He smelled like lemon, or some other citrus scent and she wondered if it was some exotic aftershave lotion, or simply the man himself. She felt intoxicated and immediately attributed it to the sun and the early-morning events.

Now, as she felt every nerve in her body awaken, each one of her senses came alive. Skye knew she should try to stop him, knew she should remove herself from his embrace, separate her lips from his, but she no longer had the strength to do any of those things.

Moments passed, their kiss deepened and a new need arose. Terrance used the narrowness of the hallway to his advantage by moving Skye's body so that she half stood, half leaned against the wall. With both his hands free, he managed to hold her to him more evenly, savoring the feel of her body against his. When the kiss ended, they were both breathing heavily.

Skye looked at him, her eyes smoldering, and smiled shyly. "I feel like I did when I almost fainted back at the intersection," she said huskily.

"Don't worry, I have no intention of letting you fall. Come on, let me get you to your room," Terrance said. The statement, issued innocently, suddenly became fraught with sexual implication as Skye once again leaned against him, her throbbing body a significant reminder of the kisses they'd just shared.

She remained silent, allowing Terrance to take her weight against his side as they moved in unison toward the room she occupied. The house seemed unusually silent, with all of its occupying guests now totally immersed in poolside activities.

They reached Skye's room and Terrance walked her toward the bed. Skye sat down heavily, her own weight having become a burden in the last few moments, as the blood coursed through her veins swiftly, hotly.

Terrance weighed his next words and actions carefully. The kiss held the promise of much more, but he did not want to take advantage of the situation. He turned toward the door.

"Listen, I'm gonna change, too. Just yell my name when you're done. Is there anything I can get out of a drawer for you?" he asked, realizing that it would be difficult for her to move without his support.

"No—I'm fine. Thanks, though, you've been a sweetheart."

Her words echoed in his ears and he watched the smile on her lips, knowing that if he kissed her again it would be more than difficult for him to stop. He turned toward the door.

"Terrance."

Turning to face her, the question in his mind almost making its way to his lips, he hesitated for a moment. In

Skye's eyes, he recognized unwavering desire and suddenly, without speaking the words, he knew. He closed the door.

Terrance took one huge step toward her, lifted one of her hands into his and then lowered himself gingerly onto the bed. Taking Skye's face into his hands, he kissed it softly, beginning at the temple. Slowly, he made his way toward her mouth, placing tiny kisses at either side. He felt her tremble and pulled her more firmly into his embrace. Suddenly, he wanted her to know that he could and would protect her at all costs. The thought caught him off guard, but not enough to make him pull back.

Skye felt the flames of passion which Terrance's kisses kindled and knew that she was unable to stop what was taking place. She was powerless to do so, caught in a torrential flood of feelings and need that she suddenly became acutely aware of.

Terrance's hands slowly created patterns on her back which became achingly sensitive to his touch. Slowly, deliberately, he raised the flimsy cotton T-shirt she wore until her skin was exposed, then placed soft, wet kisses along the expanse of skin just below her breasts.

Skye gasped when his hands found her breasts, his fingers circling sensitively, teasing and awakening them to peaks of ecstasy as she moaned softly into his mouth.

Time ceased to exist as the moments passed, each filled with a rising torrent of desire. Need replaced all rational thought and both surprise and delight filled them both as they made love slowly, deliciously, as the afternoon approached.

An hour later, no one seemed to notice that when they

returned to the pool area they both appeared to be either substantially refreshed or marginally exhausted. They were all too busy either swimming, eating, chatting or talking about the storm.

Skye had managed to put on a dusty-lavender two-piece which did amazing things to the color of her skin and the shape of her body. She knew it emphasized her breasts, highlighted her long legs and did little to hide the ample bottom she often tried to minimize.

Terrance watched her make her way to a lawn chair and swallowed hard. He'd helped her to the pool area with her leaning most of her weight against him but Skye insisted on making her way for at least part of the journey. It seemed the ankle was indeed improving, the swelling having substantially gone down, the pain now almost entirely gone. He was sorry that he would no longer have the excuse of needing to accompany her everywhere. At the same time, he realized that after having made love to Skye only moments before, he wanted to hold her in his arms again.

It seemed the weekend was off to an interesting start on all fronts.

Chapter 8

Skye had no appetite. Not for the food which had been grilled and served as she and Terrance rejoined the guests surrounding the pool, not for the idle chatter which seemed to hum all around her, nor for the nagging thoughts which buzzed incessantly inside her head.

She had no excuse for her behavior, but she questioned why she felt one was necessary. Her reaction to Terrance, her response to his lovemaking, had caught her completely off guard and that bothered her. A lot. The torrent of desire she'd felt and the passion their lovemaking had evoked was something she'd only felt one other time. And that had proved disastrous. She'd vowed to never again let hormones rule her actions, which was what made the morning's events so totally unacceptable now.

Sunglasses in place to shield her eyes, a tall glass

filled with iced tea by her side, she lounged in lieu of congregating. Her hope was that by indulging in a self-propelled isolation, no one would ask any questions which could prove embarrassing, or at the very least, shed light on a situation she found hard to describe.

Even as these thoughts possessed her mind, her body betrayed her. Thighs that still remembered the feel of his weight, breasts that still bore the sensitivity his lips had brought forth and a body that ached sweetly from the intensity of his deep thrusts were vigilant reminders of her own physical betrayal.

Nita, noticing the quiet composure of her friend, sauntered over, hoping to cheer her up. She figured she was still mentally processing the morning's ankle occurrence and was nursing it to be on the safe side. Nita came bearing a plate of sliced pineapple and grapes in one hand, and headed toward Skye determined to pull her into the activities.

"Girlfriend, here. Try some of this. You didn't eat much. Are you feeling okay?" she asked, her brow furrowed with concern and a slight tinge of curiosity.

Skye removed her sunglasses, placed them in the valley of her two-piece bathing suit top and smiled uneasily.

"No. I mean, yes," she stammered, wondering how much longer her emotions would roller coaster between yin and yang.

"I'm fine, Nita," she lied. "Just doing a little thinking and trying to allow this ankle to heal quickly. I still want to be able to take advantage of some of Fort Lauderdale's hot spots. I know you and Branch probably have a great evening planned and I, for one, don't want to miss out. I feel awful that I've basically spoiled it for myself by being so clumsy," she added, a note of irritation creeping into her voice. Her answer hadn't been a total lie, but the untruth annoyed her and made her wonder why she'd felt the need to hide her true feelings from the best friend she had on the planet.

"Look, stop feeling sorry for yourself. Nobody is to blame for an accident that happened just because you were trying to keep on top of physical fitness. Girl, you know stuff happens—don't trip."

"I'm not tripping. But it couldn't have happened at a worse time. I guess I'm just annoyed." Skye looked down as she noted Nita's direct glance at her lower extremity. At that moment, she wondered if her answer had more to do with Terrance than to a rapidly healing ankle.

"It's getting better." Both Nita and Skye now nodded in unison as they noted the improvement.

"Yeah, the swelling has gone down but when I stand on it, it still aches a little."

"Okay, so we won't allow you to stand. Branch is excited about all of us going out this evening. I know you won't be able to dance or stand for long but don't even try to opt out."

Nita's smile softened her words, but Skye knew her friend. When it came to socializing, Nita was a serious participant. She and Branch prided themselves on giving great parties and hosting legendary functions, even when they'd only been dating. The weekend was, thus far, turning out to be one event-filled occurrence in Skye's estimation.

On the other side of the patio, Terrance watched as Skye and Nita laughed like little girls. He liked the sound of it, and wondered if Skye was thinking of what had just taken place between the two of them. Then, just as quickly, he erased the thought from his mind. The last thing he needed was a lover who lived so far away. He hadn't thought of that earlier, but in hindsight, the prognosis for any continued relationship between them was slight. He was still reeling from the revelations which his ex had made in their last conversation. His feelings were clear on that issue; there was no chance of rekindling the marriage.

He hadn't intended to make love to Skye, but things had gotten out of control pretty quickly when they'd entered her room. He realized that he had wanted her in a way that he was unaccustomed to experiencing. But he would have waited. Now, as he watched her place dark sunglasses over her eyes as Nita gave her a high five, he wondered just how much the moments they'd shared had meant to her.

With all that he'd only recently gone through with Brianna in the past year, the last thing he wanted or needed was to become involved. His thoughts were interrupted by Roger, who was laughing as he spoke.

"Man, I don't know who or what has gotten into you, but you were about a thousand miles away. Is everything okay?" he asked, mild concern written on his face.

"Yeah, I'm fine. You know, just trying to sort out some things. Between you and I, my divorce just became final. Now, my ex seems to be having second thoughts. I don't need that stuff, you know. It messes with your head." Terrance realized as he spoke the words that it was true. Part of his confusion over what had just taken place with Skye hinged on the phone call he'd received the night before. Women. He wondered if he'd ever figure out just what it was they wanted.

"Wow. I'm sorry to hear that. Do you think she was serious?"

"Not really. Brianna can trip if she wants to. If it wasn't for our daughter, Jacqueline, I wouldn't even entertain her phone calls. The scars are too fresh for me to turn around and start all over again with her. I'm done."

His words sounded final, his voice convincing. Roger just shook his head in agreement, figuring he was better off single. Thus far, it worked.

"Anyway, on a positive note, I also recently finalized the paperwork on a private practice with two other physicians. Looks like we'll be starting our practice in about six months. My residency with the hospital ends the month before. The timing is perfect."

"Hey, congratulations. Have you told Branch?"

"Not yet—in fact, my plan was to announce it tonight at the official dinner party. So keep it under wraps. He'll be just as psyched as I am. He knows I've always wanted to have my own practice."

"Man, I'm proud of you. Ever since college days, you always were a go-getter. Always knew what you wanted and how to get it. Worked hard, did your thing and now, look at you. Come here."

With that proclamation, Roger circled Terrance in a bear hug that lasted for seconds but still left a lasting impression. Both men laughed and grinned, solidified in their efforts to keep at least one choice secret from the group at large.

Meanwhile, the pool was the hub of activity for the remainder of the afternoon. Some swam, many lounged and everyone present enjoyed the Florida sunshine and warmth. In direct contradiction to the weather projections, there was not a single cloud in the sky, and no sign of rain or wind, either.

Terrance walked slowly over to the side of the patio which housed the lounge chairs and pulled one up beside Skye, who appeared to be reading a book. She glanced at him as he lowered his body into the chair, smiled briefly, then returned to her novel.

He wasn't at all sure why he suddenly felt compelled to just be by her side, but it felt comfortable; it felt right. They fell into an easy silence, each acknowledging the other's presence without words.

Skye watched him out of the corner of her eye at small moments, her pulse quickening as she traced the muscles of his thigh with her eyes. She could not help but notice the muscular arms which had held her tightly earlier. She silently marveled at their strength. She remembered how his breathing had sounded in her ear as they made love, the scent of his cologne still somehow in her mind. Then she realized that with the short distance between them, she was actually inhaling his scent again. The realization made her heart beat faster, causing her breath to come in shallow bursts.

As the afternoon wore on, many of the guests revisited their rooms, deciding to rest up for the evening's festivities. Terrance and Skye remained on the patio as the sun slowly lowered itself in the afternoon sky. Each was conscious of the other's presence, but neither was willing to break the comfortable silence they'd fallen into.

Terrance marveled at the peaceful existence which seemed to fill him as he sat beside Skye. There were things he wanted to say to her, but felt it was premature on his part. He wanted to caution her, wanted to commend her, wanted to let her know his life was more complicated than she realized. What he really wanted to say was thank you, although he recognized that it would seem inappropriate for him to even refer to the morning's events.

At the same time, Skye was filled with longing. She wanted to again be held in Terrance's arms, wanted to hear him say her name in the same breathless way he'd spoken into her ear as they made love. What she didn't want was to be told anything less than the truth. If he was incapable of being honest, she didn't want to know it. And that was what held her to the silence she now embraced.

Moments passed and suddenly, Terrance reached over, grasped her hand softly in his own and began to speak hesitantly.

"Look, Skye, I think we both were honestly taken by surprise this morning. I, for one, don't feel the need to apologize and hope you understand my stance. I'm not sorry about what happened, although I can handle it if you are having some second thoughts." He waited a few moments, stole a glance at Skye's face and forged ahead.

"I can't tell you how much this has meant to me, how much it caught me off guard. We just met but, I want to get to know you better. I hope the feeling is mutual."

Skye listened intently but held her composure. She wasn't at all sure of what his next words would be, nor could she predict her response. The one thing she knew to be true was that she, too, had been swept up in the swell of physical need which had consumed them both. She wondered if he realized that his non-apology was, in fact, painting him as sensitive, even intuitive.

Moments passed as they each searched for the next words they would speak.

Finally, Skye sat forward abruptly, turned toward Terrance and removed her sunglasses. Looking into his eyes, she spoke softly, yet the words carried significance and a self-imposed weight. "I'd rather not discuss this. Not here, not now, not ever."

Her words hung in the air like a sword used to sever and slash anything in its path. Terrance was stunned, then angry. He had never known a woman to be as direct, as cold, as definitive as Skye had just been with him. It went against everything she'd shown him that morning. He watched her as she sat back, put her sunglasses in place and exhaled slowly. Her skin glowed with the recent sunlight and it brought to mind the softness she'd exhibited while in his arms. He remembered how they'd fit together as if by design, and desire filled him. He wanted to pull her into his embrace again, feel her response, see her reaction and incite the desire he knew was simmering just below the surface of the calm facade she wore.

"You should let me love you," he whispered softly. He waited for her response, and when none came, repeated himself.

"You should let me love you. Again. You need it," he added this time.

Skye's face remained expressionless, then in an instant, everything changed. She again removed the sunglasses, turned to Terrance and the anger which had suddenly overcome her was keenly apparent.

"This can't be happening between us. You're barely divorced. I'm…well, I'm not in a place to be in a relationship. And a weekend fling at Nita and Branch's party shouldn't be happening. I got carried away this morning. I don't… I mean, I can't…" Her words trailed off and she shook her head.

"You know I never expected any of this to happen." Terrance turned toward Skye, sincerity etched on the handsome plains of his face.

"Neither did I, but now that it has, I think we should both just get over it. The weekend is almost over. If it hadn't been for my clumsiness, none of this would have happened anyway," she ended.

"You're wrong on both counts. The weekend is in full swing and what happened between us was inevitable from the moment I saw your photo as part of the wedding party. I asked Branch who you were, if you were married, even if you were involved seriously with anyone. There was something about your face that spoke to me. I don't usually talk this way, Skye, so don't write this off as some kind of player's move. I know my situation is complicated, but don't minimize what took place between us. I know I'm not perfect, but you probably have some skeletons in your closet, too," he added, then fell silent, wondering if he had revealed too much.

Skye wondered if it was at all possible that Terrance could be the honest, sensitive type he was doing one hell of a job portraying, then asked herself why he would go to the trouble, put out the energy and put in the effort to perpetrate a fraud. The answer was not forthcoming. What if he was the genuine article?

"You scare me," she admitted.

"You have nothing to be afraid of, Skye. I would never hurt you intentionally. Relax."

The vulnerability and confusion she felt at that moment engulfed her entire being, flooding her senses with a yearning so strong that it almost made her cry out. Instead, she reached out toward him and Terrance took her hand in his.

"So, you liked my photograph, huh?" She smiled slightly then, looking at him sideways with one raised eyebrow.

"Yeah, I did. You know, although I hate to admit it, I'm kind of glad you had that spill this morning. Otherwise, I never would have gotten the opportunity to play doctor to you. And I have a small confession to make."

"Okay, go ahead. What is it?" Skye asked.

"Well, it's just that making love to you was like receiving a huge bonus—one that I'd like to receive over and over again," he admitted, a mischievous glint in his eye.

Skye laughed, leaned over to brace herself as she struggled to her feet and was shocked as waves of pent-up desire overcame her as Terrance took her weight against his, helping her up. The hardness of his body reminded her of everything that had already taken place, making it impossible for her to ever forget.

Terrance helped her to her feet, his body braced solidly against hers as a buffer. Skye stood, put half her weight on both feet and nodded positively.

"I think it's going to be okay," she added.

"Damn, there goes the need for my services," Terrance offered, a smile playing about his mouth.

"Not so fast—no one said anything about disruption of service. We don't want to push the patient too quickly and have her relapse, now do we?" Skye delivered the question with a laugh and a quick toss of her head as she continued to lean against Terrance's muscular chest.

He laughed then, wondering how long they would each play games with one another. Then, they moved toward the house, Skye with a slight limp and Terrance with a grin on his face.

"Well, since you are still under my care I have to revise my earlier prescription."

"What prescription?" Skye's question was delivered with pure innocence and a healthy dose of curiosity.

They entered the corridor which led to their respective bedrooms, but Terrance guided her toward his.

"Where are we going?"

"Nowhere special. It's just that I practice medicine best when I'm on my own turf," he added as Skye allowed herself to be drawn into the web he wove with his words.

"You are incorrigible—and obviously insatiable," Skye responded as she stepped into his embrace. He lowered his lips to hers in a kiss that left little discussion. When they broke apart some moments later, both were breathing heavily.

"Are you sure this is okay? I know I kind of pushed it, but if you're uncomfortable, please just let me know. I know how I feel but I don't want to rush you," he added, backing away from her as he looked down into her face for the answer.

"Whatever you do, don't stop looking at me like that."

"No problem. Just pay the bill you're gonna receive on time," Terrance added, smiling as he once again closed the distance between them.

Skye's laughter was cut short as his lips touched hers. There was no more conversation, no more smiles, no more threats. Nothing but the rustle of clothing being removed, soft whispers of desire and the shorthand which lovers sometimes use when passion is in control of their minds, bodies and hearts.

Chapter 9

The marina which Branch pulled into later that evening was filled with cars of every make and model. BMWs, Mercedes, Volvos and convertibles of every magnitude were present in good quantity. The *movers and shakers* of South Florida were obviously aware of the reputation of the hottest spot in Fort Lauderdale. Base-pumping music, name-brand liquor, mouthwatering codfish cakes served nightly, as well as the prestige of being the only late-night enclave with an incredible live band confirmed the location as the stuff of South Florida's legend. They also served legendary Jamaican-style rice and peas, red snapper and curried chicken.

The Harbor Club had been carved out of the numerous warehouses lining an inlet which, up until now, had largely been used for commercial import/export business. Dockworkers whose main focus was usually either loading or unloading their catch of the day had long ago left the area for parts unknown. Now, the only *goods* which were in sight belonged to the young men and women who made their way to the doors of Fort Lauderdale's hottest and most intriguing club scene.

Branch, Nita, Roger, Simone, Skye and Terrance all made their way carefully through the crowds surrounding the bar area. Led by Branch, they snaked their way through the thickest part of the evening's attendees, taking in the stylish outfits, trendsetting hairstyles and overall ambiance.

Lorenzo and the other guests were on their way in another vehicle.

Branch already knew that the remainder of the evening would fully support his theory that the Harbor Club was the place to be—on any night. He and Nita had partied here together several times before their marriage. Each carried fond memories of those evenings.

He remembered that it was here that he'd realized that Nita was somehow different from most women. She seemed to stand out from the crowd, seemed to rise above those whom he'd either dated or befriended in the past. And Nita remembered the Harbor Bay as the place in which Branch had first taken her into his arms, whispered into her ear, "I love you," and then kissed her softly on her neck just below one ear.

"Man, the dance floor is packed and they're still coming. What's their secret?"

The question had come from Roger, but others in the party were also wondering what drew so many people to this one single club scene.

"You'll see—in a moment, the secret weapon should come out," Branch answered, checking his watch. It read 12:00 exactly. "Until that time, let's find a spot, order some food and wait for the unveiling."

Branch's mysterious attitude was intentional. He loved surprises, loved unveiling some unsuspected entity on friends or relatives while he feasted on their reaction.

"Let's just say it's gonna be off the hook," he added as Nita nodded her head in unison.

"My husband is right—if I do say so myself. But then, he's always right," she added, lifting her lips to his in a quick kiss.

"Man, you guys are getting to me. All this love and happiness is enough to make a man challenge some of his former attitudes," Roger said, a look of seriousness on his face. The remaining members of the party laughed either in disbelief or discomfort. They all knew Roger to be a monumental flirt and a commitment phobe. Even Simone, his most recent conquest and current date for the weekend, brushed off his statement.

They found a table, which was really a round, stool-height cable spool which had been converted by simply stapling navy-blue vinyl to the top. Imitation grass had been attached to the table's circumference, giving the appearance of a large cylindrical grass hula skirt with a waterproof surface. A large glass bubble containing a single votive candle sat squarely in the middle of each table, providing light as well as an additional design feature. A waitress took their drink orders, then sent a guy for their food.

Leafy vines and palm trees, both real and imitation, were also laid out throughout the club, providing a relaxed, island-like atmosphere complete with grass huts for both the bars and a thatched roof over the band's stage area. Two large saltwater aquariums were at opposite ends of the room with several different species of costly tropical fish swimming within. The owner prided himself on these in particular, but realized they did as much for the club's ambiance as any other design feature. Even the nearby inlet provided just enough of a water feature to secure the whole island theme.

The group crowded around the one table they'd been able to secure, ordered drinks and made ready to begin an evening of pure enjoyment.

Nita sat on Branch's lap and he wound both arms around her to keep her steady as the chair was wobbly. Roger and Simone took up residence in the corner, obviously in conversation about some newly developed hiccup in their rapidly deteriorating alliance.

Terrance made sure Skye was situated comfortably in the only available chair, then headed back outside. His phone had begun to vibrate moments before.

"Hello—hello, I can't hear you," he repeated. The line disconnected as he reached the parking lot. He pressed a button and the number which was stored in the memory came up. It was Brianna.

Terrance thought for a moment, almost reached for the door to reenter the club, then thought again. Jacqueline could be ill. Or maybe there had been some other kind of problem. He realized that no matter what happened, they would both always be his family. He also acknowledged he would never be able to enjoy the evening if he did not resolve whatever was on the other end of the phone. So, he dialed.

She picked up on the second ring, sounding breathless and more than a little anxious.

"Hey. Is everything okay?" Terrance asked quickly, hoping that his voice did not betray his inner feelings. He'd never liked hurting anyone's feelings, even going back to his college days. He wanted to end things on a clean slate knowing that it would do no good to offend Brianna. But he acknowledged that it was becoming more and more difficult to keep up a charade of tolerance. This was the second call in less than a day and his patience was wearing thin.

"Yes. I mean, no," Brianna stuttered, then fought to regain her composure. She hadn't expected Terrance to return the call so quickly. Leaving her original message, she had only known that there was no one she'd rather talk to than Terrance. Now, as she realized that she had probably interrupted him and quite possibly intruded on something private, she was suddenly uncertain and more than a little embarrassed. But even that couldn't stop the torrent of emotions she'd been holding back for longer than she cared to admit.

Brianna took a deep breath, got up from the oversized chair she'd been seated on and began to pace the floor.

"Look, I don't want to play games with you. And I'm sorry if I interrupted something important. I just had to talk to you about us." She stopped then, wondering if Terrance's silence on the other end was as a result of surprise, denial or just plain disgust.

"Brianna, can we have this conversation at another time? I'm away for the weekend. I thought I made myself clear on this last night." The suddenly recognizable anger in his voice was on simmer, bubbling just beneath the surface and Brianna realized that her timing could not have been worse.

"Yeah, sure. I mean, I didn't know what you were doing in Miami, or Fort Lauderdale, so I just figured I'd call. You know how it is when you have something important on your mind. It doesn't feel as if it's too soon, too late or not the right time. It just feels urgent and I went with it. Sorry."

"Don't apologize. There's really no need to. Isn't it a little late?" he asked, noting the hour on his watch. It was after midnight.

"Yeah, actually this was going to be a booty call," Brianna laughed into the phone, her breath coming in waves of nervousness and a bravado she was not really feeling.

"Brianna, listen, now is *really not the time*," he repeated, ignoring her attempt at humor. In actuality, he wondered if there would ever be a good time to discuss a reconciliation he had absolutely no inclination to participate in.

In Brianna's mind, this was a last-ditch effort to hold on to a marriage that had shut down too quickly and with too little effort. "Okay. I guess that means there are no more chapters to the Terrance and Brianna story," she added quickly, then hung up.

Terrance wanted to redial, but knew that it would only make matters worse, so he hung up, too. It was the second time in the past two days that he'd had to stop, reconsider the life he was exiting and reevaluate the life he was now starting. For some reason, the moment he realized he was trying to reconcile the past with a future which was unknown, his head became clear. He closed the phone, put it into his pocket and walked back into the crowded nightclub.

The first round of drinks had been received and everyone was listening to Branch's recollection of some of the honeymoon which he and Nita had just returned from. What they really wanted to sample, though, was the legendary food.

"Now I don't remember when the snorkeling became more of a sea hunt but I do remember when somebody yelled, 'Shark,' and everybody quickly exited the cove we were all swimming in. It was more than hilarious when the shark sighting turned out to be nothing more than a nervous landlubber who'd never seen a large tiger fish," he ended as the others cracked up. Some of them didn't know the difference either but were reluctant to point that out in mixed company.

Nita leaned back into her husband's chest from her comfortable position between his legs and smiled up at him, just as the "secret weapon" stepped onstage. The five-piece steel band was welcomed enthusiastically by the crowd. "What Branch is forgetting to tell you guys is that he knew I had a deep-seated fear of sharks from the time we'd talked about going snorkeling. So when this guy starts yelling, 'Shark, shark,' Branch practically broke his neck getting to me. That was when I knew that I'd married the right guy," she said, turning into his arms and placing a small kiss on his lips.

"Was there ever a doubt?" he whispered to her.

"Not even a small one," she answered, smiling as she nestled back into the protective custody of his arms.

"Looks like I came back just in the nick of time.

Where's our dinner? Don't they realize we're starving at this table? Don't let me have to go back into the kitchen."

Roger shook his head at Terrance's threat and held up one hand in feigned surrender. The others laughed at them both.

"Don't have to worry about me, bro. I'm not going down like that," Roger suddenly added.

Simone watched him and laughed nervously. "You got that right," she said, then laughed.

It took a moment for the joke to be understood, then Terrance laughed, Branch nodded his head in recognition and the rest of the group laughed as they turned away in embarrassment.

"See, that's why I never trust a woman. They're always quick to give a brother up," Roger said, a half smile on his face. Apparently, he and Simone were not getting along any better in the bedroom than they were in mixed company.

"Well, did anyone order anything for me?" Terrance asked as he scanned the makeshift table for an unassigned drink.

"Yes, I ordered a beer for you. That's what you were drinking this afternoon, so I figured it would be the safe bet," Skye responded and wondered why the revelation made her feel like it meant something more.

"Thanks. That was a good guess." He picked up the open bottle and turned it up to his head for a long, cool drink. He watched Skye as she laughed at something Nita whispered to her, then realized that the band was starting to play. The strains of Bob Marley's "No Woman No Cry" began and the dance floor became a magnet for those who were now ready to express themselves. Roger and Simone headed toward the crowd as Branch and Nita watched.

"I think we can sit this one out," Terrance said as he took the vacant seat beside Skye.

"I love reggae, always have. When I was a teenager, I went out and bought my first reggae album. Of course, it was by Marley. That thing almost drove my parents to drink with the volume pumped up, but I was determined to get them to like it, too. Beres Hammond was my second album and that's when they started to listen. They liked the calmness he communicated, not to mention the common-sense kind of lyrics."

"So, you're well-rounded. I like that. Not too many folks are into different kinds of stuff but it truly makes a difference. I like to think it builds character," Terrance added. Throughout the past two days, he'd managed to see Skye from many different angles. He also realized that the more he knew about her, the more he liked her.

"In college, I listened to lots of different kinds of music. Rap, of course, but rock was also one of my favorites. You can't tell me that reggae, rap and rock don't have some kind of intrinsic appeal to any intelligent young person who is deep in the process of defining his or her own identity."

"That's one way to put it. I like to think of it as experimental. You know, you're trying new things each and every day, you're experimenting with your life at that moment, trying stuff on, so to speak. Musically, you just have to listen to stuff that no one else wants to hear. It's a rite of passage," Skye said, laughing.

Terrance watched her and knew he wanted her again. She was funny, smart and interesting. He had had absolutely no intention of becoming attached to anyone so soon after divorcing Brianna. He also had had no intention of sleeping with anyone so soon, had not realized that he could become so deeply aroused, nor so forcefully, and that fact puzzled him.

Sitting next to her in the darkened nightclub, he wanted to hold her hand, wanted to kiss her deeply and wanted to feel her body against his as he had only hours before. The band slowed its tempo and Terrance made his move.

"Let's dance," he suggested, reaching for Skye's hand.

"I don't think that would be a good idea. I'm not sure about putting my weight on this foot," she said, uncertain as to just how much healing had taken place.

"Don't worry. I don't plan to let you put any of your weight on that foot," Terrance responded. He quickly helped her to her feet and walked her to the club's patio, which also had a smaller dance floor, with one arm around her waist, taking more than half her weight onto his, and then she was in his arms.

It was heaven. Skye leaned into him, as if she'd been born there, as Terrance held her tightly.

"Thanks—you're right. I'm hardly putting any weight on my injured ankle," she said softly. Her face was only inches from his own and he wanted nothing more than to touch his lips to hers. He reluctantly held back, knowing that it was too soon to allow the others to realize how far they had come in the short period of time they had known each other. There would be time for that later. Right now, he just wanted to continue to hold Skye in his arms, feeling the warmth of her body against his, moving rhythmically to the reggae beat which was being pumped out firsthand by a darn good band.

"I had to hold you in my arms again," he whispered suddenly into her ear.

"That was a mistake—one that won't happen again if I have anything to do with it," she said evenly.

"It was not a mistake. It was wonderful and you know it. Don't feel you have to justify what happened between us, Skye. Some things are meant to be. Face it."

His words resounded with more emphasis delivered amidst the pounding beat of the reggae rhythms and Skye wondered for a moment if she'd entered some primitive environment where her emotions were no longer in her control.

"I didn't say it wasn't wonderful. I said it can't happen again," she responded feebly. She did not know what else to say, having been a willing participant in a sexual encounter that had been something like spontaneous combustion.

Now, as she realized that her attraction to Terrance was taking hold in a whole new way, she knew it was time to put a halt to whatever had gotten started. Their connection was a temporary one in her mind.

"Do you always try and destroy things that are good for you?" he asked suddenly, no longer willing to tiptoe through the conversation.

"Terrance, be real. I mean, sure, we had a nice time. A *very* nice time, but that's it," she ended, while still holding on to him for balance.

"Nice time, hmm," he said, looking into her eyes. Although Skye did her best to appear unfazed by Terrance's determination, he could feel her response to him. He knew he still wanted her and by the way her body was molded to his, knew that she felt the same way.

"We'll see."

"What's that supposed to mean?"

"I just meant that we still have another day here at Branch and Nita's. I don't think you can ignore me for that long. And I definitely don't plan to ignore you for a single moment."

Skye watched him as he drew her back into his embrace, their bodies naturally meshing together, following the beat designed by the music.

She felt his gaze caress her face, her neck, her breasts, then felt his hands as they continued to hold her to him and wondered if she'd ever tire of the passion they inspired.

"You should let me love you," he whispered into her ear for the second time that day. He thought for a moment that she would laugh and turn away. But the look which came across her face defied description and certainly didn't come close to amusement.

They continued to look at one another for a long time, then looked up as a shooting star appeared and disappeared just as quickly.

"That's an omen—"

"Really..." Skye's hesitation was not lost on him but Terrance knew that he was not the one to convince her. If and when it happened, it would be of her own volition.

"Yeah—the hurricane has passed farther south of us. And we're no longer under tropical storm watch. It's all working out. Just like I knew it would."

His words unnerved her, but still she said nothing. She was too afraid he might be right.

Chapter 10

Somewhere around three-thirty, the crowd began to thin. Only those who were die-hard regulars and a small number of first-timers, obviously mesmerized by the combination of exotic music and island environment, still lingered.

Branch, Nita, Roger, Simone, Terrance and Skye were in no hurry. The band was phenomenal although they had already taken several intermissions. Each time they returned to the stage, the applause was even more enthusiastic. The familiar strings of a Jimmy Cliff hit, "The Harder They Come," filtered through the air and Terrance helped Skye to her feet once more as they headed toward the dance floor. Their bodies swayed to the incessant beat, leaving the real dancing to those who were unbelievably just arriving or not impaired by recent injury.

Lorenzo and the other guests had come and then gone to another club. Terrance was painfully aware that although he and Skye had managed to share the entire evening with one another, she'd somehow maintained a comfortable distance. The phone call he'd received at the beginning of the evening had done more damage than he'd realized. He felt more than a little responsible, but wondered how long it would take for him to be ready to free himself of the guilt which Brianna still seemed to be able to incite. Inwardly, he acknowledged that ambivalence played an important role in transition. Transition was the perfect description in his mind of his current mental state, although until that very moment, he had been reluctant to admit it, even to himself.

Skye watched him. She wasn't at all sure about the chain of events which the weekend had inspired. The one thing she did know for sure was that in Terrance's presence, she felt almost light-headed, unsure of her next move and decidedly affected. It brought to mind another time in her life when she'd felt similar emotions and made her want to shut them and him out. Even now, as she moved into his arms, their bodies molding together as the notes of the familiar song set both the tone and the flow of their rhythm, she winced inwardly at the memory of Aldon.

She thought they might get married someday. At least, that's what she'd thought at the time. Now, in retrospect, she realized that he'd never fully committed to the idea, the concept or the actual reality of marriage. Sure, he'd said the magic *I love you* words. He even talked about marriage. But Skye later learned all that was while he was still married to another woman. The divorce had never been finalized although they lived separate lives and occupied separate homes.

She couldn't forgive the fact that he'd kept such a huge part of his life secret, most importantly, the fact he still had a wife.

As Skye remembered the conversations, the confrontations, the recriminations, her heart seemed to ache accordingly. Even now, as she did her best to focus on the man whose arms held her tightly, whose body she had responded to time and time again in the last twenty-four hours despite the memories, she knew that in some small way, she'd been forever changed by the experience.

Would she ever love again? Could she forget the pain, the mistrust, the denial of self that she'd lived with for four long years?

The answer was not forthcoming but, in that moment, Skye knew that Terrance's arms offered a haven, a sanctuary for the meanwhile. She was comforted knowing that in his arms, she could shut out the world and focus solely on the feelings his nearness inspired. Skye gave herself up to the experience and relished in the welcome feel of his hard, muscular body against hers.

Willing herself to focus on the moment, she leaned into him more heavily and felt his response immediately. Luckily, her ankle no longer hurt very badly, but at the moment, her mind was no longer focused on anything other than the man who held her, as her body reacted accordingly.

Terrance felt the change in Skye's demeanor and held her even closer. He knew that without a doubt he wanted to make love to her again. He thought back to his conversation with Brianna earlier and wondered if he was traveling down a dangerous road. He leaned away from Skye and looked into her face, seeking answers, confirmation and something else. He was unsure of his question but knew that the answer lay beyond either of them.

Skye's eyes closed. Terrance saw a look of peace and serenity on her face and wondered what her thoughts were, wondered if he ranked at all in her mind. He leaned forward, kissed her softly on the forehead and drew her back into the close circle of his arms. Something in her expression tugged at him, made him want to consider her feelings, causing him to examine her needs in a way that shook him to his core. This was no ordinary woman. This was no casual weekend.

She relaxed into Terrance's arms and they spent the next several minutes locked in a tender embrace. Terrance could feel the tips of her breasts against his chest through the lightweight silk shirt he wore. He wanted to pull back just enough to touch them lightly but knew it would be totally inappropriate in a public forum.

As the song ended, without a word spoken, he led Skye from the dance floor toward the other side of the nightclub. The harbor's lights shone against the sheen of the water and many of the tables had already been abandoned by guests who had early-morning business. The moonlit night offered an unexpectedly intimate haven and Terrance smiled in the darkness.

Skye remained silent as Terrance led her to a table in one corner, sat down and pulled her into his lap. She wanted to ask what he was doing, but the question was unnecessary. She knew. She, too, felt it.

They remained silent for a moment, then without

words, without gestures, Skye lowered her lips to his. The kiss was a searing testament of desire which had remained in check for too long. In a day which only held twenty-four hours, their passion was running into overtime.

Terrance loved her mouth. Lips that were soft, succulent and unafraid to explore answered his every measure.

Skye wanted to exercise caution, but it was too late. Memories of their lovemaking overshadowed any hesitation and rekindled her desire to once again feel the torrent of emotion Terrance's kisses elicited. She kissed his forehead, then his eyes, then his cheeks, separately, deliberately.

"What am I going to do with you?" he asked, breaking their kiss.

"I don't know. Maybe you should leave me alone and let me go home," Skye breathed.

"Not on your life. Anyway, we're staying at the same place so your home is mine," Terrance reminded her between kisses that smoldered.

Skye had worn a short flared skirt, and the moonlight shone down on her thighs, sending vivid thoughts through Terrance's mind.

He wound his right hand around her waist and placed his other hand lightly on one thigh. Silky smooth skin greeted him and he almost groaned with the recognition that he wanted her again, right now.

Skye lowered her lips to his once again. The darkened corner provided just enough privacy that only someone walking directly into the area would observe them. At this time in the morning, most of the remaining club goers were busy on the dance floor, or making sure to get their last call refills.

Roger and Simone were deep in conversation at the table, and Branch and Nita stood at the bar amongst a couple of dozen other patrons waiting their turn for a final nightcap.

"Do you think we should head out after this?" Branch asked, wondering if their guests had had their fill of Fort Lauderdale's nightlife.

"Honey, I'm sure they're probably just as ready to leave as we are. Everyone woke up pretty early this morning, especially if you take into consideration that we all went to bed well past two a.m. It's got to catch up with them sometime," she added, doing her best to stifle a yawn.

Branch loved to watch his wife's face, even if it was only doing something that came totally naturally. He put his arm around her, nuzzled her neck and whispered into her ear.

"You know I just want to get you home, whether we go to sleep or not, I don't care—I just want to hold you in my arms."

"Then you must really be drunk, honey." Nita's accusation hung in the air for a moment, stunning Branch into a moment of surprise.

"Now, what makes you say that?" he answered, slight annoyance in his voice.

"'Cause normally you would have a lot more interesting things in mind. Either that, or the honeymoon is definitely over," she added, turning her face up to him in a questioning stare.

"Honey, you are really something. I just figured you would be tired after taking care of houseguests for the past couple of days, cooking a great breakfast early this morning and all that goes with that. But, listen up. If you're up for it, then look out 'cause I am definitely not drunk."

Branch's statement was delivered with all the seriousness he could muster while still reaching over to twirl his fingers with Nita's. He really didn't care what they did when they got home, as long as they were together. He suspected she felt the same way, but also knew that women could be pretty sentimental about things like honeymoons and such, so he let the subject drop.

It was at that moment that he realized he hadn't seen Terrance or Skye for a while. Concern flooded him, then he relaxed. Terrance could definitely take care of himself and he suspected Skye could, too.

"Honey, where's Skye? I thought we left her at the table."

"I don't know, but I think Terrance is missing, too," Nita answered, turning around to give the immediate area the once-over. Neither party was visible. Nita knew they could not have gone far. They had all come together in Branch's Escalade and would all leave together.

"Maybe they went outside to get some air. It's a beautiful night," Branch said. And it was. The moonlight streamed down on the harbor, leaving a trail of light reflected by the ripples on the smooth surface of the water.

At that moment, deep ripples of passion were coursing through Skye's body. She could no longer predict what her responses would be, no longer control the outcome of the encounter. Terrance's hand continued to stroke her thigh, moving higher as their kisses ignited a passion that cried out for satisfaction. Through swollen lips, Skye tried to once again gain some semblance of control. But it was no use. She could only moan as he reached the tops of her thighs and began to caress her intimately.

Sky's breathing came in short gasps and though she realized the precarious nature of their behavior, she was powerless to stop it. Desire surged through her body as Terrance's fingers stroked her softly, murmuring into her mouth.

"Skye, you are so soft, so warm." He knew he should stop. Knew that at some point, he had crossed the barrier of impropriety, but he no longer gave a damn.

Skye moaned softly, her throaty sighs encouraging and confirming.

The band started up again then, the strings of a striking reggae beat reaching their ears, reminding them of their whereabouts. Terrance, with great difficulty, broke their kiss. He looked into Skye's passion-filled face, kissed the tip of her nose and pulled her skirt down, smoothing it into place gently.

"This is not the time nor place for this. I apologize. I got carried away," he added, his voice seeming to come from far away.

Skye nodded as she did her best to reign in her emotions, but her heart was still racing.

"You're right—I don't know what's wrong with me," Skye said then, her breath coming in short gasps. She smoothed her hair back, stood on shaky legs and reached out one hand to Terrance.

He laughed, took it and stood on his feet within a half inch of her. Skye turned to him, wound her arms around his neck and he lowered his mouth to hers again. Slowly, deliberately, he allowed his tongue to touch hers, but only for a single moment.

He stepped back, put one hand out in a gesture of civility and said, "Not one single solitary thing is wrong with you. Come on, I'm taking you home."

Skye laughed and headed toward their table, her eyes adjusting quickly as she sought Nita, Branch or anyone in their immediate party.

"You guys about ready to make the move?" Branch asked, noting for the first time that his buddy seemed to be forming quite a fondness for his wife's best friend.

"Yeah, whenever you guys are ready," Terrance responded, pulling out a chair for Skye.

Roger and Simone remained silent, obviously still caught up in whatever drama had ensued earlier. Simone looked sullen; Roger appeared to be bored. Neither was talking and eye contact was definitely out of the question.

Nita and Branch felt uncomfortable trying to negotiate a truce so they'd vowed to stay out of it.

"Okay, let's hit the road then," Branch offered and Terrance nodded in agreement.

The six of them left the nightclub and headed for the Escalade. As they made their way in the darkened parking lot, Terrance noted that many of the cars present earlier had now been removed.

As they approached Branch's vehicle, out of the shadows, two men approached.

Branch noticed them first, wondering if he was overreacting, but was on guard just the same.

"What's up, guys," he said quickly. It was more a statement than a question and both Roger and Terrance noticed that.

"Nothing—we were just wondering if this is your

ride. It's hot," one of the men responded, his voice filled with hostility and something else which Branch would later identify as fear.

"Yeah—it's mine. Thanks for the compliment," he said, hoping to avoid confrontation or anything else these two might have in mind.

"Well—that's nice—it's yours and all. We was wonderin' if you would mind giving us a ri-i-i-i-ride and all…you know, li-i-i—i-i-ke a test d-d-d-d-drive," the other one said, stuttering. His words sounded ridiculous, like a bad joke, but his request held an icy edge.

Both men snickered then, but their demeanor was anything but comedic and the humor which they'd attempted to display was even more chilling.

Branch and Terrance instinctively stepped forward, ready for combat. Roger pushed Simone to the side and also joined them. The women now were more in the background as the men formed a barrier and appeared to set a formidable defense mechanism into place.

"Does this look like a freaking dealership?" Branch spat out, anger rising in his body like a torrent of hot lava. He hated confrontation, but knew that in some circumstances, it was unavoidable. This would be one of those times. Every bone in his body said combat. He also knew that Terrance read the situation the same way. They stood almost side by side, with Roger only slightly off to the side of them.

The two men looked at one another, silently judging the situation.

"Look, I don't think you guys really want to do this, so just turn around and walk away. Trust me, the three of us will splatter you all over this freaking parking lot before you even know what happened," Terrance growled, unable to contain his anger any longer.

Roger spat on the ground then, adding to the tension present and Branch knew that he, too, was not taking the threat lightly.

One man whispered something to the other, they both laughed and did a half turn.

"Yeah, we don't really like Yankee-made cars anyway," one of them said over his shoulder as they turned away.

"Not li-li-like the R-r-r-ange Rover," the stutterer said with perfect imperfection as they made haste to leave the area.

"Good decision," Branch said under his breath, but loud enough for the members of his party to hear.

"Yeah, 'cause I was gonna hurt one of them—bad," Terrance added. He was more than certain Branch would have mopped up the parking lot with the other.

"And I probably would have damn near killed the other one," Branch said, anger still etched in his voice.

"See, this is what gets me. You can't even have a decent ride without folks trying to do you harm. Those guys were gonna try and jack us. Can you believe that? Despite the fact that there was only two of them, and six of us. Ridiculous," Roger said, the impropriety of the statement sinking into everyone's conscious simultaneously as they hurriedly got into the Escalade.

"Man, there's always somebody who wants to relieve you of your stuff, somebody who ain't doing nothing for themselves, but who want to look like ballers. Those guys were a prime example of where we don't ever want to be," Terrance added. His statement was filled with contempt as he helped Skye into the vehicle.

"You got that right. Punk mothers…" Branch spat out angrily. He hit the steering wheel, frustration and tension evident. Nita reached out to him then, rubbing his back soothingly.

"Honey, you were magnificent. Those guys knew not to mess with us. You were like some kind of conquering hero. I mean, it was scary but you were beautiful to watch," she added, pride evident in her voice.

"It happened so fast, I didn't even realize we were really in danger," Simone said quietly. Her anger and frustration with Roger had left her the moment they were all confronted with danger from an outside source. Now, as she thought of how Roger, too, had stepped forward when they were all being threatened, she realized he was not as irritating as she'd thought earlier. Theirs was an uneasy alliance though—one she figured would never outlast the current weekend. Still, she somehow found herself positioning closer to Roger's side as they entered the truck.

"We weren't in danger. Those two were in danger if they hadn't taken a hike when they did. Man, is this the kind of stuff you have to deal with around here all the time?" Terrance asked, incredulity in his voice.

"Not really. Usually, the riffraff is content to stay on their own side of town. This is kind of far north for them. I have a feeling they were just testing us."

Skye remained silent, her body shaking suddenly. Terrance noticed that she hadn't spoken one word and put his arm around her, pulling her close to him. He whispered something into her ear and she turned to him, nuzzling her face into his neck. He could feel the wetness of tears on her face and realized she was crying.

"Shh, shh, it's okay. Nothing happened. Nothing was going to happen. We know how to take care of ourselves— and you ladies, too," he whispered into her ear softly.

Skye laughed then, the double meaning somehow lifting the cloak of fear which had enveloped her during the encounter. She'd never liked violence, never had a tolerance for confrontation. Just the thought of violence was enough to shatter her composure, though it had been years since she'd had to give any consideration to that aspect of life. Those few moments spent in the parking lot had been enough to bring it all back. Memories of Aldon's violent threats and the time he'd slapped her came vividly to Skye's mind.

Terrance reached for one of her hands then, entwining his fingers with hers, which comforted her further.

The vehicle was quiet for the rest of the ride home, each occupant filled with his or her own thoughts.

As they arrived at the house, Branch and Nita said their good-nights and headed off to the master suite. They were exhausted both mentally and physically and wanted to get a good night's rest for their guests' final day.

Roger and Simone headed to bed, as well, one following the other without speaking. Too much had happened in too short a period of time for either of them to want to address the evening. Tomorrow would come soon enough.

Terrance followed Skye down the hall toward where their rooms were located. Turning toward him as she reached her doorway, Skye made a decision.

"I want you to know that I need some time to think about all of this... You, me, all that's happened this weekend..." she said, her voice filled with emotion.

"I can handle that. Listen, for the record, I never expected things to go this far myself. It's been wonderful, don't let me neglect to say that. But, it's also been kind of frantic 'cause I've got some loose ends that need tying up, if you get my drift," he said candidly.

"I figured as much. That's only one of the reasons I'm going to open this door and not invite you in. I've got some issues that need to be cancelled, too. Let's both get a good night's sleep. We'll see what the morning looks like," she added before turning the knob.

Terrance watched her with regret. He'd wanted to make love to her again, wanted to feel her in his arms once more before they both had to leave for cities which were hundreds of miles apart. But, in his heart, he also knew that the space Skye was instigating between them would be important if there was to be any future.

"Good night. I had a wonderful time this evening," he added as she stepped into the room.

"So did I. That's why I'm doing what I'm doing," Skye admitted. She raised her hand to her lips, kissed two fingers and reached out to place them against Terrance's mouth. She no longer trusted herself to have a higher level of contact with him—he did things to her that rendered her incapable of rational thought, things that made her body crave the release she knew he was more than capable of giving.

"Good night," Terrance whispered and crossed the hallway to his door. He didn't turn around, didn't wait for her response. The night was over in his mind. Stripping off his shirt, he sat down on the bed heavily, his body still reminded of the intimacies they'd exchanged inside the club. Suddenly, he felt the vibration of his pager and he retrieved it from one of his pockets.

He scrolled down to the message, noted the time, noted the name and cursed under his breath. Brianna had called again. It was four-twenty in the morning.

The clock on the nightstand read 5:35 a.m. and the sky was beginning to lighten as Skye tossed and turned. Unable to sleep, her mind was filled with thoughts of the evening's events, including the encounter in the parking lot. Quietly, silently, she left her bed. She turned the knob of Terrance's door slowly, entering his room without making a single sound.

He lay turned on one side, his arm behind his head acting as a cushion, the pillow thrown to the floor. Skye climbed into the bed slowly. Without waking, Terrance instinctively moved to allow access and Skye fit her body into the curve of his.

Finally, she fell asleep with Terrance's arm thrown protectively across her body.

At 6:45 a.m., the National Weather Center issued a report which stated Tropical Storm Charley had just passed the coastline of the state of Florida, headed into the Gulf of Mexico. It seemed one storm had been diverted.

Chapter 11

Terrance awoke abruptly as bright morning sunlight streamed into the room. Although he'd been sound asleep only moments before, Skye's warmth assaulted his senses. He awakened fully as his body responded to the nearness of the woman who slept in his bed.

He didn't remember, nor did he care how she'd come to be there. He thought of all that had transpired the day before, the evening before that and in their last encounter at the nightclub. Every instinct signaled that he should stop things from moving forward, that he should stop their liaison, but his body dictated differently. The last thing he'd thought of before falling asleep was Brianna's number on his cell phone. That final call signaled that in Brianna's mind, the case had not yet been fully settled. Chastising himself for his behavior in the past forty-eight hours, he closed his eyes as he fought for control.

Cautionary thoughts were fleeting as the heat generated from both their bodies grew. It was a heat that he could not ignore.

Skye began to stir, coming to full wakefulness under Terrance's watchful gaze. He found himself unable to turn away as she opened her eyes sleepily, threw one arm up over her head and yawned softly.

"Hi," she said shyly, seemingly unaware that one of her legs was wrapped around his.

"Hi, yourself," he responded. He couldn't bring himself to say anything more because he was determined to control his body. He wasn't at all sure what had prompted Skye to come into his bed, but the reason didn't really matter. He wondered if she had been spooked by the incident in the parking lot. With that thought, he moved away from her in an attempt to untangle their limbs.

Skye smiled shyly, jumped up and said, "Excuse me," as she ran to the bathroom in his room. A quick glimpse of white panties, and she was gone.

Terrance turned over then, placed both hands behind his head and stared up at the ceiling. He let out a deep breath, wondered what the heck was going on and closed his eyes. Mentally, he sought clarity. Physically, he wanted connection.

Moments later, he felt the bed shift as Skye returned. Apparently, she was as unpredictable as his thoughts were unsettling.

When he opened his eyes, she was watching him. Slowly, softly, she lowered her lips to his. The kiss was tentative, but the passion that flared was anything but that. There was no hesitation now, on either of their parts. Last night had set the stage for them both and unknowingly, there would be no turning back.

All resolve disappeared as Terrance trailed smoldering kisses from her mouth to her shoulders. Her breasts were warm from sleep and he teased the nipples as his tongue touched them through the filmy nightshirt she wore.

Skye thought her heart would pound through her chest. Ripples of excitement coursed through her body as each tug of his mouth sent a corresponding message to her womb. She felt herself moisten in anticipation of receiving him and marveled at her response to a man whom she'd been total strangers with only two days earlier.

Skye wound her arms around Terrance's head, caressing his back, his arms and finally, lifting herself so that she almost came off the bed. Terrance responded by lifting her so that she now straddled him. The shift in power added another level of heat to their passion. There was no longer any rules, no longer any restrictions. All bets were off.

The nightshirt was quickly lifted above her head and thrown aside. Trailing kisses from Terrance's neck to his navel, Skye took control. She couldn't explain it, but something about Terrance increased her desire more than she'd ever experienced before.

As Skye continued her not-so-timid exploration of his body, Terrance held his breath for long moments, letting her have her way with him.

A soft knock at the door startled them both, rendering their bodies motionless. It was as if time had been suspended while they struggled to catch their breath.

"Terry—man, are you still asleep?" Branch's voice reached them and Skye dove under the coverlet, embarrassment spreading throughout her body. She wasn't at all prepared for the world to know that she and Terrance found each other irresistible—not yet anyway.

In the next second, Branch opened the door slightly.

"Terry—man, come on. You only have until later this afternoon here. Come on out and have some mano-to-mano time, dude! Breakfast is almost ready, too."

Branch's statement almost made Skye laugh, but she held her silence hoping the shape of an additional body beneath the coverlet would not give her away. She felt slightly ridiculous resorting to such measures, but knew that Terrance was probably not yet ready to announce to the world that he was sleeping with the best friend of his buddy's wife.

Feigning sleepiness, Terrance lifted his head, rubbed his eyes and said, "Man, don't you believe in folks getting some rest? You do know we only went to bed about four hours ago," he said before yawning convincingly.

"Yeah, and I also know that in medical school, you had to handle your business on four hours and less, so get moving. We only have about half a day to catch up. You can sleep when you get back to the Bahamas."

"You know, you're a pain in the neck. Always have been," Terrance grumbled. "Well, do you mind if I have a little privacy? I'll be out in a minute. Oh, and you'd better have some *really* strong coffee to accompany this *mano-to-mano* conversation," Terrance wisecracked, knowing that Branch would have done that already. "*Very* strong java," he added, motioning for Branch to leave.

"Okay. At least you're up. See you in a minute— kitchen central—coffee coming up," Branch added, closing the door softly. He whistled as he headed toward the kitchen, glad that the two of them would have a little time to catch up on old times. Then, he stopped, shook his head and smiled.

Terrance threw the coverlet back, drew Skye up alongside his body and kissed her softly.

"I'm sorry—it seems we've been preempted by my buddy's need to have a one-on-one. Maybe it's best," he added, meeting Skye's eyes.

"Yeah, I know what you mean," she responded softly. "Things seem to happen quickly between us. Sometimes that's not a good thing, you know?" The rhetorical question hovered between them and remained unanswered, but registered just the same.

"Yeah, Branch's intrusion probably was a good thing," Terrance said, his voice sounding unconvincing even to himself. His eyes remained focused on Skye's breasts, still warm and rosy from their interrupted foreplay, as she reached for the discarded nightshirt. As she pulled it over her head, Terrance wondered just what the heck was so important that Branch had to discuss it at that very moment.

"Look, you know I was looking forward to making love to you, but Branch's interruption may have served a very real purpose. You and I seem to have a strong connection when it comes to certain things," he added carefully. He stopped then, fearful that if he said any more, he would damage the fragile beginnings of a potential friendship. He wanted to be up-front, wanted to clarify his current situation, but he also wanted to do everything in his power to give whatever was building between them the chance to grow.

Skye sat on the edge of the bed, staring out of the

window, wondering how it had been so easy for her to cross the corridor in the middle of the night and enter his bed. She wondered if she were becoming something of a whore, then almost laughed. She had never taken sex casually—and realized now that she probably never would. The connection she felt with Terrance was something different, something special. Whether or not they would ever explore it to its fullest was up to the universe.

Terrance watched Skye and wondered why he had connected with her so easily, so quickly. It was as if their liaison over the past couple of days had been preordained. And he acknowledged that if that were the case, it would be the first time in a long time that he felt blessed.

He went into the bathroom, brushed his teeth, threw water on his face and returned to an empty bedroom. Skye was gone.

Branch was eager to share the wedding memorabilia he and Nita had accumulated, knowing that Terrance would be suitably impressed. Theirs was a competitive friendship, one marred by the occasional kind of rudimentary rivalry which often plagues any healthy relationship of equals.

"Man, where is that coffee? My body is definitely in need of a jump start this morning," Terrance admitted as he walked into the kitchen. After hastily showering and dressing, he'd managed to stop himself from knocking at Skye's closed bedroom. She'd emerge when she was ready.

"Yeah, man, I even pulled some bagels together," Branch responded, nodding to a platter filled with bagels, butter, cream cheese and jelly. "You're on your own though if you want anything else. I'm done playing chef."

Terrance laughed easily and poured a cup of coffee, then smeared a poppy seed bagel with cream cheese, then jelly. He wondered if it was only wedding memorabilia that had prompted Branch to get him up at the awful hour which now stared back at him from the kitchen's clock face. Eight-thirty had never seemed quite so early and he remembered that they had all gone to bed sometime past four, after having been up from early in the morning.

"Okay, so what's so important that you had to get me up at the crack of dawn to talk about?" he asked impatiently. Knowing Branch, it would be something that nobody but him would appreciate, so Terrance waited patiently for his best buddy to break it out.

"Dude, I just wanted us to share some quality guy time. You know, before the rest of the team awakens and joins us. This is the last day of your visit, it's my last time to be able to bring you up to speed on a couple of things. You know the drill, man. Nita is great and all that stuff, but guys can't really do their thing with the women in our midst. It's almost like we're a tamed version of ourselves in their presence. I mean, I love Nita to death but, dude, even I know I'm not the same. Marriage has changed me, probably for the better, but that doesn't mean that I'm not missing my old dog days—and when your homey's come around, it's hard not to revert back to some of that nonsense we like to tout."

Branch's explanation was delivered with deliberate speed, as though he recognized that he was on a limited time-out and wanted to make the best of the moments he and Terrance now shared. He poured himself a cup of the strong brew he'd just prepared, pulled up a bar stool to the counter and sat down.

Terrance wondered if the stuff going through his mind would blow Branch away, or if he would understand the difficult decisions he faced. He felt as if his entire future was being decided in the space of a few days, but knew that couldn't be true. Still, he felt pressured to know the right thing to do and the answers were not forthcoming.

"Man, you go first, 'cause I've got a bombshell to lay on ya. I don't want to trump you or anything, but get ready," Terrance warned. The stubble on his face which had accumulated in the past seventy-two hours itched and he scratched it periodically, knowing he'd have to shave sooner or later, and relishing how much he'd been able to relax and let go in such a short period of time.

"Man, whatever you have going on is probably more traumatic, more devastating and even more serious than what I have to say, but I got you up, so it's my turn," Branch said heavily. His words had been serious, but the look on his face was still relaxed which meant he was only playing up the dramatics. Terrance knew his best friend well, and also knew that the quality man time that Branch had referred to was long overdue in coming—for them both.

"Look, what I really wanted to say was that I'm really in love with Nita—I mean, man, she makes every day a day worth living. I guess what I'm getting at is that I just don't want to screw it up. You know, back in college, we used to run through women like there was no tomorrow—well, at least in the beginning." He laughed good-naturedly. "Man, I don't feel like that anymore. I want to keep my woman, keep her happy, keep my marriage and all the stuff that we talk about each and every day. We're even talking about a possible addition to the family."

Terrance watched his friend, heard his words and shook his head. He was the last one to offer advice, especially in his current frame of mind, but cautionary bells sounded off and he could not help himself.

"Man, you sound happy, but deluded. You guys just tied the knot. Why don't you let the rice settle before you talk about having kids and stuff. If I had to do it again, I'd wait a while, get to really know my partner and then wait a little more," he added, shaking his head as thoughts of Brianna and her unexplained absences, overnight disappearances and the general chaos that his marriage had become ran through his mind.

"Who said anything about kids? I'm talking about us getting a puppy, man. We're not ready to settle down and start our family just yet. Nita and I both want to travel a little, enjoy ourselves and buy a bigger house before adding any rug rats," he added, smiling.

Terrance let out a long breath and realized he'd been holding it all this time. "Whew—you had me going there for a minute. A dog is one thing, kids are a whole other level. Promise me that you two will wait a while before taking that major step."

"Don't worry, we will. What's more, I know that when the time is right, we'll embrace moving to that next step with open arms, but not right now. Right now, we're talking about getting a puppy, training it right and then making it the family mascot."

"Good. You know I wanted to say a couple of things to you, too. Set the record straight, so to speak. I know you were somewhat aware of my situation with Brianna. The divorce is final. I can officially say my marriage failed." Terrance's statement sounded so final, so devastating that Branch took a moment to respond.

"Terrance, man, I am sorry, so sorry," Branch responded. The coffee had somehow become cold and he reached for the pot, pouring both himself and Terrance another cup of the steaming brew.

"Are you ready to talk about what happened? You kept the whole breakdown to yourself. I guess I don't blame you—I can't imagine how I'd feel. But I've been worried about you." Branch wanted to ask many questions, but that was all he could blurt out at that moment.

"Life happened, man. You know, the day-to-day, insignificant things that happen to people and that cause them to change overnight. One day you think you want to spend the rest of your life with a person, the next day you can't stand being in the same room with them."

Branch remained silent then, not knowing what to say or what to do.

Terrance hesitated, then looked at Branch for a moment. "Actually, that was only the beginning." His tone changed then and emotion filled his voice though he hadn't realized that just talking about Brianna would upset him to this degree.

"What do you mean? Go on, man, you need to let this stuff out," Branch encouraged him. He could see that his friend of many years was struggling with pain he had obviously become adept at keeping bottled up inside.

"What I mean to say is that things started out fine,

then they got a little rocky and then it became beyond repair. Some nights, Brianna would go out, not return until the morning and didn't feel that she had to be accountable. Man, I was her husband," he said loudly, standing and raising both arms toward the ceiling. He pointed at himself when he said the word *husband* and Branch knew that no matter what happened going forward, his friend would never forgive the woman who had so cruelly taken him to task.

"Damn. She must have lost her mind. I mean, even that's no excuse but the woman has got to be insane. There are some brothers that would have seriously hurt her behind that stuff. I know you though, Terry—that's obviously why she's still breathing."

"Yeah. That occurred to me, also. Brianna tested me so many times, tried my patience in so many ways. I never touched her, man, and I never will. But you know sometimes I would awaken in the middle of the night in a cold sweat. I'd be dreaming of us in an argument and then, suddenly, I'd just snap. I didn't want that to happen, so I moved out. I filed for the divorce."

"You did the right thing. No man has to tolerate that kind of behavior. Whatever reason she was trying to conjure up to give credibility to her actions, man, that had to be some foul stuff."

They both remained quiet for moments, the air charged with emotion. Then Branch spoke.

"So, I guess that's why you were flirting so hard with Skye. I was wondering what was going on with you two. Now I understand," he added.

"Actually, that's the thing I was getting to. Brianna and I are done, it seems. I mean, she's still trying to get me to hear some stuff that she's trying to put out there, but you know, man, when it's over, it's over. I feel that way and I can't change it."

Terrance then went silent. He started to speak, stopped, then began slowly.

"Man, believe me, I had no intention of starting up *anything with anyone*. Meeting Skye this weekend has been a demonstration of bad timing. Unfortunately, we seem to like one another, so it's a little more complicated than that," he admitted.

"I see. So that would explain why she was in your room this morning when I stuck my big head in," Branch offered, a subtle smile playing around his mouth.

"Man, you don't miss a beat. I don't know why we tried to hide that from you. It was really very innocent."

"Sure, sure it was," Branch laughed, wondering why he was putting his buddy through such embarrassment.

"Man, I'm telling you, nothing happened. She was a little spooked after that whole thing in the parking lot and just needed someone to be there for her. We've been talking, hanging the entire weekend. You know the drill. So I figure she just felt comfortable with me. She's a nice girl, an intelligent woman and a beautiful lady. That's it, or maybe I should say—she's all that," he ended, laughing now.

"Yeah, that's how I felt about Nita when I met her, too. She was and still is the total package. Look out, man, you may be right in the midst of a love TKO—you're already one of the walking wounded. It wouldn't take much for you to hit the mat again," Branch warned.

"Nobody is hitting any mats, nobody is getting knocked out, nobody is going for the sucker punch—

not in this life, not in this go-round. Brianna offered up her best and it wasn't enough to destroy the kid here. I've been dealing with her nonsense for the past two years now and I tell you this—that's the final countdown for this kid. No more nice guy," he finished, his voice raised, one arm in the air to emphatically confirm his position on the matter.

Unfortunately, it was at that moment that Skye walked into the room overhearing the last portion of his speech. She'd clearly heard the words about his intention of no more nice guy. Clearly, it was more than she'd expected to encounter as a breakfast side order, but she'd already walked in.

She quietly poured a cup of coffee, said an almost inaudible "Good morning" to Branch and quickly left the area. Her greeting to Terrance was noticeably absent and he realized that she had probably jumped to a lot of wrong conclusions. He'd never meant for her to overhear his words, but it was too late for that now.

Branch watched his buddy wrestle with the next uncomfortable moments, then spoke up.

"Listen, man. You have a lot of decisions to make, a lot of stuff to handle. Skye is a nice lady, she's my wife's best friend. For all I know, she'll be godmother to our unborn children. What I'm trying to say is this— don't mess with her head if you know you're not ready. It would make for a lot of uncomfortable moments in the future. You're my buddy and I don't want to have to quarantine you whenever we throw something for all our friends."

"Thanks a lot," Terrance said, sarcasm coating his words as he fought for control. He wanted to tell Branch that it was too late for consideration, that he'd already opened Pandora's box, but knew a gentleman didn't kiss and tell. He'd die before he'd detail the intimate encounters which he and Skye had enjoyed over the course of the past couple of days.

"Look, man. You don't have to issue any precautionary warnings. I'm an adult and so is Skye. What we do is our business, and you know that no matter what, I always handle mine."

Branch watched the way Terrance delivered the line and wondered why it smacked of defensiveness.

"Hey, listen. I can't tell you who to sleep with anyway. That's not in my jurisdiction." Branch laughed then, knowing that his best friend would find the reference both funny and relevant.

"No, you can't, now can you? But just the same, let me reassure you that I have no intention of screwing this up. I'll handle my stuff just like I always do." Terrance ended the sentence with a note of seriousness in his voice, wanting to both reassure and convince his friend of his true intentions. He'd managed to get through the past days without incident and fully intended to continue the remaining hours of the weekend in the same good shape.

"Look, man. Don't ever say I said it but just know this. If you think Skye is the *one,* do everything in your power to keep it and her. There's nothing else that is truly important. Not in this life anyway," Branch added.

Terrance listened to his friend deliver this last line and wondered how long it had taken for him to come to the realization. Instead of asking, he simply said, "Thank you," and walked out of the room.

Chapter 12

As the afternoon progressed, the photo album was put away with the wedding pictures having served the purpose of bringing a reminiscent moment for all time to the surface. The photographer had captured the pure essence of Branch and Nita. Everyone agreed they were incredibly lucky to have found one another. Everyone exclaimed over and over again how beautiful the photos were. But not everyone wanted to be in the same position and yet, no one wanted to let that fact be known.

By half past five, most bags had been packed, hugs exchanged, kisses planted. The weekend guests all had luggage in the foyer and were ready to be driven to the Fort Lauderdale airport by Branch in the seven-passenger Escalade.

Goodbyes were exchanges which came easier for some than for others. Roger watched as Simone hugged

Nita and he wondered what had possessed him to bring her in the first place. He wondered about the interaction between the two women who had been strangers before the weekend.

"I want you to know that I had a wonderful time. Your home is lovely, the hospitality was great and you and Branch are the best," Simone gushed emphatically.

Nita hugged her even tighter, aware that Roger looked on from across the room.

"If there's anything I can ever do, don't hesitate to give me a call. Men aren't always as sensitive as we'd like them to be," she added under her breath, winking at Simone.

Simone nodded quickly, the conspiracy at once confirmed and concealed, both women acknowledging that there were circumstances which were sometimes beyond control. Simone instinctively knew that Nita realized the weekend had been stress-filled at times, even though Roger was a longtime friend of both Nita and Branch's. The fact that their friendship superseded her arrival on the scene made it sticky when it became clear that she and Roger had probably agreed on spending the weekend together prematurely. Now that the weekend was drawing to a close, she only wanted to make it clear that she'd enjoyed herself and the hospitality offered.

"Thanks—I mean, for everything," Simone added meaningfully.

In another part of the room, Branch was speaking to Lorenzo, something he'd been unable to do the entire weekend. His brother's absence had gone unnoticed by many of the guests, but it had been blatantly obvious to Branch. It, in fact, angered him immensely.

Branch wondered if he'd disappeared out of contempt or to just plain create a mystery and he intended to find out. It wouldn't be the first time that Lorenzo had shown himself to be unpredictable and unreliable. Branch did his best to push those thoughts from his mind, not wanting to prejudice his next words in any way.

"Man, you were here one minute, then the next, you were gone. I tried you on your cell, at your crib, even at the job. What exactly is your problem?" Branch's voice had risen with each successive sentence as his frustration became apparent to everyone in the immediate vicinity.

"Look, Branch, this was your thing—yours and Nita's. I didn't really see the need for my attendance. I mean, I came early on Thursday night, helped you get the place ready, spent the night and then I realized it wasn't my gig. It was yours, so I left. Why are you getting in my face about it?"

Lorenzo's voice carried. His six-foot frame matched his older sibling's, but he was a bulkier version. Lifting weights, consuming tons of carbohydrates and drinking more than an occasional beer helped put additional pounds onto his body. Fortunately, his frequent workouts had produced more muscle than fat. At the moment, he stood toe-to-toe with Branch without an inch between them, and managed to hold eye contact for a very long moment without flinching. He avoided looking at Skye, hoping that she would not notice the exchange. In his mind, she was more than reason enough to either remain with the group or to be conspicuously absent. He'd chosen the latter after he realized that Terrance was making a move when he'd seen them kissing in the corridor on the day of the pool party.

"Look, Lorenzo. Nobody asked you to be here if you felt uncomfortable, or if you had other things to do. I just figured you would want to be here, is all."

Branch wanted to make a point, but he was unsure that his younger brother would really get his meaning. Lorenzo had been right when he'd said that the party had been his and Nita's. That much was certain. But, what he hadn't seemed to comprehend was that in his mind, Lorenzo was part of their union. He'd always been such an integral part of Branch's life that he couldn't imagine leaving him out.

As he watched his younger brother struggle with the weight of confusion, Branch suddenly realized that none of it really mattered. It had been a weekend filled with friends and love, a weekend celebrating the union that he and Nita had recently formed. If his younger brother, single and unattached, felt the need to make himself scarce after at least showing his face, then who was he to make a big thing about it?

Branch reached out his hand toward Lorenzo, pulled him into a long embrace, then stepped back.

"Man, it don't really matter. What's really important is that we're here for one another when the chips are down. There's no discussion on that one, so forget the rest," Branch said.

Lorenzo was glad to do just that. He could not bring himself to even begin to try and explain his dilemma. His attraction to his sister-in-law's best friend was his burden and he'd done his best to keep it to himself since her arrival days before. He knew that it was the best thing to do. He figured she would probably laugh in his face before writing him off as a young man with way too many growth hormones.

Nita watched her husband with his younger brother and was filled with pride. They were both handsome, virile and she loved them. She, too, had noticed Lorenzo's absence, but figured he'd found something better to do. In her mind, a single man without an agenda on a long weekend was a rarity, especially a single man with Lorenzo's looks.

Roger came toward Branch then, shook his hand, hugged Nita tightly, whispering, "Thank you for everything," into her ear, and began to gather both his and Simone's bags.

Meanwhile, Terrance placed his oversized leather duffel bag into the Escalade's rear space and came back inside to help with the others.

Skye watched him, wondered how she'd get through the next moments and took a deep breath. She walked over to her best friend, hugged her fiercely and they relaxed into one another's arms for several long moments.

"You know I had a great time. I can't tell you how good it is to see you married, happy and giving your husband hell at the same time," Skye said quickly.

"Damn right. I'm determined to keep him honest, at least as long as I can," she added with a wink and a smile.

Skye shook her head and both women laughed. Branch cast a glance their way, sensing they were probably in the midst of some intimate female scam.

"When are you coming back to visit us again? This was just a preview."

"Well, I've got to get some things going in the next month or so, but whenever there's a three-day weekend, let's discuss the possibility. The flights are reasonable between Atlanta and Fort Lauderdale, so it's definitely doable."

"I know. We'll stay in touch, figure it out and hope that when the next holiday comes up, you're not in the midst of a work crisis."

"Tell me about it. Mortgages come with a serious tag attached. If things are too quiet, you're afraid that you're losing business. And when it's crazy busy, there's no time to do anything else. It's what I call the mortgage catch-22," Skye said, her brow furrowed slightly.

Nita watched her, knowing that Skye had always been a hard worker.

"You and I both know that spells a recipe for becoming a workaholic, so be careful. I want you to be happy, too, not just successful," Nita said with genuine concern.

"I will. I just have to be sure that things are flowing the way they should first. You know there never seems to be the time to fit everything in. This weekend was the first time in a long while that I was really able to relax and enjoy myself in a social setting. I had fun." She ended the statement with a quizzical look on her face and Nita knew it was not the time to ask any questions.

She'd noticed that Terrance and Skye were spending more time together than two strangers with nothing in common would have. Watching Roger and Simone muddle through their difficulties had been stressful enough and she and Branch had both agreed not to interfere in any way. Terrance and Skye would receive the same neutral handling no matter what was or was not going in, in Nita's mind.

"Okay, well, you know how to handle your

bidness, girlfriend," Nita said, now laughing at the absurdity of it all.

"Darn right I do. I also wanted you to know that I fully intend to take you up on your offer for a return visit. Since me and Aldon…" Her voice trailed off. "Let's just say there doesn't seem to be enough quality time in my life. I don't enjoy things as I used to. And you know that I used to enjoy a lot of stuff," she added quickly, looking toward Nita for confirmation.

She continued. "Now, it's my time to handle my business correctly. Many guys try and date someone like me but they find it too challenging. They want an interaction with someone who hasn't a clue as to what the ropes are, much less hasn't ever been up against them, or had to even employ that in their past relationships. Brothers these days are spoiled. I don't think that will change in any positive way any time in the very near future."

"You're probably right. I have to say that I'm kinda glad I don't have to try and guess what's up out there 'cause I'm definitely off the market," Nita returned. "One thing though—don't try and figure out everything before it even happens. Give things a change to unravel in due course. That way, you're not second-guessing each and every thing that happens."

"Nita, I know where you're going and believe me, it doesn't work that way anymore. I read *The Rules* and I'm not sure if it's a recipe for disaster or a bible to today's dating world. Some of it makes sense, some of it seems a bit overdone."

"I remember all the press that book was given. I figure if you have to read a book to date effectively, it's over anyway. Things should happen naturally, not ac-

cording to a chart, or a game," Nita said, a look of seriousness on her face.

Skye knew that her friend's opinion was one borne
of her own experience. She also knew that she wasn't
altogether sure it was valid. If her past experiences were
to be given consideration, the natural order of things had
been severely damaged.

"Don't worry about me. I'll be fine. I'm pretty busy
right now anyway and don't really have a lot of time on
my hands for dating and the rest of it," Skye added.

"Look at me, girl, and listen to me. If someone comes
along that's worthwhile, you be sure to find the time.
Nothing in this life is more important than love and I
mean that. The weekend may be over, but life goes on."

Nita's proclamation caught Skye off guard. She had
never heard her friend speak so frankly nor so forcefully
on the subject of relationships. Even Branch, who
couldn't help but hear her, thought her words were a bit
harsh under the circumstances. Skye wondered if she'd
always been so passionate, or if her stance was solely
due to marital bliss.

"Okay…I mean, I'll try. For you, I'll try." Skye's response was an honest one. She'd been caught off guard
by Nita's frankness.

"Good. Now, let's get you to the airport before you
miss the flight."

Skye, Roger, Simone and Terrance all rode to the
nearby airport together bound for different destinations.
The Escalade's interior was quiet as its occupants either
reflected on the weekend or began the readjustment into
the week approaching.

Skye sat beside Terrance and wondered if she would ever see or hear from him again. His thigh leaned into hers from time to time as the vehicle sped along U.S. 595E headed toward the airport. Her own muscles tensed in response to the connection and Skye chastised herself for continuing to want him.

He was a man just like any other, or so she told herself. She wanted to know more about him, wanted to interrogate him, wanted to feel him deep inside her again, all at once. And at the same time, she wanted nothing at all to do with him. The complexity of this made her remain silent, her face turned to the window as the route to the airport became a thing to be engrossed in without conversation.

Branch turned to Fort Lauderdale's R&B station 93.4 and the sounds of Kem's latest urban mantra filled the interior. "I Can't Stop Loving You" filled the space with emotion, sensitivity and imagined pain, making its occupants suddenly sit up and take notice.

"Man, that guy sure can sing," Roger exclaimed. "Can you turn it up?"

"Yeah, and he writes all his stuff, too," Simone added, suddenly feeling as if the weekend's commencement might make Roger more tolerable.

Branch hit the control panel of the steering wheel and the words and music became even more haunting enhanced by the interior of the vehicle.

"I think he writes from a place of pain and experience. You know, they say that life makes the songwriters churn out their best stuff. If that's true, I'd better start putting pen to paper," Roger added, shaking his head with a rueful smile.

It was the most sincere thing she'd ever heard him say and it actually caught Simone off guard. Here, she'd been willing to accept that she'd spent the entire weekend with a jerk and at the twelfth hour, he somehow seemed to be transforming himself into a human being.

She looked at him and smiled. An unspoken truce passed between them.

Terrance liked the feel of Skye's thigh against his, liked the way she seemed to be soft, vulnerable, yet solid at the same time. It made him think of the way she'd responded when he'd kissed her, the way she always smelled of pineapple. The thought of all that they'd shared during the course of the weekend only confirmed to him that she was, indeed, a paradox which made him want to know more about her. That created another problem. Unsure of his next move, Terrance wondered why the dilemma seemed to loom darkly over his head as the vehicle sped toward the airport. Then, he realized it was because in the next moments, he would decide if they would simply have shared an incredibly passionate weekend, or if the possibility of a future existed.

Terrance made a decision. He glanced at Skye and realized that if they were to move forward on any level, he needed to set the record straight.

Skye remained silent, quietly watching the hustle and bustle of the airport's comings and goings unfold before her eyes. She thought of the intimate moments they'd shared and realized that things between them had more than gotten out of control, even from the very first kiss. For a long moment, she wondered if she should feel guilty about what had occurred, then realized there was no need. That was the honest truth. It had been beautiful, sporadic and entirely without guile. For once in her life, she'd acted entirely on impulse and it felt good. She realized, suddenly, that she may never see the man sitting next to her again. The finality of the thought set her free.

She closed her eyes and tried to clear her mind of the thoughts which seemed to overtake her in waves. When she opened them, Terrance was watching her.

He smiled, reached for one of her hands and whispered, "We have to talk."

At that same moment, Branch pulled the vehicle into the dispatch area for passengers at the departure terminal, jumped out and began to unload the bags from the trunk.

"Okay," she replied quietly and let her hand remain clasped within his for a long moment.

Simone and Roger were busy getting out of the vehicle, grabbing the bags from the trunk and exchanging pleasantries with Branch. Neither noticed Skye and Terrance.

"Come on. Let's get checked in."

Terrance's words broke the heavily charged moment and propelled Skye into action. She slid out of the seat, then walked to the back of the vehicle. She hugged Branch briefly and whispered, "I love you guys a lot. Tell Nita she should have ridden with us even if it was just a short distance." She turned toward her luggage at the curbside.

"I know, I will tell her. She just wanted a head start in straightening up the house. You know it's like her baby at this point and she prides herself on keeping it just so. She loves company, but Nita always cleans up immediately. I love her, but we both know how she is.

She's just the opposite of me 'cause I won't clean up for days," Branch said, laughing at the thought.

"Well, you've certainly got that right." Terrance hugged his buddy tightly, whispered something which only the two of them could hear, and stepped back.

"Take good care of my buddy. She's the best," Skye called over her shoulder as she hugged him briefly again, then began to walk away.

"Don't worry, I will. She's my buddy, too. Hey, take care of that ankle," he called quickly.

"I will. It feels fine for now. Thanks."

Branch watched Skye wave and wondered if the weekend had been good for her. He only knew that there had been times when she'd been extremely quiet and seemed withdrawn. His thoughts were interrupted by Terrance who walked toward him with a huge grin on his face.

"You've done well, my brother. I'm proud of you and your bride, maybe a little jealous even. You two seem to have it made on all levels wherein I've definitely made a mess of things. Anyway, just wanted you to know that I look up to you for what you've been able to accomplish. Keep it up!" With that, Terrance waved one arm in the air, grabbed his bag with the other, then walked away.

The words echoed in Branch's ears as he watched his best friend walk toward the terminal behind Skye. He wondered if what Terrance had said was just a response to the events of a weekend gone by too fast.

Branch stepped back into the vehicle, watched the last of his guests enter the terminal and hit the accelerator. Nita was right, the weekend was over.

Chapter 13

"Damn, my flight has been delayed. Looks like there's some weather backing up in the Caribbean," Terrance said as he checked the flight schedule board which flanked the lobby.

Standing next to him, Skye immediately sensed his frustration. She looked up, located her information and breathed a sigh of relief.

"Mine appears to be okay. Thank goodness. There's nothing more depressing than having to hang around an airport without any clear-cut idea of when you're going to be able to leave. I'm sorry about your flight," she added. They continued to walk toward the security checkpoint and noticed Simone and Roger ahead of them walking apart.

"What do you think went wrong for them?" Skye asked out of curiosity. They'd appeared to be miserable for most of the weekend and it was painfully apparent that neither had enjoyed the other's company.

"Who knows? Maybe he just asked her because she has a pretty face and a nice body. Unfortunately, without a personality to go along with those attributes, it can get kind of rough. I think most guys pick women for all the wrong reasons, then suffer the consequences when it blows up in their faces."

"Are you including yourself in that, Dr. Marshall?" Skye asked boldly.

"Hey, it's one of the most honest things I've ever said and yes, I've definitely been guilty of doing that very same thing with the expectation of getting a different result."

"I believe that's the definition of insanity," she said quickly, unable to stifle the smile which immediately crossed her face.

"Yeah, actually it's also the definition of a guy's approach to romantic love. We all just want to be wanted. You know—needed, desired, loved. Whatever. But what happens instead is that we choose a woman who looks like she will offer those things readily but it's all a fluke. Women who have great bodies, who are dressed provocatively and such, always offer the greatest challenge when it comes to sex."

"Are you sure you know what you're talking about?"

"Absolutely, and I think I know why, too."

"I'm listening."

They had already gone through security, received their boarding passes and were headed toward the departure gates.

"Well, because women who are extremely attractive

and sexy also seem to know that men are always going to seek them out. But they also know that oftentimes, it's for the wrong reasons. So, instead of them being more secure about the various offers they get, they are more insecure. And suspicious."

"That doesn't make any sense. Are you sure you're talking about the average African-American female—like ages twenty-four to forty-five?"

"Yes, I am. You see, those are the same women I would be dating. The only reason I'm out of that league is because of my ex-wife."

When he'd added the title portion of his statement, Skye felt herself freeze, despite the fact that she'd refrained from reacting on the surface.

There was nothing more to be said in her mind, but suddenly, there were also many questions which remained unanswered.

Terrance sensed her unease, but hesitated. He knew he only had moments to make a lasting impression, only had minutes to say the things which he felt would somehow matter and only had one last chance to connect with a woman whom he'd shared several intimate moments with over the past weekend. He also knew that if what he said seemed canned, or ill-prepared, she might reject it as part of some rehearsed jive talk. Still, he had to take that chance.

They reached Gate B9 at that moment and the opportunity for discussion on either of their parts became even less of a possibility. The flight was boarding.

"Listen, I know hearing me mention my ex-wife is probably, well, uncomfortable for you."

Skye looked away, afraid to meet his gaze as she took in his words.

"We're both getting ready to board planes which will take us to different parts of the country. We never have to see each other again, never have to speak to one another and definitely face the possibility of never coming together again. But that's not what I want." He stopped speaking then, looked into her eyes and held her gaze.

Skye blinked from the force of emotions that seemed to fill her entire body, threatening to spill over into her eyes and out onto her face. She would not allow herself to shed tears and willed them back down her throat and into her heart.

"Listen, I have no claim on you, or any of this. We shared some moments, had some fun. That's the gist of it, that's all of it. You don't owe me any explanation because there were no promises made—there are none to keep," she ended, turning away.

His eyes were too intense for her to keep the connection. She felt as if he could see into her soul, and if that were true, then he would know the words she had just uttered were lies of mythic proportion. She did care, she did want to know more about him. But she also knew that the possibility existed that this would be the last time she would ever see the man standing across from her. At least for a long, long time, until Nita and Branch brought the gang back together again.

"Say something," he urged, taking one of her hands into his. She'd placed her bag on the floor and her pocketbook hung on one shoulder.

"There's nothing for me·to say. You have a complicated life. We all do. That's why weekends are a perfect time for folks to get away and experience a break from all the things which life hands us. This weekend was a little more special than others, perhaps. At least I'd like to think so," she said, then looked away.

"Skye, please don't trivialize what happened between us. There is no need for you to do that. Yes, I was married. My marriage didn't work. But it doesn't necessarily mean I'm damaged goods. And it has absolutely nothing to do with how I may possibly feel about you or what we may mean to one another."

His words sounded forced, but somehow, they still carried an element of sustained relief for her. She felt as if she were injured and in a kind of elemental shock. His words seemed to be a necessary first aid and for a long moment, she just stood there, feeling the weight of his hand as it held hers tightly.

"Flight 543 to Atlanta will begin boarding now. All passengers traveling with children, first class and anyone requiring assistance, please approach Gate B9 with your boarding passes and identification out."

In an instant, everything changed. Skye's heart beat faster, her blood coursed through her body more rapidly and she felt as if she couldn't breathe.

Terrance watched her face change as she grappled with the emotions that were so obviously affecting her behavior. He wondered why he felt compelled to make a further connection and then realized that it had been a long time since he'd felt anything for anyone other than his daughter, Jacqueline.

"I have to go…."

The words hung in the air as Skye bent down to pick up her bag but Terrance covered her hand with his own.

She looked up quizzically, wondering how much more they could say in the moments which remained.

"I know you do. But unless you're traveling first class, you still have a moment or so. I want to give you my number. I'd like yours, too, if you want to share it with me," he added.

"Oh…okay," she replied, reaching to take her handbag off her shoulders. She reached inside, pulled out a business card holder and handed him the connection he'd been unable to leave without.

"Thank you. And here's my card, too. The number at the hospital will take you into my office voice mail, but if you leave a message, I'll get it immediately."

As they exchanged business cards, each wondered if the other would actually use it or if the gesture was a meaningless ritual being done for the sake of appearances.

"Listen, I want you to take good care of yourself. You know, eat right, sleep tight and all that good stuff," he added as Skye reached down for her bag.

She smiled, and Terrance thought he saw something in her face that he'd recognized only one other time. There was an innate shyness about her, a timidity which belied her business persona and defied the outgoing part of her personality.

He stepped closer to Skye, tilted her chin upward and, without a word, kissed her softly. The passion which they'd shared over and over again flared despite the hundreds of passengers around them, the noise of a busy airport and the hustle and bustle of a huge passenger terminal.

"I will. And you do the same. I mean, take good care of yourself."

"Don't worry about me. I will use the card. I will call you." He bent his head toward hers once again and brushed her lips once, then again. She was unable to turn away and equally powerless to stop the flow of warmth which filled her entire body as she reacted to the nearness of him. The flight was announced again, with Skye's seat number included in those passengers now being called to board. It was time to go.

Terrance's words echoed in her ears as she walked through the Jetway some moments later and she wondered why they seemed to repeat themselves over and over again as the roar of the jet's engines revved up.

Delta Air Lines flight 543 took off moments later as Skye relaxed into the seat and closed her eyes. She was exhausted, but sleep eluded her. Instead, her mind fixed on warm brown eyes, a definitive walk and a smile that challenged her.

Finally, as the plane left the airspace over the state of Florida heading north toward the state line of Georgia, Skye Thompson drifted off to sleep, her mind still thinking of the man who'd turned her weekend inside out.

Chapter 14

Terrance remained awake during the entire trip back to the Caribbean. So much so that his entire body seemed to tense as the plane approached the tiny island of Nassau. His mind stretched itself and its capacity, still he could not stop thinking of the woman who he'd come to know first as a patient, then as a lover. It did not seem comprehensible that in so short a time frame, she could have come to mean anything more, but he realized that he had been changed by the encounter. He wanted to talk with her, wanted to see her face, hear her laugh, touch her skin all over again. And yet, he knew, that at the end of his journey, he would have to face the very thing which had compelled him to accept the weekend getaway in the first place.

Brianna. He could not escape her, nor could he forget her. He did his best to avoid acknowledging the disappointment that their marriage had become. He'd never expected the liaison to become a hellish nightmare. Her bold admissions had sickened him to the point of nausea. In the end, he'd been unable to sleep, unable to work effectively and in a sense, rendered himself incapacitated. But, that was before he'd come to his senses.

When he'd realized that he was losing money, time and credibility, he'd pulled himself together and returned to work, scheduling more appointments than usual.

In time, he found that work comforted him in some small way. Seeing patients whose medical difficulties were helped by his practiced hands made him feel useful. And somehow soothed his soul.

Brianna's lack of compassion toward both him and, at times, Jacqueline, had moved him to doubt himself. Medicine erased that doubt and put into its place something which he'd lost. Purpose.

Trying to put the reconciliation Brianna so eagerly sought—and would never happen—out of his head, he thought about the successful practice he and his partner were building. But he couldn't keep the demons at bay.

He'd never forget the morning his daughter had awoken in her crib and looked around for her mother.

On that morning, Brianna's absence was painfully apparent as he'd tossed and turned during the night expecting her to slip into bed and turn her back to him like she'd begun to do months before. The light of early-morning dawn softened the room and bathed it in just enough illumination for him to make out the empty space next to him. He then went into Jacqueline's room to check on her.

"Mommy?" Jacqueline had asked in a half cry as she

rubbed the sleep from her eyes with one hand while holding a scruffy gray-and-white stuffed tiger in the other.

It was 6:30 a.m. and the sun shone brightly in the morning sky, almost as a reminder that a new day was dawning, one not riddled with any of the transgressions of the day before.

"Did you have a bad dream, honey?" he asked, smoothing her hair in the hopes of diverting her attention from the obvious absence of her mother.

"Uh-huh," she uttered, looking up into his face for a reassurance he knew went further than any dream could suggest.

"Honey, I want you to forget about it. You and Honey Tiger should go back to sleep. It's pretty early, even for you. We'll get up in a little while and I'll make your favorite breakfast. Okay?" he asked soothingly.

Silently, she nodded her head. Moments later, she closed her eyes, relieved by her father's words. He watched her, his heart filled with emotions too heavy for him to acknowledge. In that moment, he knew that no matter what happened, she would be his first consideration when the time came.

He'd kept that promise. Even when he'd confronted Brianna sometime later and she'd thrown all that she'd done up in his face, almost as a backlash to his complacency, he'd still kept Jacqueline's fate uppermost in his mind.

The lies, the deceit, the infidelities, all of it soon had come out one rainy morning when she'd returned from being out on another all-night jaunt. He'd been numbing himself with work, trying to get the medical facility that he and his partner envisioned up and running. It helped him forget what his wife was putting him through. There were times, however, when he would wonder just how long he could continue to keep silent as she flagrantly flaunted her disrespect for their marriage and for him in his face.

The rain had begun during the night, accompanied by thunder, lightning and intermittent downpours so heavy that flooding had occurred within the first two hours of the storm. Terrance knew then that there was no way a person could be out partying in weather so severe that it shook many of the low-rise apartment buildings on the island.

He also knew that nightclubs, bars and other social establishments would close in the face of such weather. Which made it pretty clear that wherever Brianna was, it was not a public domain.

He'd tucked a scared Jacqueline back into bed and stayed with her for a period of time, reading her stories and making hand puppets on the walls of her bedroom. It had only taken her minutes to fall asleep and for that, he'd been grateful.

Terrance walked into the kitchen, reached into the cabinet for a glass and poured himself a half glass of orange juice. He then filled the glass with seltzer water and took a long drink. It was his favorite drink, one which he'd discovered back in college. It had always calmed his nerves. Sitting on the sofa, he watched the sky develop a slight reddish-orange glow behind the rain clouds which filled the sky. A sense of dread washed over him. Where the hell was Brianna?

It did not take long for him to get an answer.

Brianna's key touched the lock several times and he

wondered why she didn't just come in. Then he realized she was drunk. That fact, the indecency of the morning hour and the fact that she'd obviously been driving while under the influence of alcohol, incensed him. The what-ifs mounted as the moments passed and by the time she finally found her way inside the apartment, his blood had reached a rolling boil.

"Where the hell have you been?" he asked, unable to contain his rage.

"What? Since when do you care?" Brianna replied, staggering toward him. She looked at his stance, realized he was more angry than she'd ever seen him and veered off toward the bathroom.

"You heard me, Brianna. I want to know exactly where you've been all night. Your walking in here half-drunk after driving from God knows where is not too smart, either. What the hell has gotten into you? You used to be a responsible wife and mother, now I don't even know how to describe you," he added, stretching his voice toward the direction she'd gone in.

He didn't want to awaken Jacqueline, but he also knew that if there was any way at all that they would ever be able to get over the cancer which was eating away at their marriage, all signs of the terminal illness needed to be addressed. He followed Brianna into the bathroom, demanding answers, adamant in his stance on their being honest with one another. Finally, after several awkward moments, Brianna looked coldly into his eyes and uttered the words he would never forget.

"Look, Terry, I've met someone else… I don't want to be with you any longer. I'm not even sure I still want to be a mother. I mean, I know I'll always be Jacqueline's mom. But right now, it's not where I'm at. Everything pales in comparison to what I've recently found out about myself." She stopped, continuing to wash the remnants of makeup from her face as Terrance looked on in stunned silence.

He was unable to speak, unable to move and did not respond. All of his senses were frozen and he wondered why people always spoke of hate as being white-hot, or red, or any terms which signified heat. In his mind, hate was cold, as cold as he now felt as he stared at a woman whom he'd once loved.

The fact that she'd betrayed him without so much as a backward glance, the fact that she now stood in front of him revealing her deepest, darkest secrets, without any significant trace of remorse or sorrow, floored him. It was then that it came to him. He was witnessing something which had to be seen, experienced and endured if he were to survive the coming months and years without her. It was a process. One which was painful, debilitating, horrific, but in the end, it was necessary.

"Look, Terry," she said. "You're just not my type anymore. It's funny—I always thought it was great, what with you studying medicine and all that. It's only the past few months that have shown me that being a doctor is not all that it's cracked up to be. And honestly, all that serious stuff you carry around with you day and night gets to be awfully boring at times…"

"Do you realize that you're still my wife?" The words were out of his mouth before he realized he'd spoken and just as quickly, the solution was evident to him, as well.

It was as if the question had answered itself, posted the answers and filled in all the blanks, all at one time. In the next moment, he knew it was too late for them. Theirs was a marriage that had come and gone. It was over.

Her words echoed in his ears as he watched her walk from the bathroom into their bedroom. She searched for a nightshirt, pulled it over her head and walked toward the rumpled bed.

Scrawled across the nightshirt in large white letters were the words Queen For A Day, and Terrance almost laughed. She was as far from royalty as he was from being a king in his home. He hadn't been respected, revered or admired in such a long time that he wondered how he would go about reestablishing his core sense of self.

More importantly, he wondered how he would get through the next moments without destroying everything in his path, including the Hippocratic oath he'd taken. His job was to save lives, his mission to try and help heal. At that moment, he wanted to tear something or someone apart with his bare hands. It took all of his willpower, all of his strength, all of his commitment to medicine, to hold back the natural instincts which bombarded him as he walked back into the bathroom, closed the door and violently emptied his stomach into the cold porcelain bowl.

He rinsed, swished mouthwash, splashed cold water on his face. Finally, he turned on the shower and stripped down quickly. Stepping into the barely warm spray, he turned the spigot to hot and stood directly under it, doing his best to absorb the warmth from the cascading water. He was still cold when he stepped from the stall some moments later and realized that the lack of warmth came from within. Somehow, Brianna's words had eclipsed the natural warmth from his body even though the hot shower steamed the entire bathroom.

Terrance wiped the mirror with his towel, looked at himself critically in the mirror and wondered what had gone wrong. From his medical training, he knew that the lack of warmth he was experiencing was borderline shock. Shivering, chills and slight nausea were all present, but he did his best to ward them off. Pulling a pair of clean but wrinkled boxer shorts out of the laundry basket, he walked into the kitchen, put on the kettle and made himself a cup of hot green tea. It was only after drinking half the cup that he realized he'd finally stopped shivering. That realization came to him at the same time that he acknowledged that he would, in fact, survive the loss of Brianna. He had to—for Jacqueline's sake.

Two months later, Brianna moved out of the three-bedroom apartment, leaving him to wonder why they'd ever married in the first place. The weeks leading up to the move were nightmarish, with Brianna staying out until all hours of the morning on many occasions. When he confronted her, she ignored his questions. She'd remained cold and unresponsive toward him. Even her interaction with Jacqueline had become rudimentary and robotic, a fact which bothered him more than anything else.

In a small way, he feared for his daughter in Brianna's care, knowing that she now had a pattern of focusing only on what she felt was important. Based on the behavior he witnessed in the weeks leading up to the departure, his soon-to-be ex-wife was in full throttle on her way to becoming an extremely self-involved whore. There was no other way for him to describe it even in his mind. He suspected that she was involved with an in-

dividual whom she'd referred to once, but he also
realized that she'd probably never possessed the loyalty
gene. Apparently, monogamy was no longer part of her
vocabulary or her lifestyle.

And so, on the day in which he came home from the
clinic, checked the condo for his wife and daughter, then
sat down with his customary glass of orange juice and
seltzer, he'd been surprised when the telephone rang.

"Hello… Yes, this is the Marshall residence. Yes,
this is her father." Moments passed and Terrance inhaled
deeply. His eyes burned, his heart beat faster and he
knew pure rage for the first time in his life.

"Yes, I'll be there in about ten minutes." He put the
receiver into the cradle, walked quickly toward the
bedroom and opened the closet door. Brianna's clothes
were gone. Hangers were askew, there were several
scarves and belts on the floor and the shoe carousel
which hung on the back of the closet door no longer held
any of Brianna's shoes.

He closed the closet door softly, picked up his car
keys and headed toward the day care center where Jacqueline awaited him. The child care attendant had
warned him that his wife had said she would not be there
to pick up their daughter at the end of that day. That's
what the caller revealed, which told him in one quick
sentence that it was, in fact, done.

For three weeks, he and Jacqueline ate dinner
together, her with a bib and a bottle, him with a quick
prepackaged dinner taken from the oven. In that time,
their relationship progressed to a point where she no
longer asked, "Where's Mommy?" before being bathed
and put to bed. She no longer seemed to notice that only

Daddy spent significant amounts of time playing with her, sniffing her hair, poking her chubby knees which she found extremely ticklish, or reading her favorite bedtime books to her.

Terrance refused to take Brianna's calls and filed for divorce. He began to relish the time spent with his daughter and it was this that made it doubly difficult for him. He wrestled with the thought of losing her, but found it difficult to handle being a single parent who also was in the midst of building both a practice and a medical center.

The divorce straightened some things out and finalized others. Custody was awarded jointly, which meant now Jacqueline came to stay on alternate weekends and holidays. The remaining time was spent with her mother who now only lived forty-five minutes away.

It was exactly three months and two and a half weeks after the final papers were received that he'd received the invitation to Branch and Nita's weekend getaway. Less than a full four months had passed since the divorce had been finalized, but apparently Brianna was having second thoughts about her hastily announced flight for freedom.

Her constant phone calls while he had been away were an instant alert. Terrance realized as she rattled on and on about second thoughts, second chances and hastily made decisions, that she'd obviously been shrewdly laying the groundwork for some kind of return visit, or so she thought.

He'd refrained from asking her why the change in attitude. He'd stopped himself from blurting out, *Stop the lying, Brianna,* because he'd known that for whatever the reason, she was now in a more vulnerable state than he'd ever thought possible.

His logical mind told him that if ever there was a time to negotiate and do it well, it would be now. He'd boarded flight 343 to the Bahamas with two things on his mind. One was how to play his cards well enough to gain permanent custody of his daughter…the other was how to somehow keep in touch with Skye Thompson long enough to gain custody of her heart.

Chapter 15

Skye was burning up. The temperature gauge in her Maxima pointed toward the one-hundred-degree mark. Its high point of one hundred twenty degrees was only an eighth of an inch away. That morning, the Channel Six local television weatherman had predicted a day with outside temperatures reaching the upper nineties with increasingly uncomfortable weather.

Skye inhaled deeply. The current humidity was working effectively to create an atmosphere that spelled the three Hs in weatherman terms. Hazy, hot and humid were the order of the day, but inside the vehicle in which Skye was now frantically racing toward her office, it was beyond sweltering.

Perspiration clung to her body, causing the crisp linen blouse and skirt she'd donned some thirty minutes earlier to damply mold themselves to her. She steered the car into the building parking lot, pulled into a space and gathered her briefcase, water bottle and handbag, grateful that the car had not overheated before she reached her destination. She knew it was only a matter of time before that happened.

Walking into the atrium of the building, the coolness of the air-conditioning hit her and she realized that it had been sorely missing in the environment she'd just left. Silently, she swore under her breath. She'd just had the car serviced, changing the oil, the fluids and examining the tires. The prognosis was it was time for a new car.

She'd gotten through the previous week by throwing herself into her work wholeheartedly with the results coming through immediately. By Friday morning, five files, complete with all the documentation necessary for a full underwrite, left her desk. That meant that she could look forward to approvals and closings before the month's end.

The financial ramifications were perfect, especially in light of Skye's automobile reality. Cars were expensive and although she had her savings account, major purchases like automobiles and real estate were relegated to a special account fund she liked to dub "high-end incidentals."

Skye had always been good with money. Actually, that was an understatement. When she'd graduated from Fordham University with a four-year degree in business accounting, which she'd earned nights and weekends, everyone immediately assumed she would go into book-keeping or accounting. Her employer at that time, Salomon Brothers, even offered her a position as an entry-level financial analyst. Instead, she immediately interviewed with a mortgage banking firm, was hired on the spot and became one of the youngest mortgage bankers they'd ever hired.

Two years later, after setting record-breaking originations and closings at their Stone Mountain office, she'd been promoted to branch manager. The company treated their employees well, and rewarded those in management positions annually with a trip to either the Caribbean or to Mexico. The annual sales rally, as it had been dubbed, was lots of fun and very little work. There were only two meetings which were mandatory, both of which were designed to be held early in the morning so as to leave the entire day open for relaxation.

It was there, at the fabulously exotic Melia Cancún Hotel, that she'd met Aldon.

The Melia Cancún was beautifully landscaped. Its balconies overlooked the water, while the interior lobby was filled with exotic plants, flowers and local vegetation. Mexican tile floors, warm-toned walls and both native and modern artwork were on display throughout the lushly decorated interior.

Skye registered, was shown to her room on the twelfth floor, and after walking out to the balcony which overlooked the sea, immediately decided to go for a swim.

She unpacked quickly, put on a newly purchased aqua-blue two-piece bathing suit and grabbed a small canvas bag, filling it with a complimentary bottle of water, keys, money and her cell phone. Dinner was scheduled for eight that evening.

At three o'clock in the afternoon, the sea was a combination of rippled glass showing rainbow blues which included teal, aqua, pale blue and violet. The beach was soft, with finely-grained sand that stuck to everything, then fell away easily when brushed off. The shoreline, which stretched as far as the eye could see, was dappled by sun worshippers, bathers and children alike, all loving the waves lapping at their feet.

Skye put her things down, donned her sunglasses and proceeded to lather herself liberally with suntan lotion. Looking around to be sure of her surroundings and its inhabitants, Skye decided it was time to take the plunge. There were two couples close by, both dozing and turning periodically to be sure their suntans were even and well angled. Also nearby was an empty blanket with no one in sight. It held one lone can of Dr Pepper and a baseball cap, which for some reason made her glance around again. The cap was clearly an official New York Yankees hat and the insignia caught Skye's attention. At eight years old, she'd become a die-hard Yankees fan after having attended her first baseball game at Yankee Stadium. Even after moving to Atlanta as an adult and having been introduced to the Atlanta Braves, she still rooted for the old hometown team.

The cap moved to the recesses of her mind as she approached the water, sunglasses in place. It was coolly refreshing as it splashed against her feet, her ankles, her legs then her thighs, as she realized that several species of small fish could be seen swimming in the crystal clear water.

The sun was still midway in the sky and it shone down hotly onto her shoulders, which she suddenly wanted to submerge. Doing so, she stretched her legs out beneath her, poised her body to enter the water and dove in headfirst forgetting about the sunglasses which immediately drifted from their perch on her head.

After a while Skye swam her way inland, then walked toward the towel she'd laid out, shaking out her hair. She squinted, then reaching up toward her head, realized immediately that her sunglasses were gone. She swore silently. They were the most expensive ones she owned and her favorites, as well. Turning toward the ocean, she watched an athletically built man of about thirty-five or so as he made his way toward the shore and in the next moment, she almost called out.

He held her sunglasses in one hand. Pointing to them as they made eye contact, his body shone with wet brilliance against the late-afternoon sun. Skye nodded her head, indicating yes, and the man smiled. His even white teeth contrasted brilliantly against his tanned brown face and her breath caught for a short moment.

As he approached, Skye's heart beat faster. She felt flustered, she felt hot. Sunlight bounced off the lenses of the sunglasses and she wondered why she hadn't remembered to take them off before going into the water. Then she realized that swimming midday was not an everyday occurrence; nor was being clad in a two-piece bathing suit in the middle of the week. She smiled at the thought, knowing she wanted more than anything to be right where she was—life was good at that moment.

"Hi. These must be yours," he said quickly as he handed the glasses to her.

"Yeah—they swam away from me. Sorry." Her apology had been unnecessary but she felt the need to give some explanation.

"Hey, it's no problem. It's not like I had to really fish for them," he said, smiling.

He had a nice smile. That was the thought which went immediately through her mind as she watched him and wondered who he belonged to, if anyone.

"Fish. I get it. Well, thanks anyway. I feel as if I should offer some kind of reward. These are my favorite sunglasses. I would have been pretty upset if I had lost them on my first day here," she added quickly.

"Oh, you just got here. Well, so have I. Forgive my manners," he added, extending one hand. "I'm Aldon. My friends call me that anyway."

"Okay—Aldon. I'm Skye. Skye Thompson," she replied, grasping his hand firmly. The glasses had been returned, the connection made.

They sat and talked for a while. She learned he, too, was a mortgage broker, but based in New York—her original hometown—and that he was a total flirt. She had no intention of becoming involved with a handsome, flirtatious industry colleague at an out-of-the-way business conference.

"Look, thank you so much for returning the glasses. It was great meeting you. Enjoy your stay."

Unbeknownst to her, Aldon had noted the change in her demeanor, saw the difference in her body language and realized he was being given a brush-off. He'd almost laughed but stopped himself. In his mind, it was refreshing to meet a woman, a very attractive woman at that, who obviously had it together and who did not behave like a desperado.

"Hey, it's really no problem. It was great meeting you, also. Maybe we'll run into each other again. I don't leave for a few days so it's always a possibility. Keep your eyes on those glasses," he added as he turned to walk away.

Skye smiled and gathered up her towel and beach bag. "I most definitely will." She'd watched his well-toned derriere make its way down the beach and sighed with relief. Somehow, she'd instinctively known that if she ever ran into him again, walking away from him would not be as easy next time.

That night Skye dressed in a white wrap skirt, white halter top and silver sandals which tied around her ankles. Two silver hoop earrings adorned her ears and she applied a liberal amount of mousse to her hair. She allowed it to air-dry, which created soft curls. At 7:55 p.m., she walked to the elevator with the walk of a goddess and the mind of a mortgage banker. The combination was lethal.

She stepped out into the hotel's lobby which was now filled with people, activity and a sense of excitement. It seemed Cancun's legendary nightlife was just about to get under way.

"Well, I see you found your way to our little hideout in the Yucatan." The voice was familiar but the face was totally one Skye did not recognize so she smiled graciously and extended her hand.

"We haven't met but I'm sure I should know who you are," she said tactfully.

"Absolutely. I'm Mike Towers—the Houston office. We worked on a deal together for one of my brokers who was buying property in Atlanta recently."

"Yes, and if I remember correctly, you were extremely good to work with," Skye added, smiling.

"Thank you. You were a pleasure to do business with,

too. Good thing we both work for the same company. I'd hate to be up against you as a competitor," he added, shaking his head.

She nodded in agreement, then in another moment, Skye's breath caught in her throat. Strolling directly toward her was Aldon. Only now, instead of being clad in bathing trunks, he was fully clothed which only seemed to compound his attraction. Khaki pants that seemed to emphasize the length of his legs and a soft blue windowpane checked shirt lay open at the neck, both instantly transforming him into one fine specimen. He'd parted his hair on one side, slicked it back and the golden brown of his face looked amazingly bronze in the muted sunlight of the lobby.

Aldon strode up to Mike, the two embraced heartily and Skye did her best to manage her surprise.

"And how's business in the top portion of the northeast corridor? I see your numbers have increased substantially," Mike said, congratulating Aldon.

"Well, if President's Club will have me, I'm ready to join. Looks like we just hit the two hundred million mark," he added as Skye did her best to remain unimpressed.

"Oh, excuse me, but have you two met? Aldon, this is Skye Thompson. She's a new convert in our Atlanta office. I worked with her once on a deal and she's pretty strong," Mike added.

Aldon turned to Skye, smiled politely and held out his hand, never once mentioning the encounter on the beach, which she found strange. She followed suit and acknowledged him, wondering what the game was.

Just as quickly, she surmised that there would surely be no escaping or avoiding him during the trip. That revelation made Skye unsure if a nightmare had just been unleashed, or if she'd just hit the jackpot. She decided to do her best to give the appearance of being unaffected by Aldon's presence. And to everyone else present, it worked. Everyone except Aldon.

The remainder of the evening passed in a blur. Mike introduced everyone, the entire group left for dinner, separating into four cabs, and the night became amazingly special.

Aldon had a way of making Skye feel as if she, and only she, existed for him. Their conversation that night and on many nights thereafter, although via telephone, closed out the world for her. She became attached to him emotionally without realizing it. It was the first relationship that she could honestly say took her breath away.

Some months later, when she found out he was still married to a wife he could not—or would not ever—divorce, she'd found it difficult to breathe. The ache which established itself in the center of her chest mimicked coronary thrombosis, but after a series of medical examinations, including an EKG, she came to know it simply as heartache.

Skye chastised herself many times thereafter, thinking she'd been too easy a target for him, that she should have seen all of what was to be coming, that she'd ultimately been silly and naive.

Now, as Skye thought back to the time she'd just spent with Terrance, she realized that she wanted nothing to do with another complicated relationship—no matter how special the man might be.

In the days that passed, she came across Terrance's business card and had, literally, been tempted to tear it into tiny little pieces. But, something stopped her, something prevented her from throwing it away.

Skye admitted to herself that it probably should all be simply reduced to the memory of a fantastic weekend at Branch and Nita's Fort Lauderdale home.

Which is why exactly two weeks later, she did throw the card into the trash receptacle under her desk after tearing it into tiny little pieces.

The following morning, one dozen tulips were delivered to her desk with a note inscribed *Terrance,* and another tiny message which was printed neatly on the other side of the card.

It read: *Thinking about you.*

Skye lost her breath for a moment, then inhaled deeply as she realized that her heart had begun to beat wildly in her chest. He hadn't forgotten, hadn't taken the moments spent together for granted and had reached out to her in the one way that he suspected would mean the most.

She was immediately assuaged by the thought that he'd cared enough to not only reach out to her, but also with a gesture that clearly signaled an intense interest.

Unfortunately, he had neglected to include any contact information. Skye cringed remembering how she'd taken the time to tear his number into tiny irretrievable pieces before committing it to the trash can.

She placed the beautiful orange tulips on her desk. Their fragrance filled the room intensely. She found herself looking up periodically throughout the day, glancing at their beauty and marveling at the strength and urgency of color which added another dimension to the otherwise dull office space. Each time she did so, she thought of Terrance and hoped that sooner or later, he would reach out to her so that she could thank him.

She figured she'd blown all chances to pursue anything further with a man who obviously was special. Then three days later, she received a phone call from Terrance.

Chapter 16

Brianna paced back and forth, her right thumb finding its way into the edge of her mouth intermittently. She bit the back of her thumbnail, forced the hand down when she realized what she was doing, then began pacing the floor again.

"If he thinks he's going to get off this easily, he had better think again," she muttered under her breath. The venomous statement was almost whispered despite the fact that there was no one within hearing distance.

Jacqueline was asleep in her room, the door left ajar in case she awakened. Brianna's return to work after her daughter's birth had been a welcome escape from a deteriorating marriage.

The schedules, the details, the nuances of juggling being wife, mother and busy nurse in a hectic environment all worked against one another. The additional stress of coming face-to-face with the reality of a waning relationship did not help the situation. Now, amidst the marital chaos which had become her everyday existence, all that seemed to matter was getting from one day to the next. Still, divorce seemed the easy way out.

By court order, Jacqueline was required to visit her father periodically, and to even stay overnight whenever he requested it. That decision, and the final numbers associated with child support and spousal alimony, were the fine points which still irked Brianna. She felt Terrance owed her a lifestyle and compensation for the pain and suffering which she'd endured in the past eighteen months. She no longer counted the first two years in which they'd been relatively happy. In her mind, that period was now categorized as a mere fluke or the dazzling honeymoon phase.

She'd never dreamed that their marriage would only last three years after they'd walked down the aisle, nor that it would end like this. But the reality of it was that she'd also never believed they'd go the distance and grow old, gray and feeble together. The catalyst was a chance encounter. Sometimes she wondered if she had left earlier that day, or taken a different route, if things would have shaken out differently. A chance encounter with a total stranger had done it. After that day, Brianna's life had taken on a different hue, an enhanced significance. Nothing was the same, nothing ever would be.

Devon Reid had seen to that. She'd tried, on several occasions, to rationalize the feelings and reactions he inspired but it was to no avail. Each time she was in his presence, her senses were heightened, her body reacted and she felt a keen sense of being alive, something that she thought she'd lost with the birth of her daughter.

They'd met quite by accident. Two automobiles entering into the same intersection at the same time, both drivers certain that they, and they alone, had the right of way. One making a left turn, the other intending to continue directly through the intersection, both encountering an abrupt meeting of automobile fenders.

Brianna remembered that her hands shook as she wrote out the contact information to exchange, and she wondered if it was because she was nervous about the accident, or if the total stranger had caused it. His eyes were the strangest color, almost an olive-green set in a face which was just short of remarkable, his skin tanned burnt-umber from the sun, though she suspected that he was really a good deal lighter. His hair was cut short but the grain was indicative of his having taken care of it at some point. At the moment, it appeared that he'd left somewhere in a hurry and had not bothered to brush or comb it. For some reason, that fact intrigued Brianna and endeared him to her. His clothing fit as if it had been tailored by a custom shop and Brianna recognized his loafers as Gucci. That single piece of information seemed to embed itself in her mind, standing out as a defining characteristic. She remained silent as he continued to take notes from the insurance card she'd handed to him.

Nervous about the whole ordeal, Brianna found herself unwilling to engage in conversation. But she recognized that under the circumstances, a degree of silent decorum was probably more in order anyway. Then she realized that she wanted to know something about this total stranger who'd inadvertently crashed into her life.

Still, she watched him quietly, knowing that he was probably a good deal younger than she was and less than interested in women whom he felt could not operate a vehicle and chew gum at the same time.

At that moment, dusk was approaching and the sun filled the sky with perfect symmetry against a blood-tinged backdrop. For a moment she was mesmerized by the impact of the colors, then realized that he was speaking to her.

"Hey, look, I hope that we can clear up any damage and repair work on our own. I hate to go through the insurance companies," he said quickly, putting his license and other information into the back pocket of his khaki pants.

"Sure. I mean, well, the car doesn't seem to be too badly hit. Thank goodness for that much anyway," she added, looking at the small dent on the left fender of her Volvo. The bumper also hung slightly askew, but was not totally detached nor was it badly dented.

"I'm sorry about this. I mean, don't take that for an admission of wrongdoing or anything. I just wanted to say that it would have been good to avoid all of this." He ended the statement with a sheepish grin, and Brianna's heart thudded loudly in her chest. She didn't know if he was flirting, was sincere or if she was just overreacting. Whatever the case, she found herself rooted to the spot, unwilling to move her feet or to tear her eyes away from his face which was handsome, tanned and bore a striking resemblance to someone she'd never met, but who was probably every woman's dream.

"I'm not sure whose fault it was. I mean, one moment I was making a turn, the next you were right there and it was just too late to turn away," she added quickly. Then just as quickly and in total contrast to how she actually felt, tears formed in her eyes and she found herself sobbing uncontrollably.

Devon was immediately contrite, reaching into his car for tissues first, then offering them to her while speaking soothingly.

"Look, please don't cry. I absolutely hate to see anyone cry. It makes me feel totally responsible. Come on, it's not that bad. I promise not to cause any problems and make a lot of nuisance about this. Come on. That's it. Here, blow your nose."

With those words, Brianna's sobs subsided, her fears allayed. She was instead filled with another emotion, one more powerful than its predecessor. Unexplainably, she felt she could trust this man, felt she could be who she was with him, with total acceptance and approval. There had only been a few moments of exchange, but it had been enough.

"I'm sorry. It's probably just the shock of knowing that either of us could have been seriously hurt. I'm on my way to work at the hospital so bodily injury is something I see on a daily basis. Automobile accidents can be the cause of some pretty horrific damage. We're both lucky," she said.

"Are you a nurse?" he asked, suddenly noticing the white outfit and shoes. It was his first direct question and she was caught off guard for a split second. All kinds of things ran through her mind before answering, then she responded with candor.

"Yes, a nurse at Regency Hospital on the north side of the island."

"Great. I pass there almost daily. Never knew they

had angels at work there," he said as he turned and walked toward his car.

The remark hung in the air as Brianna entered her vehicle. She hadn't felt the need to mention a husband, but her wedding ring had been clearly visible. On the one hand, she hoped that Devon had seen it and recognized it for what it was. On the flip side, she wanted to go on feeling the way she did right then forever.

He'd called the next morning, set up an appointment for them to exchange the remaining information and the rest became a blur.

Reid, as he'd instructed her to call him, had a way about him, something which defied description. It called for the use of more than your imagination and more importantly, set Brianna's heart on fire. Little by little, day by day, encounter by encounter, their time spent became more about them as individuals and less about the unfortunate collision of two ill-fated vehicles.

What began as an accident at a busy intersection, soon moved to lunch, then on to short walks at the pier. Whatever it was brewed quickly and Brianna realized, almost immediately, that she was powerless to stop it. Even after she pointed out that she did, indeed, have a husband and a child, they continued to make feeble excuses to see one another. To Reid, it absolutely made no difference.

The first time they made love, they'd driven to a small beachfront area on the far northern side of the island after Reid had insisted he wanted to talk to her about something special.

The lunch they'd originally planned was picked up

at a local sidewalk restaurant that sold conch and bami, local island fare. Two bottles of beer and a blanket which Reid had stowed in the trunk of his still dented vehicle completed their beach blanket picnic.

Brianna watched as Reid spread the blanket out carefully, then took her by one hand as he encouraged her to sit at his feet. He then laid out a couple of white linen napkins which he'd also taken from the car trunk, popped the tops off the beer and settled in beside her as they each faced the ocean surf.

It was beautiful. Quiet, serene and deserted, the beach was something that Brianna rarely had an opportunity to visit. With her and Terrance's schedules shaping up to be at polar opposites, there was very little time to enjoy simple outdoor activities like picnics and such. Or so she'd told herself.

As she sat there that day, her arms around her knees which she'd pulled in tightly against her chest, she wondered just how much she and Terrance had given up in recent months. Their marriage was like a binding contract, one which neither of them really enjoyed but were unable or unwilling to negate.

"What are you thinking?"

The question was a whisper Brianna wanted to ignore, wanted to drown out with the sound of the ocean that continued to pound the shoreline. She dared not answer, dared not acknowledge the thoughts, the feelings, the need she felt beginning to take over her mind, her body. She was powerless to stop the flood of emotion which threatened to overtake her very existence.

Reid sensed her confusion and doubted that Brianna realized how long he'd thought of being there with her, alone. In his mind, there was very little time in life for recrimination. The good times, the good things were there to be sampled, enjoyed and consumed. He watched the ocean for some moments, then decided it was time.

On that day, Devon Reid became more than just someone whom Brianna had encountered in a collision. He'd become a lover, a confidant and an intrusion which she immediately interpreted as bringing extraordinary meaning to her life.

Brianna had never expected to become enmeshed in a full-fledged love affair, but there was no turning back. Not after he kissed her, moving her hair to one side of her neck as he placed soft kisses there. Certainly not after he removed her clothing without so much as a word, touched her in places she'd never realized existed and whispered her name into her mouth as she climaxed for the second time.

The afternoon at the beach was a catalyst in their relationship after which there was no turning back. For either of them. And though she was reluctant to admit it, it put her marriage to Terrance in serious jeopardy.

Two months later, when she realized that Reid did not hold a traditional job, that he actually sold illegal substances to the many seaside shops and restaurants lining the road into Nassau's capital, and that she'd fallen in love with a man who was the polar opposite of her husband, Brianna cried for two days.

Terrance had been out of town at a medical conference, and Jacqueline was staying overnight with her parents. Reid promised that he would pick her up early, they'd have dinner and then she could spend the night at his place.

None of this happened. Instead, she found herself calling him repeatedly, leaving messages and then waiting in vain for a return call. The evening progressed with an ever increasing degree of deterioration. Brianna looked at herself in the mirror for the first time in a long while. Clarity somehow made its way through and she saw what she'd been unwilling to acknowledge, unable to accept and what was unthinkable on any scale. She had thrown her marriage into a tailspin for a man who was not dependable, unemployed by all conventional markers and was a felon in the making.

Despite the revelation, she continued to see him, hoping against hope that she'd somehow gotten it all wrong. Little by little, the bits and pieces of Reid's sordid involvement with drugs, his lack of discretion when it came to his personal life, and his apparent attraction to married women came to light.

Brianna stumbled on most of this quite by accident. Once she realized that she'd fallen in love with a pusher with a penchant for unavailable partners, Brianna became incensed. It was hard for her to believe that she'd succumbed to an age-old line, a common fall from grace. Thus, she began a frantic search for a way to somehow make it right.

Brianna decided that if there was one thing she could do to try and change him, it would be worth it. She began laying the groundwork for what she felt would be a triumphant redemption of the man she now felt she loved.

At first, it seemed to work. Reid agreed with everything she said in theory, or so he said. It was only after he'd sat her down, talked to her for an hour and a half about the multileveled marketing plan he envisioned, that she'd realized there was no opting out for this man. He was committed to a lifestyle that she'd only read about in adventure novels and seen played out on the big screen, often with a disastrous ending.

It was in that moment that Brianna realized she'd made the biggest mistake of her life. At the same time, she also acknowledged that the only way to rectify any of it was to walk away. She did so with absolutely no regrets, no forwarding address and no recriminations.

Which is why on the eve of the weekend which Terrance had just spent in Fort Lauderdale, she'd done her best to convince her estranged husband that perhaps the best solution to their problems would be to give the marriage another try.

She had no idea how bad her timing was, nor did she know that Terrance had come to a final conclusion on their marriage when he'd signed the divorce papers. That conclusion included a no-return policy which was stamped *Final Sale,* front and back. His liaison with Brianna was over, all ties cut, except when it came to Jacqueline. And even in that area, there was little room for negotiation because the courts had already desig-nated a joint custody agreement and included it in the final decree.

What he was unaware of was Brianna's change of heart and her determination to somehow right the wrongs she had set forth. And if that included changing the court's mind, then so be it.

First things first—and that meant Terrance Reid Marshall. Brianna willed herself to put her hand into her pocket, fighting the urge to return the thumb to its warm, welcome place. She silently vowed to break the lifelong habit if it meant that the man she'd betrayed and lost would somehow return to her.

Silently, she issued the proclamation which seemed most appropriate, then thought of her young daughter's face.

"It's for Jacqueline," she whispered to no one in particular. Not once did she address the transgressions, not once did she allow her mind to touch upon the act of betrayal, nor did she think it necessary to recognize her part in the marriage's failure.

Her plan was a simple one. Reconnect the components of her family unit, realign the elements of their now defunct love and take it from there. It was simple, effective and quite possibly doable. Except for one element. The undefined X factor had already been unleashed.

Chapter 17

Terrance picked up the phone, dialed the number, then hung up as he heard his name called over the hospital public address system. "Paging Dr. Marshall, paging Dr. Marshall. Please check in at the second floor laboratory."

He dialed the laboratory's three-digit number, then waited for someone to pick up. He'd wanted to talk to Skye but the atmosphere at the clinic was not the environment to do it in. In their first conversation, he wanted to establish a degree of intimacy, wanted the conversation to be lighthearted and full of the promise of perhaps what was to come. As he headed toward the clinic's in-house laboratory, he decided to wait until he could speak to her from the sanctity of his own home and placed the business card she'd written her home number on back into the pocket of his white lab coat. Pale blue scrubs were beneath it and though he had not gone into the surgery suite yet that day, he felt more comfortable dressed this way whenever he saw patients.

As he approached the double doors of the laboratory, one of the clinic's newer physician assistants walked out. She stood about five feet without shoes, weighed perhaps one hundred and ten pounds, and had a pixie-like face. The short cropped haircut she'd recently adopted accentuated her features perfectly and Terrance smiled, said a quick hello and held the door as she walked past him. He was tempted to watch her walk away, then realized that there was something vaguely familiar about her. It dawned on him at that moment that, for whatever the reason, she reminded him of Skye. Perhaps it was her smile, or maybe it was her stride. He shook his head slightly, wondering what it was about Skye that had him thinking of her whenever he looked at any woman, especially an attractive one.

He spoke with the laboratory technician at length concerning the test results of a patient who exhibited signs of possible pneumonia. Both the X-rays and sputum results confirmed the worse, but Terrance also knew that with antibiotics, the patient's chances for a full recovery were excellent.

In the two weeks which had passed since he'd returned from Florida, he'd been busy. He'd done his best to make time to spend with Jacqueline. His daughter was the best thing in his life at the moment and he did not want to do anything which would further exacerbate the situation with her mother.

It was becoming more and more clear that Brianna was exhibiting signs of a change of heart. He'd called to speak with Jacqueline, told her he loved her, then just before he hung up the phone, Brianna had come back on the line, her voice sounding soft and syrupy.

"Hey, just wanted to remind you that I have plans for the weekend. What time will you be able to pick up Jaclyn?" she'd asked. They sometimes called their daughter by the shortened version of her name, but the question had thoroughly thrown Terrance off balance and immediately raised his guard.

Terrance already knew that it was his weekend to spend with their daughter. Why did she feel the need to mention that she had plans for the weekend, especially since she had twice asked him to sit down with her in an effort to discuss the possible rekindling of the relationship? His gut churned acid as he did his best to ignore the signs of game playing.

"I should be there around ten-thirty in the morning. Give my little princess a big hug and kiss for me. I missed her a lot." He ended on that note, glad to be able to focus on something other than the tension which Brianna seemed determined to initiate.

"Great. I'll have her ready." Her reply was terse, unrehearsed and short, which spelled annoyance. Obviously his lack of response to her reference to weekend plans had not played into her hand.

Terrance hung up, then did his best to concentrate on the paperwork on his desk. There was never enough time to handle all the clinical and administrative tasks that owning/operating and practicing in your own business dictated. Both he and his partner, a medical school buddy whom he'd become thoroughly attached to by his junior year, had thrown themselves into the business.

Parkside Medical would be in existence in only eight

months, but they had already gained a solid reputation amongst the people in and around the immediate area of Nassau township. Both physicians in residence had done the bulk of their studies abroad, then come home to finish the task at the University of the West Indies.

The one year of studying he'd completed in England had done wonders for his understanding of the importance of medicine to the community at large. When he'd returned to his birthplace, he immediately realized that Nassau needed an ambulatory facility which could facilitate day patients representing a number of medical procedures.

On most days, the hospital was full of patients representing a wide variety of minor illnesses and maladies. Sometimes, there was the occasional cut or broken bone which required stitches and/or a cast setting.

In his estimation, the clinic would need to bring in a resident surgeon capable of performing minor procedures on site. Hence, they would need to purchase additional expensive pieces of equipment capable of X-rays, sonograms and other necessary medical functions.

Terrance's training as an internist would enable him to cover a disproportionate number of the patients who entered their doors. His partner Vernon's specialty, pediatrics, would cover all those patients ranging in age from birth through thirteen, although he would also see adolescents up to the age of sixteen.

Both men loved medicine but for different reasons. Terrance loved the feeling it gave him to diagnose, provide the proper protocol and the difference he saw in the patient's face when all of the above had been accomplished.

Vernon Bradley, on the other hand, just loved kids. He and his wife Deborah had been told they would never be able to have them, and each time he weighed a newborn baby, administered shots or examined a precocious toddler, his eyes sparkled.

The Bradleys had discussed the possibility of adoption but both were holding out with the faint glimmer of hope for a miraculous blessing. In their minds, time was on their side.

The practice would surely require solid concentration, a steady stream of hard work and a total commitment. Terrance closed his eyes, sat back in the chair at his desk and put both hands behind his head. He had another hour's worth of work before him, but it was already after ten p.m. If he waited any longer, it would be inappropriate to place the call that he'd been delaying for days.

He dialed the cell number listed and was connected directly to voice mail. He silently swore, then went back to the paperwork on his desk. Twenty-five minutes passed and the stack of papers he'd tackled was more than halfway done. He gathered them up into a folder, turned out the lights in his tiny office at the hospital and headed for home.

He arrived fifteen minutes later, thirsty and tired. He walked into the kitchen, poured himself a glass of water, then sat down to finish the task at hand.

He reached for the pen, put it down and dialed instead. Skye picked up on the third ring.

"Hello."

"Well, hello to you, too. How've you been?"

Her voice sounded exactly as he remembered it and the force of emotions which coursed through both his mind and body made him grin widely. He was glad she could not see him, glad to be speaking with her finally and glad that he'd already accomplished much of what he'd set out to do earlier in the evening so that he could talk to her without thinking of it.

"I'm fine. Just fine. How're things in the Bahamas?" she asked, recognizing his voice immediately. It sounded warm and intimate, welcoming almost, and she realized that she'd been waiting for his call without knowing that she did so.

"Things here are fine. I'm sorry it took me a while to call but when I got back, all hell broke loose at the hospital. It was really hectic," he added, remembering the backlog of patients he'd had to see before his patient load had even allowed him a moment's peace.

"Wow, I do know what you mean. It's a totally unrelated field, but the mortgage industry has been like a bear market recently, too."

"It's probably the time of year or something. Seems like everybody is busy and overwhelmed by their commitments," he said, wondering if she was also facing drama in her personal life, as well. They'd never discussed a significant other in her life and he hoped there would not be the need for it. His mind shifted for a moment and he remembered their lovemaking. If there was a significant other in her picture, that relationship was in double jeopardy.

"So, tell me what you've been up to—don't hold anything back, either," he said, the hint of laughter in his voice.

"Oh, so you really want to know, with all the intimate details?" she asked.

"That's right—especially the intimate details." He was fishing. It would be better to know right away if this woman was involved elsewhere before he fully committed his mind, his heart and his soul to her. He'd already held her in his arms, already felt her heart beating rapidly against his as passion overtook them both. That much was a given. He was now vying for her mind, doing his best to see if what they'd shared had any bite behind it, or could be trusted to go the distance.

In some ways, it felt premature. In other ways, it represented a long overdue connection to another human being. In that moment, Terrance recognized that he'd long ago negated the connection between him and Brianna, perhaps well before either of them recognized the signs of deterioration in their marriage.

"Well, first let me say thank you so much for the beautiful flowers. How'd you know that orange is my favorite color?"

"Actually, I didn't know but I suspected you liked it when you wore those orange jogging shorts. I thought of them when I picked out the flowers. Kept thinking of you in those shorts. I felt inspired," he added, then laughed wickedly.

"I see. Well, that explains it. I'm glad I inspired you. And I loved the flowers. Thank you for thinking of me."

"You're more than welcome. So, now, tell me. What else have you been up to?"

"I've been working my tail off trying to get a greater percentage of my pipeline closed. That's the large and the small of it. I wish I could include some juicy tidbits but I haven't even been out socially since my return."

"I'm sorry to hear that you're leading such a boring

existence. But then, not that sorry. If I were living closer to you, I'd whisk you away for two-hour lunches, dinners that ended with breakfast the next morning and nights filled with lovemaking under the stars." Silence ensued for several seconds, then Terrance laughed nervously. Perhaps he'd said too much.

"Have I scared you off with my descriptive mind?"

"No," Skye replied quietly. "It's just that what you described was so lovely I wasn't sure of my response. On the one hand if you're joking around, your joke is definitely at my expense. On the other, if you're serious about that statement, then we're both in trouble. Big trouble."

"Well, consider yourself stamped with a capital T. I know it's late in the evening, and the things we say will seem out of whack in the morning, but just know this. I haven't thought about much else since my return from a most promising weekend spent in your company. Fort Lauderdale now holds itself in my mind as my number-one destination on the planet and all because I met you there."

"Wow, that's a really expansive compliment, both to me and to the state of Florida. Seriously, I guess we did share an intense experience, but I just want you to know that it was something totally out of the ordinary for me. I mean, from the time you walked out to the car as I arrived, the whole weekend was in a dreamlike state. I'm sure even Nita and Branch were wondering just what had come over two of their best friends in the world. I know I definitely had a couple of conversations with myself about the things I was allowing to happen with you." She did not want to diminish what had occurred between them, but she did want to explain her behavior so that he would not think she engaged in indiscriminate sexual encounters on a regular basis.

"You know, I never thought of what we shared as anything other than extraordinary. That's the honest truth," he replied. "I knew from just watching you that it was as intense for you as it was for me, and also that you weren't accustomed to doing that sort of thing. I think that's why it turned me on so much. It was like I couldn't stop touching you."

"I see. So, you were also feeling it. I wondered if it was just me being pushy and forward and I hated myself for that. I actually figured I might not ever hear from you again, but am so glad that you called."

"Yeah I am, too. I still want to touch you. Right now, I'm imagining that lavender two-piece you wore and the way it hugged your hips and breasts and other things. I can hardly breathe. I don't want to think like this with you on the other end of the phone miles away. It serves no purpose other than to get me totally frustrated, raising my blood pressure, pulse and respiration, not to mention other things. Then, there is no satisfactory recourse. I'll probably toss and turn all night."

Skye laughed then, totally and gutturally. She knew that he was joking, hoped he was anyway, but in all actuality, she, too, was affected by both the sound of his voice and the mental picture she'd sought to block out when she returned home. It was of Terrance when she'd first arrived, wearing a tobacco-colored silk shirt, tan slacks and loafers.

He'd looked collegiate, preppy and very much like South Florida, which is what had drawn her to him initially. That and the sunglasses that covered his eyes, allowing no semblance of expression to be gathered on this tall, handsome stranger who was a mutual weekend guest of Branch and Nita's.

"Well, I am delighted to know that you share in my dilemma. Now, what can we do about this awful situation?"

"Nothing right now. I'm buried with work, can't even think about taking any kind of vacation time," he answered quickly. "There are some official days coming up in about a month, though. Would it be too premature for me to invite you down for a three-day weekend?" He knew the risks, knew the danger, but asked anyway, hoping against hope that she would say yes.

"Wow. You know I've wanted to visit the Bahamas for some time now, but I'm not sure it's a good idea." Her hesitation was genuine. Yet, in the far reaches of her mind, Skye knew that she wanted to see him. The conversation they'd had at the airport still echoed in her mind. He was recently divorced, with a young daughter. The possibility for drama definitely existed, yet she trusted that he knew how to handle himself, his life and his situation.

"Guess you have no excuse then. Or should I say you now have the perfect excuse?" he asked.

"I'm not really sure, but I do know that I would love to see you. Let me think about it." The words tumbled from her mouth and Skye wondered what exactly had gotten into her. Sure, she'd enjoyed his company, the attention, even the lovemaking. But the venture on the table would require three real days of interaction with a man she'd spent only hours with. Her thoughts were interrupted by Terrance's voice and she realized it was almost too late to change her mind.

"Okay, that's a reasonable answer. When you do decide to say yes, I want your stay to be stress free. You deserve that. Just know that I also want it to be memorable," he added then.

"Sounds like it's too good to be true. Not only do I get to stay on a Caribbean island, but it sounds as if I'm to be looked after, too. You're a real charmer, Dr. Marshall," Skye added, addressing him by his last name for the first time.

Once again, the words were out before she'd really defined them in her head and she wondered if he would always affect her in this way.

"It takes one to know one. You're the charming one," he teased.

"Oh, so you're putting it back into my court now. Well, that's okay, too. I've been called a lot worse," she laughed.

Terrance listened to the sound of Skye's voice, noting the texture, the tone, the words she chose. He realized that he genuinely enjoyed the woman on the other line. He hoped that in time, she'd come to accept his invitation and he realized that he was excited at the prospect of showing her around his world. He'd be sure to choose a weekend when he was not scheduled to have his daughter Jacqueline. There would be time enough later, if things went well, for the two of them to meet. He thought of Brianna and what her reaction might be when confronted with the fact that he'd truly moved forward, then immediately dismissed it. She'd managed to move on at a record-breaking pace even before they'd officially separated. For his part in the breakup of their marriage, Terrance had paid a hefty price, which included the disintegration of his actual home. Weekends and holidays spent with a daughter whom he was accustomed to holding and interacting with on a daily basis left much to be desired. He'd come to terms with that slowly, unwillingly, grudgingly, which was why as more and more time passed, he held his daughter and all that she meant to him even more dearly.

"If you like, I can check the flights for you. I know all the best airlines which come into the area at the good rates."

"Whoa—slow down. Remember, I haven't really agreed to come, but I will think about it. I promise."

Skye liked the fact that Terrance seemed to be a take-charge kind of person, something she'd always admired in a man, but rarely found herself confronted with.

"Okay. You'll have to forgive me. I'm really looking forward to your visit so my mind is already moving forward to the actual mechanics of it. There are several carriers which connect in Miami creating an almost shuttle-like stream of activity between here and there. They're usually the most reasonable. By the way, have you ever flown in a twin-engine plane before?"

"Not really. I'm not usually your best person in that environment, either. It's just that once I was on a plane and the weather was awful. You know, rain, thunder and lightning, and the plane kept dropping from its altitude as we went through a really turbulent area. I swore then that I'd never fly again. It was a promise made in vain but there's absolutely no time that I am really comfort-able up there." The revelation, once stated, made Skye feel as though she'd put her innermost feelings on the table for inspection. If he was going to admonish her for being silly, immature or otherwise lacking in sophistication, now would be the time.

"Wow, I can't imagine what you went through. I've never been in a rainstorm, but turbulence seems to follow me. Twice I've experienced the oxygen masks coming unglued which is probably the silliest looking situation you never want to see. It scares everyone to death because they look like some kind of lifeline hanging from the ceiling above your head. Then you realize that you actually might need to strap them on. It's then that you remember you paid absolutely no attention whatsoever to the flight attendant earlier. That's when most people panic."

They both began to laugh at the absurdity involved and the pure mayhem which would probably ensue.

At that moment, Skye realized that Terrance was probably one of the nicest guys she'd ever met. It was then that she knew she would definitely take the trip offered, only she'd wait a little before she let him know that.

She'd originally wondered why he'd taken so long to call, then realized that with the daily schedules they each adhered to, it was very often impossible to carve out the moments necessary to reach out. She was, however, impressed by the flowers he'd sent, the intensity of their first conversation and the things they'd discussed. It was as if no time, no space, no distance had taken place.

"So, how's the ankle?" he asked abruptly.

"Actually, it's been fine. Every once in a while, if I'm wearing heels, or if I go up and down a flight of stairs, I'll feel a little soreness in it. Other than that, I don't notice anything wrong with it. Thank goodness it hasn't been swelling, either."

"Well, you're lucky. You must admit though—you had the best in medical care, which is probably why you healed so quickly." He issued the last statement with the utmost sincerity, which only made it even more absurd.

Skye laughed, with Terrance joining in. "You know you're rotten. I mean, you didn't really do anything, just had me put my leg up and stay off it," she added.

"See, that was the miraculous part of it. Remember the lovemaking? Well, that's when I practiced my best doctoring efforts on you. Now, just know that not every patient gets that kind of doctor care. Consider yourself fortunate, woman."

She laughed so hard then that she had to put the phone down for a moment. Tears filled her eyes as she remembered clearly that they had in fact managed to make love despite her damaged ankle.

"So, you're telling me that without the lovemaking, I would still be limping around here?"

"Absolutely. In fact, without that key ingredient, you may never have been able to even hobble your way home. Would have resigned yourself to the greater Fort Lauderdale area forever. Sorry, babe, but that's the truth."

His synopsis was so ridiculous that even he had to laugh, thus breaking up the seriousness he'd delivered his circumstantial evidence with.

"You are one crazy man," she stated, convinced that his imagination surely was one on the level of a psychotic inmate who'd just perhaps reached the point of no return at a local mental health institution.

"I'm so very sorry to have to disappoint you, young

lady. The truth of the matter is that what I've been telling you is the honest to goodness truth. If you don't believe me, that's on you. But I'd better warn you that your ankle can and will rebel if you decide to denounce me."

"Well, under those circumstances, how could a girl say no? Anyway, let's leave it on the table for the next time we speak. By then, I'll be more familiar with my schedule in the month of September anyway. Thank you, Terrance, for asking me. I'm totally flattered," she added, her voice deepening with sincerity.

"Just say yes. I'll call you again in a couple of days. That's all I want to hear. Yes. Nothing else, no excuses, no badly executed reasons, no recriminations."

"Has anyone ever told you that you're relentless? I promise that when we speak next, I will definitely have an answer for you. Promise."

"Okay. On that note, I'd better let you get some rest. I have to be at the hospital at seven in the morning so I'm going to hit the hay right about now. It's been great talking to you. I knew it would be."

"Well, thank you, Terrance. I've enjoyed our conversation, also. And I look forward to our next time." She wanted him to know that she did like him, did want to spend time with him, but needed to think his offer over. A long weekend was the kind of commitment one could surely interpret as either purely a sexual tryst or the real beginning of getting to know another human being.

They hung up then, both wondering if the other one realized just how much the conversation had meant.

Skye pulled up several Web sites she was accustomed to checking whenever making flight reservations and saved the information. She then printed three pages of flight itineraries and wondered when she'd made the leap from thinking about it to checking on it.

In preparing for bed later that evening, Skye realized two things. One, Terrance Marshall was an alpha male. Two, with that kind of personality, she had absolutely no chance of avoiding him if she was what he had his mind set on.

Clearly, the chase was on.

Chapter 18

Branch wanted in. He and Nita both did. They'd watched the two people whom they loved the most do a tango in front of their very eyes, then walk determinedly into an airline terminal and now knew nothing of what was going on.

"I told you something was up from the time he picked up the photographs, pointed to Skye's picture and said, 'So, who's that?'" Nita said as they had dinner the week after their weekend guests had departed.

They'd returned to their daily routines quickly, going to work, the gym and then restocking the pantry and freezer on the second day. Now, as they sat having a dinner of chicken breasts sautéed with sun-dried tomatoes, olive oil, capers and broccoli over angel-hair pasta, Branch sat back listening to his wife recount her suspicions.

"I'm not so sure. I mean, I could see that they were chatting, making eye contact and all that stuff, but I never really suspected anything. I did think it was odd that they disappeared Saturday might at the club. But I really figured Skye was dealing with the whole ankle thing and that Terrance was just helping."

Nita shook her head, laughing at the same time. "I know. I know. And they were both so cute trying to act as though nothing was going on. Even the night at the Harbor Club, they were definitely all over one another in the corner. Then, we practically had to call out an all-points bulletin to get them out of the club. But you know I didn't want to say anything, then those two thugs approached us in the parking lot and I really thought things were going to get ugly. Has Terrance always had that temper?"

"Yeah, pretty much. Even back in college, he wasn't one to be messed with. And neither was I, for that matter," Branch added emphatically.

Nita patted her husband's hand in agreement. "Honey, you don't even have to go there. I know you're no joke, especially when it comes to somebody trying to jack your ride. Those guys must have been smoking or on drugs, or something. Why on earth don't folks do whatever it is that they have to do to be on the up-and-up?"

"Honey, everybody is not structured to do a nine to five and all that. For some people, that's really hard and so is all the rest that goes along with it. That's the way of the world. But, back to our two favorite people. Have you heard anything from Skye?"

"Not since she called to let me know she'd arrived back in ATL okay. I didn't have the heart to question her about anything at the time because it was really late and all. But, I almost said something while she was telling me that she had had a really great time. I stopped myself just short of asking her if Terrance had anything to do with it. I figured if she wanted to share the details, she would."

"Uh-huh…don't I know it. Terrance is probably caught up in his practice and the kind of drama that goes along with a new divorce. He didn't have the time to go into details, just that everything was final."

"You know, I really didn't have any idea that it had gotten that bad. I knew they weren't doing well 'cause each time he'd call, she was nowhere in the vicinity. I'd always ask for her, just to say hello, but that girl was gone. I spoke to the baby a couple of times… She's so precious." Nita's voice took on a different tone when she spoke of Jacqueline and Branch noted it, but immediately dismissed it. It wasn't that he was opposed to or disliked children. It was more along the lines that he and Nita were nowhere ready to begin a family. He wanted them to enjoy one another for a while before they began to add little folks to the equation.

"I know. I knew something was wrong, but could never pinpoint it. And Terrance never spoke on it. Not until the end. Then he told me it was over, final, kaput. Whatever happened, it sounded like it was definitely ugly."

"I'm sure. It never ends until it gets just that way. I guess the weekend getaway was just the right thing for him then. But I just hope that he's not on the rebound from whatever happened with Brianna. I mean, Skye is my best friend, I love her and I do not want her to be hurt or used in any way."

"Baby, let me just say this about Terrance. I don't know exactly what's going on with him, don't pretend to know what's going on in his head right now, but I think Skye is a big girl and can take care of herself. Also, he's not the kind of guy to just use and discard a woman, no matter what the case. If they connected, which I suspect they did, it was because each of them was feeling it. That's all anyone can ever ask for. Right?"

Nita nodded silently, then put one finger into the air, solidly emphasizing her next words. "I know Terrance is your boy. I know you're going to stand up for him no matter what, but I just want it on the record that Skye is special. She always has been and always will be. So, he better not mess up." She ended the statement with a direct look into her husband's eyes, then they both leaned forward, touching their lips together quickly.

"Honey, please don't worry. It was a weekend away from home, both of them probably needed the diversion, et cetera, et cetera, et cetera. Now, let's stop talking about them and talk about something much more important." Branch pulled his chair closer to the one in which his wife was seated, closing the gap between them instantly.

"And just what is it that you have on your mind?" Nita asked suspiciously.

"Well, for one thing, we're here in our home, all alone finally and there's nothing to stop us from doing anything, anywhere we want to, if you get my drift," he said suggestively, a smile spreading across his face.

"Has anyone ever told you that you have a vivid imagination?" she said, leaning over the table as she kissed him softly on the lips.

"Honey, just give me five minutes in the bedroom. I have a little surprise planned. Don't worry about the dishes. Just pour us both a glass of wine, count to fifty and then come on back."

Nita watched her husband's face light up with a mischievous look, then shook her head.

"What about the food? It's still out—I don't want it to spoil."

"What... Okay, I'll help you. That'll make it faster. Come on," he added, picking up the plates and following his wife into the kitchen where she began putting the foods she'd prepared into the refrigerator.

They wiped down the countertops, the range and the table, loaded the dishwasher, then Branch headed toward the bedroom.

He closed the white shutters, which dimmed the sunlight still coming through them. The room was still bathed in the diminishing sunlight that the approaching dusk offered, its orange-like rays filling the room with warmth and light that reflected off the walls brilliantly.

Reaching into the bag which he'd brought in earlier, Branch removed four white candles, placing them around the garden bathtub and poured a healthy amount of bubble bath in before turning on the faucets. He lit the candles, turned down the bed and removed the bouquet of roses he'd placed under the bed earlier. Eleven stems were stripped of their petals, the fragrance filling the room as he spread them on the bed and on the floor leading to the bath. One single pink rose remained, and he placed it carefully on Nita's pillow.

He stripped naked, brushed his teeth then put on a fresh pair of navy-blue boxer shorts.

"Okay, what's going on in here?" Nita called out softly, turning the knob on the bedroom door slowly.

"Why don't you come in and find out for yourself," Branch called out, opening the door.

Nita gasped as she saw the pink petals on the floor, noted the turned-down bed and then the glow coming from the master bathroom caught her eyes. She grinned, moved toward the bathroom with a questioning look on her face, then gasped. The entire bathroom was filled with light from the candles which lined the back of the ledge, rose petals creating a soft cushion on the floor leading toward the tub. Tears filled her eyes as she looked at Branch and she quickly wiped them away with the back of one hand.

"You're incredible and I love you," she said softly before walking toward him.

"I know."

Nita wound her arms around his neck, drew his head down to hers and their lips met in a kiss that was passionate and intensely tender all at once. She began to remove her jewelry, walked toward one of the twin basins and proceeded to wash her face. Branch watched her silently, then walked up behind her, turned her around, and after placing both hands on her wet face, kissed her passionately.

"Come on, the water will be cold if we wait any longer."

His words were whispered with an urgency that Nita responded to immediately. She wrapped her arms around his neck, raising her lips to his in a kiss that was scalding.

Half an hour later, as the water cooled and neither could wait any longer, they made love without reserve, without question, without barriers.

For the first time since their honeymoon night, Nita called out his name. Branch covered her mouth with his own as he, too, found the ultimate release within her body.

Later, as they lay in bed wrapped in each other's arms, all thoughts of Terrance and Skye had been replaced with their own.

Chapter 19

Skye checked the Internet for flights, almost made the reservations, then backed out at the last minute. Basically, she wondered if she was doing the right thing. The last conversation she'd had with Terrance had caused her stomach to knot with anticipation. Fed by the rush of adrenaline, she'd gone on the Internet, found flights which were fairly reasonable and almost sealed the deal. Twenty-four hours later, she was tempted to cancel the whole thing. As a final safety precaution, she kept the reservations to herself, thinking if she neglected to share them with Terrance, she could always cancel and give some earth-shattering excuse.

He called again two days later. Although Skye could tell he was a little hesitant, he was also charming beyond belief, single-minded in his intention and extremely to the point.

"Look, there is no reason for you to hesitate or to debate this, Skye. You don't have to worry about anything—I have the entire thing planned out. All you have to do is choose when you want to come, book the ticket and the rest is a done deal. I'll reimburse the money to you when you get here. The only reason I'm not booking it is because I don't know your schedule well enough to do that. Just settle on either the second or third weekend of either of the next two months. Honestly, I'd love it if you would come sooner rather than later, but I realize that you're a busy lady so you may have to postpone the trip by a couple of weeks. That's okay. I can wait because I already know that when you do get here, we're going to have a great time no matter when that happens."

His words echoed the feelings she'd had whenever she thought of being with him and once again, she thought it would be good to see him. She relaxed as he spoke of the things he wanted to plan, the time they'd spend together and the fun he already anticipated having.

"Okay, I'll make the reservations tonight," she said, then wondered when and how she'd come to that conclusion so quickly.

"Are you sure? I mean, I don't want you to feel pressured, but I really do want to see you."

"It's fine. I want to see you, too." They talked for another twenty minutes, catching up on different aspects of their jobs, their lives and simply because neither wanted to sever the connection, but finally, they each hung up.

Skye immediately confirmed flights on the Internet, then sent the itinerary to Terrance via e-mail. As she did so, she wondered if she'd done the right thing, or if she had been so moved by Terrance's prompting that she'd gone ahead and behaved like someone who had very little semblance to the woman she knew herself to be. For the life of her, she could not decide which it was so she let it ride.

Preparing for bed that evening, a cup of tea by her bedside, a book on real estate investing in her lap, she was startled when the phone rang.

Picking it up quickly, Skye heard the now familiar static which signaled an overseas connection.

"Hello, hello… Can you hear me? Hello?" she repeated into the receiver.

"Yes, I can. Why are you repeating yourself?" Terrance asked, his voice filled with humor and something else which could only be described as anticipation.

"Sorry, but I couldn't hear anything for a moment. Good evening, Mr. Marshall," Skye said, her voice dropping to an intimate whisper.

"Good evening to you, too. So, you finally broke down and did it. It's about time," he added, laughter evident in his voice.

"Well, I had very little choice after you practically read me the riot act. I mean, a girl does have her pride," she added, exercising her right to have a sense of humor, too.

"Oh, you are so right. I am glad you think the way you do. And, it was for that reason that I did my best to suggest the trip as a way to say to you that you have a tremendous future ahead of you."

"Is that right? And just what do you have in mind?" Skye asked the question with all the innocence of a woman who was not at all aware of her suitor's real intentions or needs. Terrance wondered how she would react if he really opened up to her. Then, he realized that the telephone was no place to discuss the intimate details of a love affair, so he changed his tactic.

"Look, I realize that you have lots of things on your plate and probably loads of stuff which should even be completed tonight. For that reason and that reason alone, I am going to allow you to get off the hook easily. Just know that when I have you all to myself in a couple of weeks, there will be no such shortcuts. We will both have the luxury of dealing with each other and our individual idiosyncrasies without diversion or delay. *Comprende?*"

"Oh, yes, I do absolutely understand your intentions, Mr. Marshall. May I remind you that I may have a few agenda items of my own? Let me just say that I can hold up my end of anything you are able to direct. Just know that I am not a pushover although you might get that impression from my hesitancy about the whole weekend thing. What you have to understand is that some of this is relatively new to me. I'm not so sure that I'm comfortable dating long distance. Not to mention that you are a board-certified physician. It feels different for some unfathomable reason, almost as if you are a rare breed. *Capeche?*"

Terrance laughed. She'd turned his lapse into another language on its ear and thrown it right back at him. He found himself wondering what she would be like on the opposing end of any kind of challenge and realized that aside from wanting to make love to her, he also couldn't wait to just have her in his company again.

"Now, what was the first clue? See, it all started when I was back in college. I discovered I could hit the books, concentrate on what was assigned and convince my instructors that I was an A plus student."

"Really? Now, did this also include your ability to score well on exams and term papers? 'Cause if I'm reading this right, you're just trying to make excuses for being serious about your studies." Skye wasn't sure if all that he'd said was in jest or if the conversation was simply meant to be lighthearted. She looked forward to spending time with him and looked forward to their exploration of one another as well as the exotic terrain which the Bahamas would surely offer.

"Look, what I really mean is if we mesh together as well as we did in Fort Lauderdale, somebody is going to be in trouble." His words echoed through the phone line and Skye realized that Terrance was already thinking ahead toward the possibility of something much more serious than a weekend tryst.

"Let's not jump the gun, Dr. Marshall. Hey, you know I think that's the first time I've addressed you by your professional title. I like it," she added, the name having rolled off her tongue without any hesitation or difficulty.

"Yeah, I do like the way it sounds when you say it, but then I've liked everything that's come out of your mouth since the time I first met you. And, I especially like your mouth. I am looking forward to spending time with you," Terrance said, mentally calculating exactly how many days, nights and hours it would take for that to happen.

In the days and weeks leading up to the big weekend, both parties had second thoughts, both parties had major concerns. Neither felt the need to cancel or postpone, which was a significant commitment on both their parts as that kind of breach would have signaled a disappointing end to what was an eagerly anticipated event.

On the evening before Skye was scheduled to arrive, on a whim, Branch thought of putting in a call to his best buddy. Neither of them had spoken to one another since the Fort Lauderdale weekend except to exchange a brief confirmation of safe arrival and a thanks for the invitation.

Terrance wasn't sure he wanted to announce that he and Skye were going to spend the weekend together, but he also didn't want to keep anything so important from his best friend. He sat in the living room, the television's volume turned down, as he continued to watch news coverage of a breaking story taking place in Miami, Florida.

In Fort Lauderdale, Nita was preparing dinner as Branch walked around in the kitchen space, pretending to be unaffected by the delicious aromas coming from the pots and pans she handled so expertly. Curried chicken, pigeon peas and rice, along with a large pot of mustard greens simmered on top of the range. Sweet potatoes that had been boiled, sliced and sprinkled with brown sugar, cinnamon and lemon juice baked in the oven, filling the house with a delicious aroma.

Branch's stomach rattled in protest at the long wait ahead of him, but he already knew the wait would be worth it. To divert his attention from hunger and the mouthwatering fare under way, he picked up the phone, dialed Terrance and waited.

When the phone was picked up on the second ring, Branch was genuinely surprised. It was hard to connect to his buddy who was usually at the clinic until all hours and then, very often, still didn't make it home until late because he was either doing paperwork or had been called to one of the nearby emergency hospitals regarding patient care.

"Man, what the heck is going on? Just wanted to make contact with you since you, obviously, cannot seem to pick up the phone," Branch chided while holding back a laugh.

"Don't even try it. You know I called you when I got back and thanked you for the great weekend. Ask Nita if you don't remember. You're becoming senile and you're still a relatively young man. What's next for you, man? Viagra?" Terrance shot back quickly. If his partner was up for a little ribbing, he was definitely the man to deliver it. He was in a particularly good mood.

"Oh, no, you did not go there. Don't you worry about me. I'm handling my business. And as for you keeping in touch, yeah, I remember that pathetic little mini phone call you delivered when you got home. You barely said hello and goodbye—then there was a click and you were gone," Branch said, his voice scolding.

"Come on, Branch. You have got to know that with the clinic, the business end of it and the hospital duty at times, that my hands are literally full. It's a miracle when I am able to spend time with my daughter on selected weekends. Thank God her mother has established a fairly generous custody schedule, or else I'd be up the creek without a paddle," Terrance admitted for the first time since Brianna had calmed down and allowed things between them to siphon down to a cordial realm. There was no real interaction or communication and Terrance liked it that way. It would decrease the possibility of

Brianna's attempts at reconciliation which lately, had become both pitiful and degrading.

There had been no shouting, no screaming and no blaming between them the last time they'd spoken. A very simple arrangement for custody of Jacqueline had been outlined and agreed upon, almost as an afterthought to all the original demands which had been made early on. As it now stood, each of them had a shared responsibility for their daughter, one which would go on for the rest of time until she reached adulthood and even beyond.

"So, if what I suspect you're telling me is true, you and Brianna are pretty much kaput. Are you okay with that, man? I mean, it can't be easy to break up with someone you've loved, not to mention had a daughter with," Branch added, his earlier demeanor now fully checked and in its place, a glimpse into a side of him which not very many people ever recognized or saw.

"Yeah, I mean, I'm okay with all of it. I told you a little of it when I was there. Brianna put me through too many changes for it to ever work again. I'd already made up my mind. But you know, it's all worked out. I see Jacqueline on a regular basis. It's not easy, but then nothing that is worth having ever comes with an easy button. I don't miss Brianna or the drama that she brought to the marriage," he ended with conviction.

"See, I'm glad I called. You've obviously got a lot on your mind and probably need to share some of it, anyway. Who better to blow it off on than your best buddy? Even if I am several hundred miles away. Seriously, is there anything I can do to help? Anything either of us can do to make this time feel more bearable?"

Branch's question remained unanswered for a long moment. Terrance did not want to answer too quickly because he realized that Branch's offer emanated from genuine friendship. He and Nita both would be there for him when and if he ever needed it. That much, he was certain of.

"To be totally honest, man, I can say that right now, I am okay. I have my work, things between Brianna and I have settled down a whole heck of a lot and I'm actually looking forward to spending a little downtime soon."

Branch laughed. "Okay, first let me say that I'm glad you're handling everything that's going on so well, but I am not at all surprised. You always had a way with keeping things pretty much on track even when you were in crisis mode. I also have to ask, what exactly is downtime? For some reason, I get the feeling that something is going on that is a little more than simple relaxation."

Although Nita had been concentrating on seasoning the chicken, preparing the rice and cutting up onions for the curry sauce, she caught her husband's last statement and looked over at him just at that moment. Branch smiled, raised one eyebrow in a suspenseful gesture and continued his conversation. Apparently, Terrance was just as resourceful as they had both discussed only some days before.

On the other side of the phone line, Terrance realized, much to his discomfort, that he was now being grilled. Unsure as to how Branch had detected anything out of the ordinary, he now realized that his best buddy was more on to him than he'd ever imagined or felt comfortable with.

"Man, look. It's no big deal. Just know that I am going to be spending some time with someone whom I connect with on a different level. It's too early to talk about this, much too soon to discuss anything with you. And if I know you like I think I do, Nita is listening to the whole conversation, so don't try it."

Terrance knew his best friend like the back of his hand, knew that his wife was never far from his side and also knew that the two of them discussed every aspect of their lives with one another. If she wasn't already aware of whatever it was that Branch knew, she would be before the stroke of midnight.

"Okay, you've got us there, but we couldn't help it. I mean, Nita is here, cooking a terrific dinner and she just happened to overhear some of what is being said. Come on, man. You know we both love you like a brother. So, who's the nominee for spending the downtime? Anybody we know?" Branch asked.

Terrance hesitated, knowing that if he told them of his and Skye's plans, then nothing developed from it, it would sour Nita's opinion of him. She was his best friend's wife and, as such, someone whom he wanted in his corner, not an opposing one. "Look. Let's just say that it's someone I've connected with in the past and we thought we would spend a little time together for fun. That's it. Nothing more, nothing less. What're you guys doing, playing house detective?"

Branch laughed at the description, inwardly acknowledging that both he and his wife were a little curious about what was really going on in their friend's life. He also understood that the curiosity was a healthy one, not based on anything other than wanting them all to be as happy, content and in love as they already were.

"Actually, no. I mean, yes. I guess what I really want

to say is that we both just want you to be happy. No matter how you achieve the balance that allows you to sleep at night, comfortable in your bed, with or without a partner of your choice, just be happy. It's all we can ever ask for and more than most folks get in a lifetime," Branch added sagely. Terrance hung up some moments later but Branch's words stayed with him.

As he drove toward the airport three weeks later, Terrance was eager to see Skye's familiar face, hear her voice, watch her smile. He parked the car alongside the airport terminal's arrival lanes, noted that there was limited parking there and walked inside quickly hoping to avoid a ticket, towing or worse. He'd noted the signs posted which clearly stated No Parking/No Standing.

"It'll only be a minute," was what he told himself as he headed into the crowded terminal.

Half an hour later, as they approached the vehicle, a parking citation had been placed squarely on its windshield. Even that could not change the mood for either of them.

"Hey there," were the first and only words out of his mouth as he'd spotted her standing near the customs office. In that moment, everything seemed to take on a different hue, with violet hues filtering the sunlight as the pale orange of a pending sunset filled the airport's atrium beautifully.

Terrance forgot about the car, forgot about the luggage, forgot about everything except the woman who stood before him, dressed in a white linen suit, black sandals, large black sunglasses and wearing a huge grin.

"Hey there, yourself. Where's the love?" Skye asked boldly, feeling more sure of herself than she'd anticipated.

The look on Terrance's face was worth the chance she'd taken. He smiled broadly, walked toward her, then enveloped her in a secure embrace. He felt good, solid and smelled like heaven.

When they broke apart, each tried to hide the pure pleasure of the moment in an awkward silence. Then, Terrance silently picked up her suitcase, took her elbow gently and guided her toward the airport terminal's exit.

"How was the flight?" he managed to ask as they approached the car. He didn't really expect an answer, but wanted to fill the silence, feeling that it was his responsibility to make small talk at any cost.

"It was fine. Not too much turbulence and definitely a short trip in terms of time. I had no idea they had a direct flight from Atlanta until I checked."

"Remind me later to give you money to cover your tickets. You should have just let me book it but I think you were still a little hesitant. Anyway, that's all in the past now. So, what would you like for dinner?" he asked, changing the subject before it could even be registered.

"Actually, right now I'm not very hungry. Guess it's nerves and all the up and down action of the flight. Maybe later, something light. Seafood is always good," she answered.

"Great. That should be no problem on this island. We'll take your things to my place, let you get a little comfortable, then we'll head out to a good seafood restaurant. I wasn't at all sure what kind of food you'd be in the mood for but we don't need reservations at most places."

Terrance realized he was babbling. Hoping Skye wouldn't know he was nervous, he promptly shut up.

They rode the rest of the way to his apartment in silence with Skye taking in every sight there was to see along the way. The lushness of the island made her think of exotic things and put her in a vacation frame of mind. It didn't matter that she would only be there for three days. The most important thing, in her mind, was that Terrance had seemed to genuinely want her there and for that, she'd been both surprised and pleased.

They pulled into the garage at his condo, Terrance unloaded the luggage and they headed toward his unit.

Skye loved the vegetation which was a natural element to the Caribbean island. Many of the plants she noticed along the walkway, and which grew in large bush-like clusters in the front of the building, were ones which were sold back in the U.S.

A large potted cactus sat squarely in front of Terrance's doorway, giving the impression of a desert oasis and it impressed Skye immediately. "Oh, my goodness—that is so beautiful. You have no idea how much I love cactus plants, but they certainly do not love me. I must have bought at least four of them in the past two years. Ask me how many are still alive," she added.

Terrance almost laughed. He did as little as possible to the plant and often wondered how much longer it would survive, but found it amusing that Skye was impressed by it. Then he realized that it was just one of a long line of things which would be fascinating about her and he did laugh—out loud.

"Wow, you are really something. You know, I always

forget the differences between the Caribbean and the States. But, do tell me. How many are still alive?"

He asked the question just as he unlocked the door, pulled the suitcase inside and held the doorway open for Skye's entry.

She gasped as she realized that the apartment faced the ocean on the other side, filling its rooms with amazing sunlight and terrific ambiance.

"Oh, my gosh! This is so beautiful. How do you ever leave this?" she asked in one rushed sentence.

Terrance looked around, shrugged one shoulder, then calmly took her bag into the bedroom.

"Look, if you would like to wash your face, freshen up or anything, everything is in the bathroom. Help yourself. I'm going to go back downstairs for some fruits and a nice refreshing cold drink for us both. I'll be right back. Please make yourself at home," he instructed as he headed toward the door.

"Terrance." Skye called his name softly, then walked toward him. He looked at her, wondered what was coming, then braced himself for the worst. He wondered if she thought the apartment too small for them to spend time in together, then dismissed that theory. It was a perfect size for two people trying to get to know one another.

"I just wanted you to know that I'm very glad I came. Your apartment is adorable—looks like it could use a woman's touch with the decorating but the ocean view is fantastic and I love the wood floors."

Terrance watched her face as she did a quick glance around the two-bedroom apartment. He wasn't thinking of wood floors, the ocean or the apartment. He was, in fact, thinking very much of a woman's touch and wondered desperately, how much longer he could go without touching the woman standing before him.

Chapter 20

Terrance placed Skye's suitcase in the second bedroom, then wondered if he'd lost his mind. He realized that his gesture could backfire, that Skye could very well take it as a signal to sleep there, but he banked on the chemistry which had already been established between them. Their lovemaking in Fort Lauderdale had left a lasting impression on him; it had been an unforgettable experience.

Skye, on the other hand, was grateful that he'd behaved in a way that said that he was not simply taking things for granted. It had been difficult for her to come to the final decision which put her on a plane bound for an island in the Caribbean to spend an entire weekend with a man whom she had only met on one other occasion. That he'd behaved like a total gentleman since picking her up at the airport was a sign of real significance, in her book. It meant she could trust him, meant she could quite possibly relax and even meant that there was a strong possibility that the weekend would be another one to remember.

She opened her overnight bag, removed a dress, two pairs of capri pants, sandals and three tops and hung them in the small closet in one corner of the room. Several toddler outfits hung there and she remembered that Terrance was father to a small child. That fact served to remind her that he was more than just a possible lover, and that he could possibly be more than a gentleman. He had been someone's husband and was still someone's father. She sat on the bed then, wondering if by putting her things into what obviously served as his daughter's room, that he was making a statement as to the status of his marriage or their budding relationship. Skye quickly realized she was overanalyzing the situation. Right then and there, she vowed to allow things to unfold as they would. No matter what happened, she was determined to enjoy this weekend spent on a beautiful tropical island with a man whom she'd found irresistibly attractive only six weeks before.

"Is everything okay in there?" Terrance called through the partially closed doorway.

"Absolutely. I was wondering if we had time for me to take a shower. Airplanes always make me feel as if I should start all over again when I reach my destination," she explained, opening the door.

She gasped as she realized that Terrance had removed the white T-shirt he'd worn to pick her up at the airport and was now standing before her, his bare chest causing her heart to beat faster and faster.

"Sure, we're not on anyone's timetable but our own. I'll get you some towels and whatnot. Why don't you use the shower in the master bedroom—it's larger and more comfortable," he suggested.

"Sure. I hope you don't mind but I hung up my stuff in your daughter's closet. I'm sorry, I've forgotten her name. Please tell me again."

"Jacqueline. She's just turning three in a couple of months although I sometimes think she's approaching twenty. She has wisdom of the ages in that little body and mind of hers—a very mature little girl who has Daddy wrapped around her little finger."

When he spoke of his daughter, his face changed and Skye knew, without his saying so, that he'd probably done everything in his power to avoid the breakup of his marriage just so that he would not lose sight of her. The thought saddened her for a moment, then she pushed past it.

"She sounds like a dream. I've always wanted a daughter."

"Well, let me warn you they're a handful, though I suspect little boys are pretty challenging, too."

"I remember my younger brother Justin was a handful. My dad had to keep a belt around his neck as a threat at all times. Once, Justin set the carpet on fire and our house almost caught fire. Then he tried to hide it by pulling a chair over it in the middle of the living room floor. My mother was not amused." Skye laughed at the memory and Terrance laughed, too, thinking of the ingenuity of small minds and the consequences that probably followed.

"So, did he get it or were your parents the lenient type?"

"Let's just say that he never touched matches again and also never tried to rearrange any furniture knowing that my parents would definitely notice immediately," she said, shaking her head.

Terrance led her into the master bedroom, then into the connecting bathroom, which had been done in shades of sea green, brown and beige. Fluffy towels were folded neatly on a rattan bench and the shower stall's clear glass sparkled.

Skye was impressed, not only by the cleanliness she observed but also by the obvious neatness and order which his lifestyle seemed to suggest.

"Wow, this is beautiful. I'm not surprised, though," she added, looking at him with frank admiration.

"I'm not surprised, either…I mean that your being here feels so totally right," he said as he stepped forward, placing a soft kiss on her lips.

Skye wound her arms around his neck, looked into his eyes and whispered, "Yes," as she sought the connection again.

Their lips meshed in a kiss that was a reaffirmation of all that had taken place weeks before but was now being relived with fervor. Skye felt the comfort of his arms, the strength of his body and the tremors of desire which coursed through her body. There had been so little time for them to reconnect yet it was as though they had never left one another and each moment confirmed the existence of an indefinable element of oneness.

Terrance wanted to make love to Skye but also wanted, even more so, to allow enough time for them to get to know one another. The passion which existed between them flowed naturally; that much he already knew. What he now wondered was if that would be enough, or would the spectacular affinity which seemed to exist whenever Skye was in the room or in his thoughts continue to exist and even expand?

The kiss deepened as Terrance allowed his body to luxuriate in the feel of the woman he held in his arms. His hands circled her body, testing, kneading, molding her to him as desire overtook them both. Her lips clung to his, their mouths meshed in a teasing match which neither would win nor lose. Both were consumed by the flames of passion which engulfed them as they leaned into one another, their bodies fitting together as if by design.

Suddenly, the doorbell rang once, then twice in rapid succession.

Terrance stepped back, almost as if he'd been suspended in another dimension.

"Sorry. Now, who could that be?" he asked, not really expecting an answer.

Skye pushed Terrance playfully toward the doorway and said, "Go ahead, answer it. I'm going to take that shower now."

"Sure. Just know that you were saved by the bell this time," he joked, running his hands through his hair in an effort to regain his composure. He walked through the master bedroom, entered the foyer and looked through the peephole. Swallowing hard, Terrance almost cursed under his breath. Only the sight of the top of his daughter's head prevented him from pretending he was not at home.

He opened the door, patience, indignation, mild annoyance and endurance etched into his face, though he did his best to hide all of the feelings which coursed through his mind.

Brianna noted the look, ignored it and spoke quickly.

"Look, I know you weren't scheduled to take Jacqueline this weekend, but the hospital called. There's been some kind of major catastrophe on one of the bus lines. They're calling in all personnel to handle the large number of emergency care they suspect will be needed. Sorry," she offered as she coached Jacqueline forward.

The toddler quickly looked from her mother to her father, decided she liked being with her daddy, anyway, and rushed into his pants leg with giggles.

Terrance's face softened, then as he reached down and caressed her head, tracing the two braids which adorned each side of her head.

"Hi, honey," he said softly. He wondered how he would ever get beyond being a weekend father, then realized Brianna was talking to him.

"Look, I am sorry about this but there was nothing to be done about it. I'll call you later from the hospital. Oh, here's a few things she might need, too," she said, handing Terrance a small canvas bag that contained a change of clothing and several other necessary items.

He stood there, still without speaking, and simply allowed the feelings of frustration to wash over him knowing there was really no way out of the situation. It wasn't that he minded having his daughter, but he did mind that the weekend he'd planned so carefully with Skye would now be changed.

"Sorry. I'll call you later. Oh, she's already had lunch but no nap." Brianna then turned and made her way toward the stairs which would lead out toward the parking lot of Terrance's building.

"Bye, honey," she said, almost as an afterthought as she began to descend the stairs.

Jacqueline did not hear or see her. She was too busy looking up at her father, who continued to stand in the doorway, shocked, annoyed, yet glad to see his little girl at the same time. At that moment, Terrance realized that the change of plans could present a major wrinkle in the weekend. On another level, he recognized that in some small way, he was glad that his two favorite ladies would meet sooner than he'd expected.

Jacqueline was full of giggles, smiles and laughter as he led her to her favorite place in his apartment, her own special bedroom. Skye's belongings had been hung up, but the full-sized bed still held her suitcase while Jacqueline's newly purchased portable toddler bed sat in one corner with balloon trimmed wall borders all around the room.

Terrance quickly took out Jacqueline's favorite toys, headed to the kitchen in search of an afternoon snack and returned with a kitchen towel filled with red seedless grapes, which he remembered Jacqueline loved.

Sitting on the bed, he watched as she squatted in the middle of the floor and began eating the grapes one by one. She never once stopped to ask any questions in her toddlerspeak, which he often understood despite its intricate language.

Moments later, as Skye emerged from the shower, Terrance was still sitting on the bed, watching his daughter finish off the grapes he'd given her only moments before.

Skye entered the room, a yellow terry cloth bath dress in place which barely reached her knees. Terrance watched her and decided that he liked what he saw.

Skye's face lit up when she saw the small child in the middle of the floor. "Oh, my goodness. You must be Jacqueline," she said immediately, and the toddler looked from her father to the stranger, an expression of wonderment on her face.

Without hesitation, Skye walked over to her, picked her up and wiped her grape juice–smeared face with the hem of the terry cloth garment.

Jacqueline laughed, watched her closely and decided it felt better to be in her arms than on the floor. She giggled, laid her head on Skye's shoulder and reached out one pudgy finger to touch her hair.

Terrance smiled and sat back unknowingly, letting out a huge breath. He hadn't really known that the sequence of events would cause him to be on edge, hadn't known that he was grateful to postpone the inevitable but now that it had happened, he felt as if an unknown and unseen weight had been suddenly lifted from his shoulders.

"I'm sorry about this but Brianna had to go in for an emergency shift at work. Looks like we may be babysitting for a while," he added.

"Hey, don't apologize—and it's not really babysitting. This is your daughter so you're only doing what's right. She's beautiful. I love the way she smells," Skye exclaimed, inhaling Jacqueline's scent.

The small hand which had held the grapes came up to touch Skye's face as the toddler realized she was being admired.

"Ooo, coo, mah, mah," she uttered, still unable to form intelligible words.

Terrance watched from where he sat, unable to speak.

The bonding he saw taking place in front of his very eyes was emotional but it was also unnerving. He realized that he'd perhaps been shortsighted when he'd allowed Skye to enter his life and his environment so quickly; he also realized it was too late to do anything about it.

The turn of events which had placed his daughter with him on a weekend that she was really supposed to be with her mother had been unavoidable and unexpected. He continued to watch them interact with one another, then smiled.

"If I didn't know better, I'd say you're a natural. Have you ever given thought to having a family of your own?" he asked, aware that he was now asking questions which he might not have if the current circumstances hadn't occurred.

"Oh, sure. I just didn't want to do it alone. You know, you really have to have the right partner when you begin a family. There doesn't seem to be a better way to do it although many people make do," she said, still holding Jacqueline who had found her tiny hoop earrings and become fascinated by them.

"I agree, although even when it starts out that way, it doesn't always hold up," he added. The regret in his voice was evident and Skye realized that he'd probably done everything in his power to avoid the breakdown of his marriage.

"Anyway, I've always felt that it's important for kids to live in a two-parent home, but if that home is a battleground, it's definitely better to diffuse things. Otherwise, they grow up living in a minefield. And they think that's what a relationship is supposed to be…a minefield." She sat on the bed then, continuing to hold Jacqueline in her arms and smiled down at her. "You're pretty heavy, young lady," she whispered, then touched her nose to the miniature one in front of her.

Jacqueline giggled, shut her eyes and stuck her face out, a clear indication that she wanted a repeat occurrence.

Skye laughed, did it again and the game was on.

Terrance watched, shook his head and folded his arms. "Well, I guess I've definitely become secondary around here," he mumbled as he watched.

"Oh, oh—Daddy is getting jealous. We don't want that now, do we?" Skye joked, sitting Jacqueline up and tickling her softly. The tiny toddler emitted giggles that made her father smile, despite his feelings of somehow being one-upped.

"Not true—just envious of all the attention. I want to be held in your arms like that. Or vice versa. Hell, I just want you to spend time with me. That's why I invited you down here," he added.

"Terrance, you know that's exactly why I came—to spend time with you, to get to know you, for you to get to know me. It's not either of our faults that we now have precious cargo to look after. And what precious cargo this is," she added, looking into Jacqueline's upturned face. She tweaked her nose softly, then looked over at Terrance once again.

"Okay, so what should we do for dinner now? I know we were going out before—do you still want to do that?"

His question caught her off guard. His uncertainty as to how the evening should progress, now that his daughter had entered the picture, was written on his face and Skye read it.

Instead of pushing the subject, she remained silent, allowing him to process the information and form whatever opinion or response he chose. In her mind, how he dealt with the unexpected would reveal volumes to her.

"You know, I think we should still go out to dinner. We'll just take Jacqueline with us. I mean, I was opting for the whole romantic interlude thing. You know, candlelight, lobster, et cetera. If you don't mind, we'll just skip the candles. I know a place that prepares lobster so tender, so delicious that it'll melt in your mouth. We can take some food for Jacqueline with us and if need be, feed her at the restaurant, too."

Skye nodded, watching his face the whole time he was speaking. She liked the way he'd come to a decision quickly, without an extended amount of time taken to think things out. It was the natural course of things, it was a good decision, one which included all parties and would thereby cause the least amount of adjustments.

"Sounds like a plan," she responded, then looked down at the bundle in her arms. Jacqueline's eyelids were fluttering, her attempts at staying awake apparently futile. Skye gently laid her down on the bed, smoothed her clothing and slowly stood up. The toddler remained in that position and both Terrance and Skye simply continued to watch her.

"I should put her into her bed," Terrance said.

"It seems a shame to move her. She's sleeping so peacefully," Skye added, glancing over at the now sleeping toddler.

"Yeah, for now. But she's a roller. Been that way since day one. This little girl began turning over at about two and a half months. I don't want her to roll off so just keep an eye on her while I open up the portable crib I have for her," he added.

"Sure, father knows best," she responded. With every growing moment, the respect she had for the man she'd agreed to travel miles to see grew and deepened. She knew for certain that she'd originally been attracted to him physically; admiration was now being added to the palette. It felt overwhelming, yet at the same time, it also felt right.

"Very funny. Now you're a comedienne, too," Terrance said over his shoulder as he set up the crib. Pulling sheets from the linen closet, he made up the baby's bed.

Moments later, after Terrance had placed the still sleeping child into bed, Skye stood alongside him as they both watched her in silence. They stood side by side, neither wanting to move, neither wanting to say anything to break the mood.

Terrance turned toward Skye, who still wore the terry cloth wrap, and gently put his hands on both shoulders. Looking into her eyes for a long moment, he lowered his mouth to hers slowly, testing, tasting, nibbling, sipping.

Skye stepped closer to him, winding her arms up around his neck as she molded her body to his intimately. She could feel the tightness of his muscles, the strength in his arms and knew she wanted to remain there forever.

Terrance took his time, relishing in the excitement which grew steadily as his body reacted to Skye and the feelings she inspired. Touching his tongue to hers lightly they engaged in a battle of wills, each unable to satisfy the desire that was building with each passing moment.

Slowly then, without speaking, Terrance took Skye's hand and led her to his bedroom. He kissed her again, trailing feathery kisses along her jawline, the tops of her shoulders and finally, back to her mouth which was now waiting for him.

Skye felt as if she were in a familiar dream, her body singed by each lingering kiss, each softly placed subtle touch she endured. The terry cloth robe was slowly becoming a distraction and Skye put one hand on his chest, stepped back and quickly disconnected the two snaps which held it together.

Terrance's eyes filled with the sight before him and he knew in his mind, his heart and his body that the woman before him was more than he'd bargained for. He gasped then, her beauty filling him with unimaginable joy but also a tremendous surge of desire. Gently, he pulled her to him, then dropped down onto one knee as he circled her waist with his hands.

"You are so beautiful, Skye. I mean it. I love the way your body looks, feels, tastes…and I especially love that you've come to spend this time with me." His words were uttered quickly, before he began to drop small quick kisses on the soft skin of her chest, her breasts, on the area just below her breasts and finally, on the tops of her thighs.

Skye felt as if she were on fire. Her body, her mind, her heart, all had become enmeshed in a searing heat and there was no way to end it save one. She stepped back gingerly, one hand pulling Terrance to his feet, the other guiding him backward toward the bed to join her.

He followed without words. There was no longer any need for verbal communication. Their bodies had become a far superior medium of translation, their passion a conduit that surpassed any relevant known medium of exchange.

They made love passionately, lovingly, intensely, until they were both exhausted. As the sun lowered itself in the sky, they slept.

Chapter 21

Tragically, the number of patients being brought into Regency's emergency room continued to grow, even after the first ninety minutes had passed. Years before, when the go-ahead had been given to build another medical facility in the center of a rapidly growing island metropolis, no one ever suspected they would be called on to service a large-scale disaster. No one had conceived the unthinkable happening. But in a rapidly changing world, where both population and recreational travel increases, change is inevitable. Thankfully, approval had been granted and the ground breaking for the new facility was given a green light.

The bus accident that had occurred more than two hours earlier had left many pinned in their seats. According to reports from emergency workers who responded to the first calls, some passengers were still trapped at the accident site, and were awaiting heavy equipment which would hopefully free them from the twisted metal remains.

Apparently, the driver had swerved to avoid an on-coming taxi, lost control of the vehicle and plummeted down an embankment, landing in a nearby ravine. Many of the injured—elderly residents of a privately owned nursing home—were left with broken bones, contusions and lacerations. Others were simply in shock, having been pulled from the accident by quick-thinking pas-sersby or the first rash of emergency vehicles on the scene.

EMT workers in Nassau were very often young police officers who had been fully trained in medical and rescue work, as well. They'd done their best to set up an on-site triage unit, offering much needed medical assistance to each of the injured passengers as they were brought up from the badly mangled bus.

One moment, the seniors had been on their way to an all-day outing which would have included a picnic and a little fishing for those who were able to on a nearby dock. Suddenly, in the next instant, the twelve-passenger vehicle careened toward the embankment, sending most of the elderly passengers hurling through the bus's interior as they came out of their seats and landed helter-skelter in a heap amongst the ruins of metal, rubber and smoking debris. Pandemonium set in before any emergency help arrived. The closest medical facility, Regency Medical Center, received all of the most severely impacted patients and many of the minor injuries, as well.

As Brianna worked diligently alongside the emer-gency room physicians, she had no time to reflect on the things which threatened to break through her mental resolve. She only knew that her daughter was safe with her father; that much was a given.

"Nurse, check the electrolytes of the patient in 3B and change the dressings on that wound. You'd better give him a tetanus shot, too—it's not likely that he's had one recently. Even if he has, we want to be on the safe side."

The physician who issued the orders never looked up as he spoke. He was too busy monitoring the vital signs of a patient who had complained of chest pains earlier. Now, the man was eerily silent as the doctor examined him and barked out orders for an EKG, blood work and an immediate IV which would drip life-saving drugs into the patient's veins.

Brianna did as she'd been told, wondering how many more patients would come through the doors before the night was over. She was bone tired and had already surpassed the kind of fatigue which you give in to. She was almost ready to ask for a break when they brought in a patient who reminded her of herself, save for the head full of gray hair and a severely broken arm.

The patient was obviously in pain though she was strangely silent; she did not make a single sound even as the resident examined the mangled limb.

"Looks like you have done something to your wing here," the young man said, doing his best to avoid jostling or moving it from its position. There was a towel wrapped and bundled beneath it which acted as a buffer but which also helped stabilize the arm.

Brianna walked over to the gurney, instructed the EMT workers to transfer the patient to the hospital's examining table and proceeded to start a glucose IV, standard operating procedure with each patient brought into a trauma unit.

She worked quickly, methodically and efficiently, never once allowing herself to think of the things which were lurking just below the surface. After making several notes on the chart that was at the foot of the patient's bed, Brianna knew that her ability to continue working at an efficient level was swiftly eluding her.

"Have this patient taken to X-ray—the right femur looks like it's shattered. Better still, let's also order a CBC, Chem 7 and a full set on the right leg, also. I don't like that swelling," Brianna ordered as she took note of the patient's demeanor.

The woman remained silent, her eyes fluttering open as Brianna spoke, but then she closed them as if she just wanted to be somewhere else.

"Hey—you want to stay awake for now. I'm sorry but until we check things out thoroughly, it's best that you not sleep."

Brianna's words reached the elderly patient, she opened her eyes and there were tears in the corners.

"Are you in any pain? I mean, other than your arm. I think it's broken but we're going to X-ray it and check out your leg, also. Is that what's bothering you?"

Brianna's words somehow soothed the patient, although she simply shook her head no, without speaking still.

"You know, you can tell me what it is. I won't tell anyone and it's just you and I here now," Brianna offered. Her training had not really prepared her for the trauma patients exhibited when they were faced with unexpected tragedy, including broken limbs, but she was pretty sure that the patient was just scared. The thought of a bus careening out of control and then coming to rest down an embankment sounded pretty scary to her and she couldn't imagine what the experience must have been like. She wondered if she would also end up alone, afraid and unable to express her fears or her pain.

The thought shook her, so much so that she had to turn away for a moment and pull herself together. This was not her, it was a patient. An elderly patient who had had the misfortune of being in the wrong place at the wrong time. It was now her job to help restore this woman, this patient, to the best possible state that she could. The realization brought her full circle to the present and immediately removed the emotional correlation.

"Look, I know you probably don't feel much like talking, but I promise to check up on you later. Okay?" Her words sounded hollow in her ears because she knew that the thing she wanted more than anything was to get out of the hospital as quickly as she could. There were too many things pressing on her, too many what ifs which needed to be addressed. But, the truth of the matter was she suspected it was too late anyway. Terrance, for all his patience and strength, had divorced her.

And though she wanted more than anything to turn that legal status around to the tune of one hundred eighty degrees, she also realized that it was a next to impossible feat.

What she wanted most, what she felt she absolutely needed, was closure. The voice inside her head which had always made the most sense to her now seemed to be silenced. With that void came uncertainty. Brianna knew she was facing a major crossroad in her life, in the same way her marriage had ended some months ago, but without the same solid assurances. At least at the time they'd seemed solid.

This time, it was more like an accumulation of disappointments, no follow-through on Reid's part and the final realization of a dream which she now realized would most probably never come true.

Reid had not said the words, but the handwriting was already on the wall. Brianna knew enough to recognize the signs of a disintegrating relationship. After all, she'd just been the one to initiate the very same thing with her own husband. In some ways, she almost felt as if she deserved it.

In retrospect, she'd realized it wasn't the smartest thing she'd ever done when she'd ended a marriage that had become tedious for her because there was a new man on the horizon. That cold, hard truth settled in sometime after the final divorce decree and at the same time she realized that Reid's faults included smoking, drugging and lying.

In fact, there had been many days in which she'd asked for forgiveness, then picked up the phone to call Terrance on the pretense of one thing or another. He'd remained polite, receptive and distant. Sure, he answered every call but Brianna was sure that that was more about their daughter than anything she had to say.

At times, she realized she was overstepping the boundaries of a woman who had left the marriage both mentally and physically some months before. But she justified her actions as those of a woman who'd been unsure of herself from the beginning. Reid had simply tapped into that uncertainty, brought it to the surface and used it to create havoc.

Brianna finished her notes, watched as the elderly woman was taken to the X-ray department, moved on to the next patient and continued that way for the next several hours. She was unaware of how automatic her responses had become, how robotic her actions were and knew only that she needed to be engaged, busy and committed to something outside herself.

Weeks earlier, Reid had made it painfully clear that there was no good reason for them to continue. His words still echoed in her head each time she allowed herself to lose sight of the tasks that she currently performed routinely, almost without conscious thought.

"I know you wanted more, know you expected more. But, the truth of the matter is you always wanted more than I was ever capable of giving. I'm sorry, Brianna, I really am."

She'd heard him, heard his words, knew what he was saying, but it did not sink in. Not until he began to speak and used Jacqueline's name did it really dawn on her that the man she'd come to care for, enjoyed making love with, enjoyed looking at, couldn't stop kissing, couldn't stop thinking about, was actually pulling the plug on the relationship.

"I'm going to miss you, and Jacqueline, too. This is not easy, but I had to tell you."

"This comes totally out of the blue, Reid. Why now? Why when we have gone through so much to be together would you come to me with this? After all I've given up to be with you, it's just not acceptable!" she heard herself scream.

"Because I never wanted this. I never wanted to be tied down with you and a kid, and all that stuff. I mean, I like you and all, maybe even love you in my own way, but I never wanted to be tied down like this. It's more than I bargained for, more than I anticipated and way more than I signed on for," he ended, his face distorted, frustration evident in his every gesture.

Brianna watched him in horror, knowing that this was what she'd been the most fearful of in the weeks and months which had just passed. She'd felt it. That much she could definitely acknowledge, but she'd simply brushed it off, attributed it to thinking too much and had gone on with the business of living their everyday lives.

"What am I gonna tell Jacqueline?" she whispered as the reality of what was occurring reached her. The daughter she'd recently deprived of a father and home she loved would now lose out once again, if only to a live-in lover who occasionally played silly inconsequential games with her in a halfhearted way.

"Look, I can't tell you what or how you should break this news to a toddler. I think she's bright enough to actually forget about me and all of this in a very short period of time."

"I see. Looks like you have all of this worked out," Brianna said, annoyance clearly evident in her voice though outwardly, she managed to remain calm. Unsure as to the direction of her increasing anger, she tossed the small piece of coral she'd been handling back and forth between both hands, unwilling and unable to sit quietly or without movement.

"I can't believe you didn't notice this, Bree," he said stiffly. It was as if he were suggesting that she should have seen it coming, should have prepared for it, should have perhaps avoided it at all costs.

"No, Reid. I didn't see it coming. I wouldn't have signed on for it if I had. After all, I have a small daughter to care for. Although my ex-husband has joint custody, it still puts a lot of the responsibility of her care in my lap. The last thing I need is a veritable ever-changing trainload of guys who come into our lives, allow us to get to know them, then drift off into the sunset. That's not my idea of a healthy environment for my daughter nor is it the way I want to do things, so excuse me if I am just a little pissed off."

"Hey, Bree baby, this conversation is becoming redundant. I've already put most of my stuff into a storage facility. I'll come back later and gather the rest of it at another time. I'm sorry for the inconvenience but then, when would have been a more convenient time? I just figured I would come and get the main items early so that they'd be out of your way."

His calculated recital of his methodology only infuriated her further; it informed her of more than she wanted to know and confirmed that he'd orchestrated the entire event so that it would cause him the least amount of inconvenience. She had to hand it to him, he was definitely a professional at ending things. A pro. She'd never even seen it coming.

"That's fine. As a matter of fact, it's thoughtful of you to have done that. Now we don't have to see you when you come to pick up your stuff. Just let me know a day or so in advance, okay? Thanks."

Her body shook as she uttered the words but on the surface, her composure was impeccable. Brianna would not allow herself the luxury of creating a scene. It was too late for histrionics, too late for discussion and way too late for anything other than compliance.

She'd been a fool. That much she now knew but it was also too late to do anything about it. Reid left a few minutes later, his swagger a bit diminished, but his ego still intact. As Brianna watched him walk toward his car, she almost cried. Recognizing that it would do absolutely nothing to alleviate the situation, she managed to hold back the tears.

It was later that day when she received the emergency call from the hospital. She'd tried to call Terrance, gotten no answer, but had been too frustrated and deflated to allow herself to leave a message on his answering machine. She'd taken a chance that he would most probably be at home and when he'd come to the door, a look of total confusion on his face, she'd almost fallen into his arms and begged forgiveness.

Instead, she had requested that he take possession of the one tangible thing they still shared—their daughter. Brianna felt good about that, felt great comfort in the knowledge that though she'd surely messed up in many ways when it came to relationships, the one thing she had done which was inarguably a good thing, had been Jacqueline.

And now, in the wee hours of the morning, after many of the last patients from the tragic bus accident had been processed, examined and given the first line of medical care, Brianna stood outside the emergency room as many of the other medical personnel caught a few moments of fresh air in an effort to invigorate themselves. The next shift would begin shortly and they would all be free to go, but many of the support staff would undoubtedly stay on until those who were coming into the hospital could get a handle on what they were being faced with.

Brianna was exhausted—both her mind and body drained. Her emotions had been on a roller coaster all through the unexpectedly long shift. Now, as she prepared to head home, she wondered if anything she had witnessed would make sense to Terrance. In her mind, life's ultimate importance had somehow been revealed to her in the narrow corridor of time which she'd spent in the emergency room as patients had come in for treatment in various stages of duress.

She was aware that Terrance, too, had seen his share of medical tragedies, but had never before realized that they shared so much. Never before taken into account that their common bond in medicine was something which meant more than she'd ever realized.

Instead of heading for home, Brianna made a U-turn and headed toward Terrance's place. She wanted to feel her daughter's breath on her face, wanted to hold her in her arms and tickle her until she giggled and laughed all at once. But most of all, she wanted to tell the man she'd thrown away that they'd both made mistakes.

It was three o'clock in the morning, but to Brianna, that didn't matter. What did matter was that it was time to face the truth, even if she had to bare all the inner recesses of her soul.

That is, if Terrance was willing to listen.

Chapter 22

Brianna headed toward Terrance's place with thoughts of all that she'd seen and heard still in her head. It was a mindless drive. She rang the bell, then waited, wondering if she should have called first.

Terrance heard the bell, figured he had to be dreaming, then came to full wakefulness. There was only one person who would ring his bell at that hour of the morning. Only one person who would have any reason to and he truly hoped it was not her.

Slipping out of bed quietly so as to not awaken Skye, Terrance went to the door.

Looking through the security visor, he saw Brianna's pant legs, the stark white of her uniform glaring brightly against the darkness of the corridor.

Propped against the wall, she leaned heavily into one

side, tiredness coming over her in waves as she waited patiently for the door to her sanity to be opened.

Terrance shook his head, wondering if the awkwardness of the moment could somehow be avoided, or if he was to remember this night for all of time.

He swallowed, turned the latch and opened the door slowly.

"I didn't expect you back tonight," he said evenly. Wearing only his pajama bottoms, he realized immediately that Brianna was staring at his chest. She hadn't spoken but he felt her response almost as if she had. The reaction made him think of Skye, who was asleep in his bed wearing the matching top.

The realization struck him as oddly funny, though his heart beat rapidly in his chest. He realized he was experiencing an adrenaline rush, knew that his heart rate was elevated, yet there was nothing to be done about it. Not until the moment had passed and he was more in control of the situation.

"My God, Terrance. The hospital was a zoo tonight. Apparently, there was a grisly bus accident that injured a lot of senior folks. I just thought it might be easier to pick Jacqueline up, rather than go home and have to circle back sometime in the morning for her. Sorry to get you up, though," she added as Terrance unwittingly stepped aside to allow her entrance into the darkened foyer area.

"I see. Any casualties?" he asked, knowing that the hospital's emergency and trauma units were both fully prepared to handle a full load of incoming patients, even if it was as a result of an unexpected disaster. He'd planned to take the next two days off but knew that if duty called, he'd have to go in, even if it was only for a few hours.

"Yes, at least four DOAs. Then one patient coded in the emergency room, and another didn't make it out of the surgical O.R. It was tough to see all those elderly folks who were obviously set to enjoy a day at the beach suddenly face the challenge of getting out of a bus accident unscathed. Many suffered contusions and lacerations. It was awful," Brianna added, suddenly feeling as if she needed to share this one final slab of information with the man standing before her, his medical experience becoming the one thing they still shared outside the realm of Jacqueline.

Terrance watched his ex-wife, knowing that she was sitting on a powder keg of emotions, but also knowing that Skye was in his bedroom. He wanted to offer Brianna comfort, wanted her to know that she would be okay and that their daughter was fine, but he also knew that there were times when words were not sufficient.

He led her to Jacqueline's room, the night-light still on, casting balloon shadows on the wall.

"She's asleep and has been for quite a while."

"She looks like an angel." Brianna bent down, kissed the sleeping child on the forehead, then laid her hand lightly on the blanket.

"I hate to do this, but I knew I wouldn't rest until I had her with me again. I just had to see her before I could even think of going home."

"Here, let me help you," Terrance offered as Brianna picked up the baby bag, filled it with the remaining items she'd packed earlier, then reached down to kiss her sleeping daughter gently on the forehead again.

The child stirred slightly, pursed her lips and sighed loudly. Terrance looked across the expanse of the crib at his daughter's mother and their eyes met. They both smiled, knowing that this would be the thing they would share for all of their lives.

"Let me." Terrance then picked Jacqueline up as Brianna wrapped her in a large blanket which would shield her from the nighttime air, though the temperature outside was still in the mid-seventies. They quietly walked outside, Brianna holding the bag, Terrance carrying the baby, and proceeded toward the car.

Terrance strapped Jacqueline into her car seat and though she stirred, she did not awaken.

"She's amazing." He watched her little head bob off to one side and smiled.

"Yes, she is. She's the best that both of us have to offer. I'm glad we made her."

"So am I. Are you okay to drive? I know how the hospital can drain you."

His question caught even him off guard, especially when he remembered that Skye was less than fifty feet away from where they now stood. But he also acknowledged that if his former wife and daughter needed to stay over, he would make do, he would make it happen. Their safety was his paramount concern; his personal life would have to adjust around that reality, at least for now.

"I'm fine. I just need to have my baby girl with me. I think you know what I mean because you face the same reality of life and death every day. Tonight was just a concentrated version of every day at the hospital. Thank you so much for not making me feel weird about this," she added, kissing his cheek softly.

"Don't mention it. And I enjoyed today with her. She was a handful but we enjoyed her."

The moment passed quickly, but Brianna was instantly alert, picking up on his choice of words.

"Did you say we?"

Terrance caught himself, realized it was too late, then decided to face the music head on.

"I did. I have company from out of town."

"Oh. Well, I hope I didn't spoil any plans or anything," Brianna said, caution edging into her voice.

"No, not really. We were going out to dinner when you dropped Jacqueline off so we decided to stay in instead. It made things less complicated."

"Are you telling me that there is someone in the apartment now?"

"Actually, yes. I mean, I didn't know you were going to show up at three a.m. That's not something you've ever done before. It's not a problem, Brianna. I mean, you felt you wanted to pick Jacqueline up and that's fine. I'm only saying it wasn't necessary. We all got along just fine. I mean, the two of them were like best buddies immediately," he added, smiling at the thought.

Brianna looked as if he'd thrown a bucket of cold water into her face. "I'm glad to know you were so totally entertained. While I was down there handling life and death, trying to decide whether to cry or puke my guts out, you were conveniently playing house with our daughter. Honestly, Terrance, I have to tell you that I am slightly disappointed."

With that statement, she got into the car, turned over the engine and tore out of the condo's parking lot.

Terrance continued to stand there, his mouth open, as he came to the realization that Brianna still had not really accepted their recent divorce. At the same time, he also realized it was her problem and that he was standing in the driveway wearing a pajama bottom, flip-flops and nothing else. He wound his arms around his body and moved quickly toward the entrance, bounded up the stairs and entered the apartment quietly.

Skye was in exactly the same position he'd left her in, one arm thrown across the pillow, the sheet twisted around her body. She breathed deeply, sighed once and turned over as he got into the bed. The warmth from her body welcomed him and he almost awakened her just to tell her that Jacqueline was no longer with them.

Looking at the light coming in from the two large windows on either side of the room, Terrance saw that morning would come soon and he inhaled deeply. Feeling as if he could sleep all day, he turned on his side, laid one hand on Skye's hip and quickly fell asleep.

Several hours later, Skye awakened, sought her bearings, then smiled. Terrance was still sleeping deeply, the planes of his face relaxed and soft. She watched him for some moments, then decided to check on the baby.

She walked into the other room, saw that the crib was empty and noted that even the blanket was gone. For a moment, panic set in. What if someone had broken in during the night and stolen Jacqueline?

Skye raced back into the bedroom, began shaking Terrance violently, tears forming in her eyes as she did so.

"Oh, my God, Terrance. Jacqueline is not here. She's gone. She's gone," she shouted as she roused him from a deep sleep.

"No, no. She's fine. Her mom came last night— actually, this morning—and took her home," he said, mumbling somewhat, not fully awake but cognizant of what had taken place and somewhat able to articulate.

"What? What are you talking about? Last night? But I didn't hear a thing. Are you telling me that I slept through Jacqueline's mother being here? Oh, my God!"

Skye's panic now really awakened Terrance. That and the fact that she was shaking his entire body as she realized what had taken place.

"It's okay. Skye, it's okay. Brianna wanted to be with Jacqueline, especially after all that she'd seen at the hospital last night. Sometimes, medicine can affect you that way. It makes you want to draw those closest to you even closer. Makes you want to be with the ones you love, so that you can tell them how much you love and need them. That's why she came by to pick Jacqueline up."

"Well, where was I? I mean, I know where I was, but did she know that? I mean, how did she come in, get the baby and not know I was here?"

"She never came into my bedroom. And yes, I did tell her that you were here. I don't like to play games, Skye. And I especially don't play games with Brianna. She's my daughter's mother and I give her that respect. But I'll also give you the respect due as my lady. That's the way I handle myself."

Skye watched his face, heard the truth in his words and for several moments, knew the meaning of pure panic. Then, in the next instant, she calmed down.

"I'm sorry, it's just so bizarre. I mean, it's not often that you're asleep in a man's bed and his ex-wife, mother of his child, is in the next room, too. I think I'm glad that I was practically comatose from the flight and all."

"I think I am, too. I just kept hoping that you would

not hear any noise and decide to come in and check on Jacqueline. You two got pretty chummy very quickly and I knew your maternal instincts were kicking in."

"Ha-ha. Thanks, Dr. Terry. You know, you're not so bad really. I mean, as things go, you handled yourself and the situation nicely."

Skye's statement was issued with total honesty, then delivered with a quick kiss. Terrance needed no further encouragement as he wound his arms around her, pulling her back into bed.

"Uh-oh, I think I've awakened a sleeping giant."

"That, my dear, is an understatement." He kissed her neck, opened the buttons on the pajama top, then trailed kisses down the valley between both breasts as his hands caressed the soft skin at the indentation of her waist, the smooth expanse of her belly and the creamy thighs that guided him the rest of the way.

In touching her center, he found that she was already moist and ready for him.

"You are delicious," he whispered into Skye's ear as he quickly removed the pajama shirt.

"Mmm," was all that she was able to murmur as she raised up to kiss him.

"Mmm," he repeated.

The remaining garments were removed between kisses and strategically placed caresses. Terrance reached into the bedside nightstand, removed a contraceptive device and placed it under one of the pillows. He then leaned over, kissed Skye softly and ran one finger delicately around the peak of her breast.

Breathless with passion, Terrance trailed kisses down Skye's body, his tongue becoming an instrument of fine desire as he teased and titillated her, only stopping when she begged him to.

Skye put one leg over his, gained the balance she needed, and quickly turned the tables, coming to rest over him.

"Now what?" Terrance said, laughter just below the surface

"Now this."

Skye leaned down, kissed him deeply, her tongue engaging his in a battle of wills as she lowered herself onto his prone figure. The contact was electric and Terrance recognized that she'd gained control—for the moment.

Skye took hold of both his hands, raised them above his head and proceeded to worm her way down his body, trailing kisses along the way. She stopped at his chest, gave attention to each of his nipples until he began to squirm with pleasure, then repositioned her body as she continued farther down.

At that moment, Terrance could stand no more. He disengaged their hands, took hold of her body and turned the tables. Reaching under the pillow, he sheathed himself quickly.

"Heaven—you feel like heaven," he murmured as he slowly entered her body.

Skye was unable to speak at that moment, so caught up in the ripples of pleasure that surged through her body. Each movement was met by a higher degree of sensation as Terrance took his time, holding back for what seemed like an eternity, but which increased their pleasure immensely.

Skye moaned loudly, signaling an arc of spiraling pleasure she found almost intolerable. Moments later,

Terrance joined her as they each found a pinnacle of intense pleasure together.

"Heaven—oh, yes, like that," Skye whispered as she kissed him softly, then lay motionless as Terrance continued to hold her in his arms.

"Yes, like that," he repeated as they found themselves, arms and legs intertwined, breath still coming rapidly, but slowly returning to normalcy.

They awakened hours later as the afternoon sun burnt its way through the sky.

Chapter 23

Skye watched as Terrance placed a folded blanket, a cooler and an umbrella into the trunk of his car. She turned her head up toward the sky, shielded her eyes with one hand and marveled at the beauty of the day.

Terrance leaned into her, playfully touched her nose with his and drew her into his arms. Looking down into her eyes, he felt her melt into him, sending a charge of energy up his spine. She was beautiful, she was smart and she was here, with him. He wanted to shout it from the rooftops, but knew it wouldn't sit well with his neighbors, nor would it make the best impression on the woman in his arms. So, instead, he turned pragmatic.

"Did you pack your sunscreen and sunglasses?"

"Absolutely. You think just because I'm from Atlanta that I don't know how to handle myself at the beach, huh?"

"No, but I just want to make sure you're going to be

comfortable. We'll pick up the food on the way. I know a great spot that does lobster to go. They also have conch salad. You'll love it."

Terrance's excitement was contagious and Skye found herself joining in without any effort. They'd spent the entire morning in bed, enjoying each other's company as they talked about their careers, their lives and their desires. The future was like an unspoken, unacknowledged third party lying there between them, and for the first time, Skye knew what it was about him that made her afraid.

She recognized in him the things she'd always wanted, always felt she should look for in a man. There was no doubt in her mind that in Terrance, she'd found a soul mate. The frightening thing was that she was almost one hundred percent sure that he, too, felt the same way. It was neither the time, nor the appropriate place to ask the question though; not on the first morning that they'd awakened together after having spent a night consumed by lovemaking.

Dressed in a green-and-white silk halter top, white shorts and green thong sandals, her hair pulled off her face and held in place with a headband, Skye looked young and incredibly pretty. Terrance watched her adjust her headband for the second time and knew that he very much liked what he saw. Even when she fidgeted, she was irresistible.

They stopped along the way and picked up two steamed lobsters, complete with wedges of lime, a butter sauce on the side and one large container of rice and beans. The conch salad had already been sold out, but the owner of the shop promised he'd have more by the next day. Terrance promised to stop in and then quickly ushered Skye back to the car. They drove to a strip of beach that Skye had seen as they'd come from the airport, the stretch of sand extending for as far as the eye could see. A soft ocean breeze blew as they unloaded the car, walked several feet onto the pearl colored sand and spread the blanket out.

"This is beautiful. Something that you dream about. I don't think I've had a beach picnic since my parents took us. My sister and I were very young."

"Well, you're overdue, but don't expect me to treat you like you're a little girl. You've already convinced me that you're a woman—and quite a woman at that," he added suggestively. His tone took on a dangerous edge with the statement, and his eyes wandered luxuriously over her body as he watched Skye remove her shorts. The halter top remained in place and a tiny pair of brief swimming bottoms, which matched the lime-green headband and sandals, barely covered the bottom half of Skye's body.

"I'm now forewarned. Don't worry, I can handle myself," she challenged him, then fell to her knees as she sorted through the various bags and other items they'd brought to the beach.

Included were two bottles of a local grapefruit drink and a small fresh pineapple that Terrance had already cut into long slices after he'd inserted several equally long toothpicks that would enable them to hold the succulent pieces of pineapple later on as their meal became a third party to the celebration.

The lobster was succulent, sweet and messy. Terrance had packed several packages of wet wipes and one wet washcloth. Still, as they cleaned up after consuming a delicious lunch, both were sticky with lobster juice, butter sauce and even small sprays of lemon.

"Let's head for the water. We'll clean up later." Terrance's practical approach was all Skye needed to hear. She bounded up, pulled off the top she was wearing over her head and headed for the ocean.

"Last one in is a rotten egg," she called over her shoulder, her hair flying in the wind.

Terrance recognized the challenge and accepted. He ripped off the cutoff T-shirt he was wearing and tore out after her, laughing as he watched her reach the water, stop and assess his gain on her, then dip her hands into the spray.

"Okay, you made it this far and you beat me, but I meant really get into the water," he added as he came up alongside her. He easily lifted her from her feet as he continued into the waves.

Skye laughed, then squealed as the cooler than expected water temperature hit her body. She struggled, yelling, "Put me down, Terrance," then burst into more laughter as she realized he was enjoying her response almost as much as she was.

"Who would have thought it?" he said as he dropped her into the water. Skye quickly regained her composure, broke into an easy breast stroke and outpaced him as she headed out into deeper water.

Terrance watched her, noted how gracefully she handled herself and grinned broadly.

"Yeah, guess you figured a girl from New York now living in Atlanta would be a landlubber."

Terrance kept pace with her easily, matching her stroke for stroke until he was alongside. When Skye turned onto her back and began to float, he did the same as they both rested, recovering quickly from the sprint they'd just finished.

"Guess you've proven almost all of my theories wrong. So far, I'm batting zero," he admitted.

"What's that supposed to mean?"

"I'll tell you later." And with that, he turned over, began treading water and came up beside her. Wrapping one arm around her waist, Terrance easily interrupted Skye's balance. He liked the feel of her body against his in the water and found himself wondering how he would manage when she returned home. In his mind, the weekend was only half over, but he was already experiencing separation anxiety. These thoughts came and went in an instant, but they registered immediately.

Skye managed to right herself, then reached for Terrance's shoulder, finding herself locking on to his body. It felt incredibly solid and she wondered if she'd ever get over the incredibly powerful feeling it gave her when he responded to her touch.

The water felt like a warm bath to them both at that point and they stayed immersed, just above their waists, for what seemed like an eternity. Finally, they headed toward the sandy beach, hand in hand.

"Okay, tell me what you were talking about before," Skye said as she dried herself off.

Terrance looked up, cleared his throat, then tossed the towel he'd been using back into the plastic beach bag he'd brought. He remained silent, watching Skye as she finished drying off, too, then asked a single question.

"Do you think you could ever leave Atlanta?"

Skye's reaction was instantaneous but she camouflaged it by reaching for the sunscreen she'd brought.

Without blinking, flinching or giving any real clue, she simply sat beside him and looked him squarely in the face.

"Exactly what are you asking me, Terrance?"

He looked away for a moment, scanning the beach, the tiny buildings that dotted the shoreline, then came back to the woman who sat beside him.

"I'm asking you to let me love you. Just like I did the first time we met. Only I mean it for eternity this time. I know you have a career in the States, but I also know that we're good together. There, I've said it. You can practice real estate and mortgages here. We darn sure have enough of it and developers have begun several projects which will probably increase both the housing and condo markets. Isn't that what you do?" His question was rhetorical, but it gave them both an opportunity to gather their thoughts.

Terrance had not anticipated feeling the way he did when he was with Skye, hadn't expected those feelings to overcome him and force him to put himself on the line the way he'd just done. But now that he had, he felt an intense sense of accomplishment, knowing that he'd done something which would either bring him great joy or intense pain. Either way, he'd gambled, which meant he'd finally broken the emotional link between Brianna and himself.

Skye looked up, watched a puffy white cloud increase in size and knew she was at a crossroad in her life. She felt good, she felt protected. But even more importantly, she felt an overwhelming sense of calmness. Terrance's question remained unanswered, but he understood. Only a woman who was truly giving his statement real consideration would take this long. A no would have come instantaneously.

"May I ask you something first? I mean, before I give you my answer?" she said in a whisper.

"Sure." He wanted to reach for her hand, but was afraid to, not wanting to make her feel trapped but needing to touch her at that very moment.

"I want us to be clear—I mean, on all fronts. You've just gone through a separation, a divorce and even some issues with the custody of your daughter. Are you sure you're ready to commit to another relationship? I know that the heart and soul needs time to heal. I'm just wondering if you've allowed enough time for the healing process. The breakup of a marriage is almost like a death. We have to grieve for a period of time before we are able to become whole again."

Skye's words reached him, and he knew that he'd scoured his soul asking the very same questions. It was only after the situation he'd endured the night before that it came to him that he was okay. He still loved Brianna in a way and probably always would, but not in the way one should love a lifetime partner.

"You know, if you weren't so special, you'd be pretty darned scary. I'm glad you're this way, though. It lets me know that I never have to truly worry about you. The answer to your question is yes. I have done due diligence with my heart and it is free of encumbrances." He took Skye's hand then, interlaced his fingers with hers and watched her face closely.

"So, this is getting pretty serious, isn't it?"

"Yes, it is. I mean, when I saw your photo in Branch

and Nita's book, I couldn't wait to meet you. Then you showed up, blew the photo out of the box and continued to fascinate me. Hell, you dazzled me the entire weekend. And you're doing no less of a bang-up job right here on my own turf. I know it may seem premature but, Skye, I'm falling in love with you."

She held his hand tightly, felt her throat constrict, then looked away. The atmosphere was electrically charged, and Skye couldn't help but note the intensity of her feelings even though she'd chastised herself against feeling anything deeply for the man sitting beside her. She'd known about the ex-wife, the child and the messy divorce. Nita filled her in immediately, but even she had not been aware of how any of it was unfolding as time moved forward.

"Okay. I mean, I feel it, too, Terrance. I'm just not so sure it's time to start talking about the future. From where I sit, we have great chemistry, good times, an incredible understanding of what the other seems to be thinking and maybe not much else. Do you honestly think that it's enough to build a foundation on? I mean, enough that I should think about anything further?"

Terrance took a moment before answering, then plunged forward.

"Skye, obviously you haven't heard a word I've said. I know all about the right formula for a relationship to work. I'm the living, breathing proof of that particular dynamic of spinning a person around and dropping them right on their head. That's not what I envision for us. No way. I mean, of course, no one has all the answers. I'm only asking you one thing. And that is to let me love you."

Skye inhaled deeply, looked at Terrance's face and smiled. In that moment, the communication was complete—no answer was necessary. They both knew it. They both felt it. No matter what happened, they would move forward.

Terrance leaned forward and kissed her softly, slowly, then deeply. When they broke apart, she leaned against him weakly, putting her head on his shoulder. They stayed that way for a long time as the afternoon sun lowered itself in the sky and the elements of the universe aligned into their rightful order, on all fronts.

Trouble was her middle name...his was danger!

Elaine Overton

His Holiday Bride

Fleeing from a dangerous pursuer, Amber Lockhart
takes refuge in the home—and arms—of
Paul Gutierrez. But the threat posed by the man
who's after her doesn't compare with the peril to
Amber's heart from her sexy Latin protector.

THE LOCKHARTS
THREE WEDDINGS AND A REUNION
FOR FOUR SASSY SISTERS, ROMANCE CHANGES EVERYTHING!

*Available the first week of October
wherever books are sold.*

KIMANI
ROMANCE

Never Without You... Again

National bestselling author

FRANCINE CRAFT

When Hunter Davis returns to town, high school principal Theda Coles is torn between the need to uphold her reputation and the burning passion she still feels for her onetime love. But her resistance melts in the face of their all-consuming desire and she can't stop seeing him—even though their relationship means risking her career...

"Ms. Craft is a master at storytelling."
—Romantic Times BOOKreviews

Available the first week of October wherever books are sold.

KIMANI™
ROMANCE

www.kimanipress.com

KPFC0371007

He looked good enough to eat...and she was hungry!

The Trouble with Luv'

PAMELA YAYE

When feisty, aggressive, sensuous Ebony Garrett
propositions him, Xavier Reed turns her down cold.
He's more interested in demure, classy, marriage-
minded women. But when a church function reveals
Ebony's softer side, Xavier melts like butter.
Only, is he really ready to risk the heat?

*"Yaye has written a beautiful romance
with a lot of sensual heat."*
—*Imani Book Club Review* on *Other People's Business*

*Available the first week of October
wherever books are sold.*

KIMANI™
ROMANCE

National bestselling author

ROCHELLE ALERS

No Compromise

In charge of a program for victimized women, Jolene Walker has no time or energy for a personal life...until she meets army captain Michael Kirkland. This sexy, compelling man is tempting her to trade her long eighteen-hour workdays for sultry nights of sizzling passion. But their bliss is shattered when Jolene takes on a mysterious new client, plunging her into a world of terrifying danger.

"Alers paints such vivid descriptions that when Jolene becomes the target of a murderer, you almost feel as though someone you know is in great danger."
—*Library Journal*

Available the first week of October wherever books are sold.

ARABESQUE®

www.kimanipress.com

KPRA0181007

Will one secret destroy their love?

Award-winning author

Janice Sims

One fine Day

The Bryant Family trilogy continues with this heartfelt story
in which Jason Bryant tries to convince lovely bookstore
owner Sara Minton to marry him. Their love is unlike
anything Jason has ever felt, and he knows Sara feels
the same way...so why does she keep refusing him,
saying she'll marry him "one day"? He knows she's
hiding something...but what?

Available the first week of October
wherever books are sold.

ARABESQUE®

www.kimanipress.com

KPJS0141007